THE BELLEVER HAGSTONE

WICKER DOGS: BOOK TWO

by D.A. Holwill

For Kahlo, Duchamp and Richard Parker
Who we lost along the way

And for Netty – who will always be first

The Wicker Dogs Series:

Wicker Dogs
The Bellever Hagstone
Jack Sharpnails

1

A fat moon illuminated the stone circle at the northernmost tip of Dourstone Nymet, white with the first snow of winter. It was midnight, the first Saturday of December. The sound of paws crunching through snow and hot, panting breath announced the arrival of an impenetrable wall of dogs, Alaskan malamutes. Their big grey faces so beautiful, so elegant, so loveable – so wolflike.

It is time. You must do it. A voice nobody but Polly could hear.

'The times they are a-changing,' she muttered, shaking her head. *Not for the better, you mark my words.*

'Now see this,' Polly shouted. 'This is Dourstone Nymet, our Dourstone Nymet.'

She threw her arms wide, standing in the centre of the circle on a large, flat stone. She wore the purple velvet robes Dourstonian officials had always worn for the Wisthound weekend. Her hair – for so long hidden beneath bleach, hair relaxer and straighteners – now unleashed in all the glory of its African roots to hang round her shoulders in long natural curls.

A cheer went up from the people of Dourstone, all crowded round a bonfire outside the circle.

'And we won't let anything stand in our way, this is how we do things now. In the open, no secrets, no hidden figures. Do you trust me?' She turned about so all could see her.

'We do,' the crowd chanted in reply. 'We do.'

'Good, now, see this thing I do.' She held an ancient looking knife above her head, moonlight glinting along the teeth of its long, cruel serrated edge. Silence filled the space between beasts and humans until all had quieted. She would make sure this ceremony got the respect it demanded. 'We feed The Devil's dogs as the cold begins to bite,' she chanted. 'The first snows of winter stained with blood in the night.'

The second time round the crowd echoed her words.

The third time all were in perfect unison.

And the fourth, fifth and sixth.

She lowered the knife slowly before pulling it across her forearm. Once satisfied the cut was deep enough she squeezed it to drip blood on the altar stone she stood upon. The stone that had spent the last century and a half hidden from prying eyes, carted between Manor and circle at need. But Polly had decided things must no longer be hidden. The cart fuelled the bonfire.

'Blood, see?' Polly's life force dripped from her hands, spattering on snow-topped granite. There was blood, there was seen to be blood. The stone had drunk so much down the years, yet its thirst remained unquenchable.

People nodded, dogs howled.

Polly's Irish wolfhound, Fenrir, stalked to the front, his eyes glowing the same blue as those of the malamutes. No longer the comical companion of her fireside, he was different, changed since that night a year before when he saved her life. He led these dogs now, and had to accept everything that went with being part of this most enigmatic pack. He nodded almost imperceptibly to his lieutenant, Cronus, the biggest and most scarred of all the malamutes, whose usually mismatched amber and sky-blue eyes glowed the same uniform blue.

'And food,' she cried, stepping down from the rock. Two robed figures hoisted a huge bag provided by Adrian the butcher into the pool of blood. They cut it open to reveal two whole pigs, as yet untouched. Polly nodded to Fenrir, who joined her. Cronus padded to his side, and at a signal from the wolfhound, raised his muzzle to the sky and gave a fearsome howl. The moon shone down between clouds as the dogs fell upon the carcasses: yellowing teeth and powerful jaws thrust aside skin intended to keep vital components inside like it was a paper bag.

The soft innards falling on snowy ground triggered a memory Polly would rather forget, when she had run for her life from this stone circle, chased by the dogs Fenrir now led and leaving her beloved Patrick to a gruesome end. As a result she had entirely given up meat, no easy feat when you unexpectedly find yourself the figurehead of a small farming community. But her final memories of Patrick's insides spilling out left her unable to consider even the most processed and unrecognisable of meats.

She hoisted a flaming torch on her shoulder and took her place at the head of eight figures in identical purple velvet robes. Where once their identities had been hidden, Polly's open door policy had reduced the tinner's masks hanging from their belts to props. The faces of Dan, Kerry, Clive, Susan, Wendy, Lynn, Jack and Father Hearne were visible. There was no other way. The people must know who it was that acted in their name.

'It is done, the town has its heart once more. We return to the Manor!' Polly cried, raising her torch to a cheer.

It's not, it hasn't, and you've really done it now girl, the voice in Polly's head said. The procession moved off down the hill.

'I told you, things are changing,' she replied, as circle and fire retreated from view. 'Nobody else need die, nothing is going to happen.'

You don't know how wrong you are.

'Why couldn't you just stay dead Melissa?'

Because you didn't know what you were doing when you tried to kill me. You want me here, you obviously need me or you'd never have taken my ring, the familiar patronising tones of Lady Melissa Dewer rattled round Polly's head as the townsfolk followed her away from the sound of tooth crunching through bone.

The next morning, an old-fashioned caravan creaked and clattered its way along the frosty moorside road to Dourstone, drawn by four hungry-looking black horses. Its much re-panelled and patched together sides, once a glorious black, had now faded to grey; the formerly magnificent black feathered plumes at its corners were now ragged stumps and the ancient sigils carved upon it had been rendered unrecognisable by the never-ending march of time and weather. A motley crew of mismatched mongrel dogs – their coats mingled to a uniform oily brown from the dirt of infinite roads – lolloped beside it, keeping easy pace with the horses. The bizarre procession came as far as the cross that marked the boundary of Dourstone proper, one of those markers they blessed every seven years when beating the bounds.

A black deadman's hat crowned the driver, while his face hid behind a beard that was hard to distinguish from his long, straggly, silver-streaked hair. His old-fashioned black leather boots crunched in the snow as he jumped from the cab and, before even untying his horses, pulled something from the folds of his well-worn black travelling cloak, ground it against the head of the cross, then threw it to his dogs.

'It's been a long time coming,' he said, lighting his pipe and looking across to the stone circle.

After he had taken a few puffs, an enormous black dog that could easily be mistaken for a small bear gave a gruff bark and nodded.

He took a few paces past the cross, into Dourstone proper, and grinned.

'Good boy, Wotan. We're home.'

2

'I wondered where you'd got to, good afternoon,' Lynn said, coming down the steps of the battlemented walkway that ran across the tops of stables and barns to surround the courtyard of Dourstone Manor.

Polly checked her watch, half past ten. Fair enough, not early, but then she didn't pay Lynn to run the place only to come in early herself.

'Morning Lynn,' she said, manoeuvring her one-year old daughter Elizabeth's pushchair inside and past the boxes filling the great hall. 'I'll be in the kitchen if anyone needs me.'

'Fine, good, I'll be in soon to brief you. We've got three new residents coming and there's a wedding party booked for this weekend. Lots to do.' Lynn was dressed for business, Lynn was always dressed for business, in a midnight blue trouser suit with her light brown hair pulled back in a ruthless pony tail. 'Oh, and I'm already halfway through the Times cryptic, I've left copies on the kitchen table. Wendy's already on it, she doesn't think I can hear her ringing her mum for the answers but I can. There will be points deducted.'

Polly sighed, she used to enjoy doing the crossword, but Lynn had turned it into something approaching all out war between the members of the newly-founded Patrick Sumner Trust. There was a scoreboard on the fridge in the Dairy Kitchen on which Lynn was currently only in second place. Polly was tempted to fill today's little black and white square with obscenities and throw the competition, but she had a little pride left.

She looked down at her cardigan, she wasn't sure which stains were baby food, and which baby sick anymore, but it was warm, comfortable and had plenty of pockets. She also didn't pay Lynn to deal with the public just to have to dress up to the nines every day herself. She checked her hair in the large mirror beside the coat-stand and very quickly wished she hadn't. There was always so much to do.

'How did you do it?' she asked the voice in her head.

I had a better wardrobe than you, and I never left my bedroom without making sure I'd got a full face and hair. I had standards, I still do, you're letting the side down.

'Oh, ha ha. Very funny, I don't care how I look, I'm busy. I meant how did you run this place?'

Same way as you, I got Lynn to do it.

'And yet there's still so much to do myself.'

You just need to know how to handle it, Melissa replied. *Delegate more, not just to Lynn, there's a whole army of scared idiots for you to use.*

'Fine, make me a cup of tea then.'

If you insist.

Polly went into the first of the long labyrinth of kitchens that ran the length of the east wing of the Manor. This one was known as the Baking Kitchen, as it held the original ovens, great stone things big enough to roast a hippo that flanked the rayburn somebody had already stoked up to full heat. She filled an old fashioned copper kettle from leaky taps that whined as they gave up their precious fluid and placed it on the range.

'You do know this doesn't save me any time at all don't you?' she said.

Try delegating to someone with their own body then.

'Okay, I will.' She sat down, waiting for the kettle, and peered at the crossword while she jingled her keys in Elizabeth's face.

'Are you still talking to yourself?' Wendy swept in, scattering papers over the vast table.

'Maybe a bit,' Polly said, pulling her crossword sheet out of the mess. 'What have you got for four down?'

'Not telling.' Wendy tied her long black curls away from her olive-skinned face. 'I need all the points I can get, I'm bottom of the league.'

'I might give your mum a bell then.' Polly grinned.

'Oh, ha ha. Anyway, we need to go through all this today when you've got time. The weekend's been fun, but a total loss.' Wendy looked at the mass of paperwork and shook her head before grabbing another pile from the dresser.

'Yeah, sorry. I know I wasn't around a lot yesterday, it was all just a bit much, the first anniversary of...'

'You killing my wife, yeah. I remember thanks, I still turned up.' Wendy slammed the stack down in front of Polly with a glare.

'Sorry, yes, but in my defence, you did kill Patrick first,' Polly said.

'I didn't, the dogs did that.'

'We can argue semantics all you like Wendy, let's just agree it's been a difficult weekend for us all. Cup of tea?' The kettle whistled.

'Go on then.'

Polly got up and poured boiling water into the big teapot. The Wish Weekend threatened to undo all the progress Polly had made in the last year, reminding everyone of the events of the last one. In Polly's fight through the Manor to get her daughter back from Lady Melissa Dewer there had been some collateral damage and Wendy's wife Delia had caught the wrong end of a pike through the chin.

Any mother would have done the same in her position. Polly wished she had been able to give Delia a vein full of Fentanyl like she had Wendy. But the non-lethal options had run out and it was her or Delia. She really didn't want anybody to die, but there were lives on her conscience whether she liked it or not.

'Proper tea today, I think we need it,' Polly said, rifling through drawers for a tea cosy. 'The roads were a bugger to get up, all that snow's turned to slush – I could barely get Elizabeth's wheels through.'

'Why didn't you drive?' Wendy shook her head, leaning across Polly and pulling a cheerful rainbow-striped tea cosy from the drawer she was staring into. 'You've got the Land Rover, it's a piece of piss in that.'

'I left it here, Saturday night after the party, wasn't safe to drive.'

'Fuck's sake Pol, you had two drinks, you weren't even pissed and there's literally nobody on the roads at three in the morning. You could, and indeed should, have driven.'

'I was over the limit, it would have been illegal.' Polly swirled the teapot around.

'As opposed to all them people you murdered and crippled last year?' Wendy took two mugs from a tall twisting mug tree that clambered around the worktop and slammed them down.

Polly hadn't wanted to hurt anyone, much less kill them. She woke up in nightmare sweats at least every other night with the faces of her victims accusing her, but she had done what she had to do. She was not Melissa. Melissa had killed countless others in the name of protecting the town. Polly was not killing anybody else, there was another way.

'That was different, and anyway, I like the walk. My head was a bit swimmy from those two drinks and it's nice to live somewhere you can walk alone in the dark.'

'Swimmy from two drinks, you're getting shit at this in your old age. You need practice.'

'I do not, I just need to think ahead.'

'I still don't see why you don't move in here Pol?' Wendy asked. 'There's more than enough space, and it seems a bit...'

'A bit what?' Polly replied.

'A bit weird that you own all of this – well Elizabeth does – and you're still living in that pokey little cottage on the other side of town. Like you're too good for us Devon lot.'

'I only lived in London for a few years you know. I grew up in Appledore,' she said.

Practically bloody Wales up there, Lady Melissa's voice echoed round her head.

'Well, it fucked your accent off didn't it. You sound like you were born to the Manor. I'll go and find some biscuits.'

Polly did not feel like aristocracy. She hadn't even met her father, never mind being able to trace her lineage by its coats of arms. She was just a mixed-race kid from a council estate in North Devon. Her mum's four kids all had different dads and none of them had stuck around. She'd been to university, made a career and moved in with a rich boy, but even Patrick's family weren't stately home posh, even if they had turned out to be the last of the Dewers (albeit illegitimately). It may have been in Elizabeth's blood but it wasn't in Polly's and when it came down to it she just didn't want to live in the Manor. Despite finding herself in charge of all this, until Elizabeth came of age, this was where she had been imprisoned for months, before having to fight her way back in and rescue her baby from the very people she now called colleagues.

No, the tumbledown cottage on the road to the moor she and Patrick had bought two years previously was the place for her. If she closed her eyes while sitting by the fire, she could almost hear him in the other room, feel him brush past her to straighten her grandfather's old sword they had hung over the fireplace together. The cottage was enough.

Lady Melissa Dewer had lived in the Manor house alone except for her dogs. All that space, all that ground, all those rooms, for one person and an ever-increasing brood of Alaskan malamutes. It hadn't felt right to Polly, so she opened it up to the community, starting with a single women's commune in the east wing. Lynn and Wendy had moved in as soon as Polly suggested it – for which she was eternally grateful, their organisational skills had proved a godsend – and more had come afterwards. Once word got out that it was a safe space, protected by dogs and ancient magick, the oppressed, controlled and plain scared of Devon turned up. Dourstone Manor had a reputation and the moors have long memories. To be there was to be a part of something much bigger than their own lives.

Polly charged minimal rents, preferring to use her tenants' skills rather than take their money, and the old kitchen gardens would soon be teeming with saleable food. The grand reception rooms were available to hire as wedding venues – along with the ornately landscaped gardens – and would be making money hand over fist with all the bookings they had for next summer, while the west wing was slowly being converted to a luxury hotel. The members of the Patrick Sumner Trust had ideas, some of the many outbuildings were going to be made into refugee shelters, applications had been made for geothermal power drilling, a windfarm and a campsite. Polly's financial expertise from her years in the city meant they could see the enterprise benefiting the community and making money instead of swallowing it up like old buildings are so wont to do.

'How's her ladyship this morning then?' Dan rolled into the room in his wheelchair, heading straight for Elizabeth. 'I'm still thoroughly jealous of all this.' He ran his fingers across the hanging plastic figures dangling along the front of Elizabeth's car chair. 'Kerry won't let me have them, kids get all the best chairs.'

'She's fine,' Polly replied. 'And maybe Santa will bring you what you want. Have you been a good boy this year?'

'Depends what you mean by good,' he said, briefly removing his ever-present Exeter Chiefs beanie hat to scratch his bald head. 'Ker says I've got to lose weight.'

'Did she?' Polly said, diplomatically. Dan had got a little larger since he'd been confined to a wheelchair, but as Polly had been the one to put him there, she didn't think it her place to mention it. 'I think you look great. Really well.'

'Well, she don't.' He reached for the plate of biscuits Wendy had brought in. 'She thinks I'm a fat lazy bastard, I told her, "I'm stuck in this chair, what am I supposed to do, go fucking running?" So she pulled out all them stupid exercise regimes the doctors gived me last year.'

'Shouldn't you be doing those anyway?'

'Yeah, yeah, I do them, I do. But...'

'But what?'

'But they're hard, and biscuits are nice. I'll figure it out.' He munched his biscuit. 'She means well, I do appreciate her caring, but, you know...'

'Didn't realise you were on today Dan.' Wendy intervened, carefully placing more mugs on the table.

'Kerry's taking Katie off to look at another university,' he explained. His and Kerry's eldest was keen to leave the town and had been dragging the two of them on research trips all over the country. 'So I'm doing the creche. Is her ladyship going to join us today, or are you keeping her with you Pol?'

'With me, I think.' Polly didn't like being separated from her baby one bit. Especially not in this house where she had very nearly lost her forever. She did sometimes leave her with the other children in the morning room, she felt she needed to, to let the child gain her independence, and help herself feel more confident. After all, she couldn't be with her all the time and Melissa was no longer a threat. If anything she was far more helpful dead than she had been alive. 'I might drop her in later, if the meetings get a bit much. Would you like that Lizzybet?' She leaned in to her daughter, who giggled in what might well be an affirmative.

'Cool, cool, see you then.' Dan rolled back out to the hallway. He didn't seem to bear Polly any ill will for putting him in that wheelchair when she pushed him over the banisters onto the hard slabs of the great hall and severed his spine.

'Are you sure we've done the right thing?' Susan burst in without any greeting, no pleasantries. Straight to business.

'What, making a pot of tea?' Wendy joked. 'I reckon so, but there should be enough water left if you wanted coffee. Where's Clive?'

'He'll be along, he takes too long to park, so I got out. And no. I do not want coffee.' Susan grabbed the teapot and poured the first cup without waiting to be asked. 'You know what I mean. Not making the sacrifice. Will we be safe?' She had cropped her hair short and dyed it a month earlier, spikes of pillarbox red now crowning her Chinese features, in what was definitely not a mid-life crisis. With her big thick-rimmed glasses and hand-made jewellery dripping from her wrists everybody thought she was trying to appear the bohemian artist she hadn't had time to be in her youth. Flowing white clothes like priest's robes only added to that accusation. Especially on a Monday morning at the day job.

'Of course we will.' Polly replied, ignoring the shouting in her head. 'It was just to sustain whatever Melissa was, and she's gone now, so we don't need to feed the monsters.'

'Well, she always said it was for the good of the town. The thing that kept it like it is. Nice, pleasant, not full of cunts.' Susan took her cup of tea without offering the pot around and sat at the head of the table.

'It's got as many cunts as anywhere else, don't believe everything that mad old bat told you,' Wendy grinned, pouring herself and Polly two cups of tea.

Filthy little two-faced bitch, I ought to pop out of you, get in her head and tell her a few home truths, maybe get her to smack herself about a bit. Fucking turncoat, I've not been gone a year.

'Shut up,' Polly muttered under her breath. 'You've never had actual friends, only lackeys.'

'What was that?' Susan cocked her head.

'Oh, nothing, I just said she's right. Dourstone Nymet is a nice place to live because it's in a good place and has been cared for by an ancient family – the Dewers – who actually gave a shit. Lady Melissa was a lot of things...' *a lot of bloody good things, much better than you, you've damned the fucking place you stupid girl* '...but she loved this place, she loved you people and she didn't just sell it off to the highest bidder. Hence us being able to do all of this.' Polly waved her hand around to indicate everything they were trying to achieve.

True enough, nice save.

'She knew some dark shit though,' Susan rebutted. 'Maybe she was on to something.'

I do and I am.

'Maybe she was, but we couldn't keep on feeding people to dogs. It's not right, there will be no more death in this place.'

'Wo wor weth,' Elizabeth echoed, banging pudgy fists on the table.

'Easy for you to say.' Susan smirked.

'Next time, tell me before you jump out of the car,' Clive said, coming in, draping his dripping wet Grenfell jacket over the back of a chair and sitting on a drier one. 'I nearly ran your foot over, you silly cow.'

'I did tell you, you just didn't listen,' Susan said. 'And maybe you should learn to drive.'

'I can drive just fine, but the dogs are running loose and I didn't want to hit one, so I took a little care parking, is that a crime?'

'Should be,' Susan said.

'Well it's not, anyway, there are more important matters to discuss. That fucking pikey's come back, no offence Wendy.'

'None taken,' Wendy replied. 'I'm still not a gypsy, never have been.'

'Yeah, you keep saying that.' Clive reached for the teapot with his prosthetic steel hand before realising his mistake and using the other one. 'Anyway, that bloody traveller doesn't ever move on. He spent three months moving round Winkleigh and he's up by the top cross now.'

'Is that the guy who was here back in March?' Wendy asked, not bothered by Clive's language, she was used to it. The casual way the locals referred to the travelling community had nothing to do with her, but given her Romany looks she caught an awful lot of reflected prejudice. Clive may have been married to Dourstone's only nod to ethnic diversity – Susan was British born Chinese – but it didn't stop his ingrained racism anymore than being married had cured his misogyny. Wendy didn't have time to police his behaviour so just left it. Her most robust rebuttal to the inevitable gypsy slurs she received would be a tired cry of: 'I'm from Chagford.'

'And April, and May, and June. Didn't leave 'til after the festival in July. He's a total piss-taker.' Clive ran his steel fingers through his almost-ginger mop of hair.

'Is it a problem?' Polly asked. She had been treated differently since letting her hair go back to its natural afro. For her first year in

Dourstone she had continued a regime of relaxing and bleaching her hair and using just the right kind of make up to pass as white. For her second year here she had 'come out' as mixed race and been treated very differently. Conversations would end abruptly when she entered a room. Laughter would hush down, and a lot more statements were begun with 'no offence, but...' before inevitably being hugely offensive. Things that used to be said to her with no fear of reproach were no longer mentioned and plenty of Dourstonians now looked on her with suspicion where before there was none. She didn't blame any of them individually, it was the same when she was a kid. That was why she had started hiding it.

'Not always,' Clive replied. 'But it has been in the past, depends on the traveller. I remember my dad planting that big row of trees along the bottom moor.'

'What have trees got to do with it?' Susan butted in.

'Stopped 'em getting their wagons off the road. At least it was supposed to, sneaky bastards still got between them: that's why we dug that big ditch.'

'I thought it was for drainage?' Wendy said.

'Yeah, so did the gypsies, told them the same about the trees, said it was to soak away the floods. It's all bollocks, Dad told me.' Clive's face split into a smug grin.

'Why did we decide to block the travelling community?' Polly asked.

'Probably for not fucking travelling, like this piss-taking bastard, his horses leave the verges all shot to shit; and they ate Dad's crops: stuck their heads in through the fence, stretched the wire right out.'

'I'll go and talk to him honey,' Susan said, biting her lip suggestively. 'I'm sure he can be persuaded.'

'No, not you, not that way.' Clive folded his arms.

'So why did the ditch get dug? Why just stop at the bottom moor?' Polly broke the awkward silence.

'He never told me why, only that we did. You'd have to ask Lady Melissa, she ordered it,' Clive said.

'Well we can't can we?' Wendy said. 'Not since Polly killed her.'

Never you mind why, Melissa explained. *Just pray your stupid idea doesn't start it all off again.*

'Yes, alright, alright,' Polly replied. 'She died of old age you know.'

'And being eaten by dogs,' Susan added.

'Yes, but they were her dogs.'

The dogs belong to nobody. But your Fenrir was telling them what to do, not my Cronus. Don't pretend you didn't want to kill me.

3

'How's the surveillance going then?' Father Hearne pulled his herringbone coat down over his tweed suit before sitting on a log.

'Pointlessly,' The Traveller replied from the other side of the fire, his nylon foldaway camping chair out of place amongst its antique surroundings. 'I can't see what the point of it is. I've never bothered before.'

'Yes, I remember.' Father Hearne leaned forward and tipped his immaculate homburg hat back. 'And look how that turned out.'

'I think I've learned enough since then.' The Traveller smiled enigmatically, puffing away on his pipe. 'What's to survey?'

'You can't get too hasty.' The priest patted his many pockets, before pulling out a silver hip flask engraved with a crucifix. 'It's better to have a foolproof plan than roll in all guns blazing and cock the whole thing up – again.'

'Yes, but no plan is foolproof, and I've waited long enough.' He poked at the flames of his fire with a blackened stick until the flames licked the spitted magpie across it.

The horses neighed theatrically at the crackling wood and stamped their feet, eager to be off, while the horde of mongrels ran around chasing their own tails, back and forth, away and return over the moors without any stick being thrown.

'True.' The vicar nodded and took another nip from his hip flask before offering it across. 'But are you sure you really want to do this?'

'Am I sure I want to do this? It's like the two of us have never met Arthur. You've known me from the beginning, this is all I've wanted.' The Traveller took a welcome drink.

'Yes, but why?'

'I don't think that matters any more, it's the principle of the thing.' He turned the magpie slowly over the fire, watched closely by the bear-sized mongrel, Wotan.

'Which is?' The priest took his flask back and began another long pat down of his pockets in search of his pipe.

'I don't know, did you ask her this many questions?'

'Who?' Father Hearne stopped patting.

'Oh you know who, I know you've been in this town all along, helping her, keeping me away. Letting her have my dogs.' Wotan pushed into him, rubbing his head along his leg.

'They are not your dogs, they are not anybody's dogs.' Father Hearne looked seriously at The Traveller. 'You need to think about the implications. There is more at stake than just your pride.'

'This is not about my pride, this is an injustice. She stole my pack, turned them against me and locked me out. There must be a reckoning. You, of all people, should understand that.'

'The dogs are their own, just as you or I are our own,' the priest replied. 'You, of all people, should understand that.' He finally pulled his pipe from the fathomless depths of his coat and began rummaging for his tobacco.

'You are far from your own Arthur,' The Traveller bellowed, laughing. 'You've been hers all this time, don't think I didn't know. You've helped keep me away from here, pretending to be on my side, I knew. I always knew.'

'I am my own.' The priest looked into the fire. 'I have always been my own, I make decisions for the good of all. I have always helped you, I've always been on your side.'

'And hers?' The Traveller pointed his pipe.

'And hers, yes.' Father Hearne nodded, having located his tobacco pouch in a waistcoat pocket. 'I am on everybody's side, I want the world to be healed, I want this place to be healed.'

'I want my revenge. I want my town.'

'What good will revenge do you? You have the loyalty of the pack again. What more do you need?' The priest filled his pipe, carefully tamping tobacco into the bowl with his little finger.

'I do have my dogs back yes. But they were always mine, I made them what they are, without me there would be no pack. She must pay for keeping them from me.' He scrubbed at the huge dog's donkey-like ears.

'And what does Wotan make of his upgrade?'

'It's what he's trained for his whole life, he knew it was coming. He's a good dog.'

'He is a good dog, but he is no more yours than any other dog.' A match flared in the hollow of the vicar's hands as he put flame to pipe.

'Dogs are dogs, their loyalty's cheap. But they are mine and she won't trick me out of them again.'

'I think we'll have to agree to disagree.' Father Hearne knew better than to try and argue the point with somebody who refused to listen.

'Fine, but you'll help me now she's gone to ground?' The Traveller said.

'Have I not been of help to you?' Father Hearne puffed out clouds of acrid blue smoke and lowered his pipe. 'Despite my reservations, I agree with your objectives, you are in the right for once.'

'Sorry, yes, of course you have. I should never have doubted you. It's just now I'm so close, I feel...'

'Paranoid?'

'Yeah, probably. Can I nick a pipe-full from you?'

'Of course.' The vicar passed his tobacco pouch over. 'Now what's your plan?'

'I think you're going to like it...'

'I doubt that.'

4

It was December the 22nd and while Dourstone might lean more towards the winter solstice, it was not a town immune to the charms of Christmas.

A massive tree had been erected in the centre of the square, lights carefully aligned to match those threading round lampposts. Shop windows were filled with fake snow and winter scenes while woolly-scarfed children ran excitedly through puddles that had replaced the crisp snows of Wish Weekend.

A German-style Christmas market filled the rest of the square, wooden sheds containing every kind of artisan tat an undeserving relative could ever want to receive. Tables and chairs were dotted between tree and market sheds for those choosing to partake of some festive food.

'How's it going girls?' Polly asked, putting Elizabeth's brakes on as they reached the food van.

'We're doing alright,' Kerry, Dan's wife, answered, straightening a white paper chef's hat over her unruly brown curls. 'Plenty of hungry people about, people who love a bit of thick, tasty sauce.' She nudged Lynn in the ribs.

'There's light mayo, guac and tempered bean sauce as well – half the calories and just as tasty.' Lynn waved her hand over an array of barely touched sauces by a full basket of wholemeal buns.

'Yeah, you know, just in case.' Kerry went back to the stove where she was cooking up more of her trademark hot sauce to refill the empty bowl next to her massively depleted bags of white buns. 'There's people who don't really like food here I daresay.'

'It's not not liking food to look after yourself, to not want to be full of sugary crap,' Lynn said. 'I've brought falafels as well, do you want one Polly?'

'Not right now,' Polly answered. 'Maybe later, I ate before I came down.' Since Polly had turned vegetarian, Lynn assumed she was on the same healthy eating trip as her. Polly had not confided her reasons for it in anybody.

They danced around the uncomfortable truth that Polly had run Lynn through with her grandfather's sword and left her bleeding to death on a cold cellar floor the previous year but, in her defence, Lynn had been instrumental in Patrick and Polly's separation. She was a devious actor and Polly was under no misapprehensions about her perceived friendliness. Polly held all the power and Lynn knew which side of her home-baked sourdough was covered in low-fat vegetable spread. Polly was cautious about trusting her entirely, despite Lady Melissa's insistence Lynn was as loyal as the dogs to whoever held the Manor.

'Of course she don't want a falafel,' Kerry spat the word. 'She's a vegetarian, not a goat. I've got some Linda McCartneys on the grill if you want a decent one Pol.' She pushed a tube of pretend meat up against the bubbling fat of Adrian the butcher's best Cumberlands.

'No, you're alright,' Polly said. 'Like I said, I've eaten.'

A screeching of tires announced Jack's arrival. 'Is there any music for this shindig?' he said, as he pulled up in his silver convertible MX5, roof down even in freezing December drizzle to let his shaggy brown hair look artfully windblown. He flicked it back from his eyes and flashed a smile.

'It's not a shindig Jack, shush Lizzybet, shush.' She sighed, pushing Elizabeth's pushchair back and forth as she woke up and started howling. 'It's a market, a lot of which is for charity. You were supposed to be here an hour ago to take over the barbecue.'

'Yeah, sorry, you don't mind do you girls?'

'No, we're fine Jack, we're good at this. We don't mind.' Kerry fussed over the meat on the grill, turning sausages and burgers this way and that with a raised eyebrow.

'And I'll stay with you when you're on. You can't do this on your own,' Lynn added, pushing forward.

'Don't put yourself out Lynn, I'm alright here. I'll stay,' Kerry said, pouring more hot sauce in the empty bowl. 'Since Jack's too useless to hold it down.'

'Ladies, ladies, I can cope, don't put yourselves out, I'll be back in a minute, just need to ditch the car.' He flicked his blue and yellow striped Oxford scarf over his shoulder. 'Anyway, Polly, would you like some music?'

'What do you mean?'

'I ran into the boys from the Artful Badgers while I was in town, the Kings Arms cancelled on them tonight with no notice, so they're at a loose end. I said we could maybe get them a gig.'

'Did you now?' Polly tilted her head.

'I did.'

'And how much will they cost us?' She jiggled the pushchair with her foot.

'Nothing, I told them I'd put them up for the night at mine – Gav's an old mate – feed them and get them pissed and that they'd have a good night.' Jack wiggled his fingers over the side of the car, trying to get Elizabeth's attention. 'Hey Lizbet, how are you? How are you?'

'Really?'

'Yeah, I mean I said we'd have a whip-round at the end of the night, see what we could get for them, but they didn't mind. Said they had some new material to try out anyway.' Jack pulled his hand back into the car. Elizabeth wasn't going to stop screaming for anybody.

'Fine, sounds good, tell them yes, and ask them nicely if they can play some Christmas songs on top of the usual.'

'Awesome, thanks Pol, you're a brick.' Jack drove off, dialling his phone as he accelerated round the corner and scattering market goers towards pavements.

Any grudge he held against Polly for killing his wife stayed well hidden, as if it had never happened. It hadn't been her fault, Edwina had run at her and slipped. It was her own fault she'd been impaled on that pike. Polly never wanted to kill anybody.

'Bye Jack, see you in a bit,' Lynn called after him, despite his being already long gone. Kerry rolled her eyes and opened another pack of buns.

'Catch you later girls.' Polly pushed Elizabeth over to a free table.

She patted Fenrir on the head as she sat down and he nuzzled in closer, prompting Cronus to push in harder on the other side. She hadn't realised both of them had come back from scouring the square for dropped food. They'd been much soppier these last weeks since the pig incident. Polly could only surmise they were grateful for not having to be involved in ritual murder anymore.

In the last year, Cronus had re-established himself as head of

Lady Melissa's malamutes (but answering to Fenrir, so more of a middle-management dog) and had become fiercely attached to Polly and Elizabeth. He knew, of course he knew. That weird bond he had with Melissa would have told him where she was. Polly was under no illusion that this gnarled old wolf had any affection for her. After all, he had chased her through the woods and tried to kill her just a year ago. But when he dropped his chin on her lap and wooed softly for a head scratch it was difficult to remember that. He was just a saggy old vicious killing machine, but Polly loved him.

'I'm here, I'm here, don't worry.' Jack came running back through the square, perfect smile in place as he waved to every eligible female he passed. 'Ladies, consider yourselves relieved.' He doffed his hat to Kerry and Lynn and waved them off to take over at the grill.

'Are you sure you can cope all alone,' Lynn said, licking her fingers to open a tricky plastic bag.

'Yeah,' Kerry said, spreading a white bun with a generous helping of butter. 'I know you blokes all think it's man's work cooking outside, but…'

'It is. I am man, this is fire, I can cope. Also, it seems to have died off a bit. Go.' He tied on an apron with Kiss The Cook writ large across the chest, snatched Kerry's bun and slammed it onto a paper plate.

'Fine. Try not to burn the flipping van down, it ain't paid for yet,' Kerry said, shunting sausages across the grill before leaving him to it.

'Well, okay. But we'll be back,' Lynn said, leaving her hand just a little too long on his arm. 'Can I get you a drink to keep you company at least?'

'Thank you, that would be very kind. Get me something alcoholic, hot and fruity please.' He held Lynn's gaze and clasped his hand over hers.

'I think you had enough of that last night,' she whispered under her breath, not as quietly as she'd hoped.

Kerry snorted back a laugh and rolled her eyes again.

'Never enough,' he whispered back. 'Anyway ladies,' he continued, louder. 'I'd love a mulled something, surprise me, and take a load off.'

'Mull yourself, you pranny.' Kerry threw her apron at him and wandered off into the market.

'I'll get you a drink,' Lynn said, carefully removing the apron from his face and looking into his eyes a little too long before going to the mulled wine bar outside the Drop of Dew.

It was obvious to everybody what was going on between them, Polly had no idea why they were keeping it a secret, but she'd play along with it, if it made them happy.

'Hi Jack,' a girl who couldn't be more than twenty-one said, blowing on her hot chocolate and sidling up to the barbecue in a way that suggested she had been waiting a while for Lynn to get out of her way. 'I'm thinking of going into property, any chance we could meet up for a drink and a chat about it sometime?'

'Sure Anna,' Jack replied, grinning from ear to ear as he looked her up and down.

'How about tomorrow afternoon?' She twizzled a blond plait behind her ear and batted her eyelids.

'Day after would be better for me really,' Jack said, fiddling with his phone.

'But that's Christmas Eve, don't you want to spend it with your kids?' Anna said, eyes wide.

'Oh, yeah, yeah, of course. I'm sure I can move some things about for you.' Jack grinned and put his hand on her arm. 'Tomorrow it shall be. In the pub?'

'Drop of Dew?'

'It's not like there's another pub,' Jack said.

'No, of course not, sorry.' Anna giggled and slurped the bottom of her hot chocolate, getting froth over her top lip.

'Okay, it's a date. I'll see you about two o'clock then.' Jack leaned in and wiped the froth from her lip before she walked away. Polly tutted, Jack shrugged and got back to the barbecue.

The market was going well. It was a new initiative for Dourstone. In previous years there had been a Christmas fair in either the town hall or the community centre (and one year, notably, in the Drop of Dew but the less said about how that ended up the better). It had always been a bit of a damp squib: a few trestle tables of jumble, horribly home-made cards and decorations and some well-meaning but untalented amateur providing mulled refreshments. There was only so much glitter spattered cardboard and wine with all the alcohol burned off anybody could take and its only being for one evening was generally seen as a blessing.

Dourstone was not a town that liked to be kept indoors, which was probably why it had never taken to its miserable Christmas fairs. Given that Christmas came so hot on the heels of their more traditional Wish Weekend celebrations it was no surprise this staunchly pagan town hadn't really taken to the Christian tradition.

But Yuletide was Yuletide, and Polly had felt the best way to win over the locals would be to give them more excuses to party. She wasn't wrong. This market had run every Saturday since the Wish Weekend and, on Christmas Eve, the sheds would be turned out and used as both bonfire and shelters for a special Midnight Mass in the ruins of the church. Father Hearne had jumped at Polly's suggestion, and the whole town was looking forward to it. In the meantime they were milling about the square in festive jumpers, drinking mulled alcohol and buying a better quality of tat they didn't need than usual. Tat produced by professional tat-creators, rather than bored old ladies with too much time, glitter and PVA glue on their hands.

A pair of dirty black dogs appeared at the top of the square. Unsupervised, they stopped, sniffed at the air and looked about as if hunting for something, or someone, specific. They sauntered down the hill, snarling at a Jack Russell that dared yip at them. Its owner pulled it away quickly, tutting at the unruly dogs as they fought over a discarded sausage. Polly tried to see if she could spot an owner. Fenrir and Cronus tensed up, hackles raised.

Lynn kicked at one with her big furry boots as she returned from the bar.

'Horrid things, here's your drink.' She handed a huge glass of mulled cider over to Jack. 'I didn't think one of those tiny glasses would be enough for you, so I got you a pint.'

'Thanks,' Jack said, eyeing the unusually large fruit filled steaming drink. 'I'll try and get it down me before it goes cold.'

'I do like a large warm one inside me,' she said, after looking around to check nobody was listening.

'Oh, I know.' Jack laughed. 'What are you doing later?'

'You hopefully.' She looked round again, grabbed his groin under the counter, and busied herself with the falafels.

Polly shook her head.

Dogs materialised two by two from the top of the hill, until a whole pack spilled past the hairdressers. The assorted populace stopped to look, wondering where they had come from. The dogs paid no attention as they tried to empty the bins.

'I know those dogs,' Kerry said, coming over to Polly with a steaming mug of tea. 'They're that bloody gypsy's, where is he?'

'The one Clive keeps moaning about?' Polly asked.

'Yeah, I can't believe you haven't come across him, he's been here weeks.'

'Well, I've been busy, and the dogs and I don't really go anywhere other than home and the Manor,' Polly replied. It was true, Fenrir, Elizabeth and her walked from cottage to Manor and back every day for work, occasionally stopping in town for anything she needed, and that was it. She rarely needed to leave town and when she did get out on the moors it was never on a path, definitely not a road. So, while she had heard of this mysterious traveller everybody was complaining about (or enthusing over if they were of a certain romantic bent) she had yet to meet him.

'You need to get out more girl.' Kerry nudged her in the ribs.

'Probably, yeah.'

The dogs stopped their rampaging as one and pulled themselves together, forming up in neat lines to move down the street as if they owned the place. Cronus and Fenrir put their paws up on the granite wall, standing on back legs to watch. Then came a black horse, with a rider, black cloak flowing behind him.

'Good afternoon ladies and gentlemen, thank you for welcoming me into your town after such a long time. I've missed you.' The Traveller waved his arm like a visiting monarch as he passed through the square, dogs flanking him like an honour guard.

Whispers ran round: 'Who is that?' 'Do you know him?' 'I've never seen him before in my life,' 'No idea,' 'Is that your granddad?'

He looked familiar to Polly, but she couldn't place it. She had a niggling feeling she'd seen him somewhere before. Most of his face was obscured by a scarf and a deadman's hat, and what was exposed was mostly beard. But there was something familiar about the curve of that nose.

'Take what you want boys, it's all yours.' He laughed, finishing his circuit. Then raised his arm and said, 'I'll be back,' before spurring his horse to a gallop and disappearing in a clattering of hooves.

The dogs split apart and followed his instruction, the illusion of order now utterly broken. If they had seemed threatening before then they were twice as bad now. They began taking donuts and hot-dogs from children's sticky hands, pushing past any that tried to stop them. Then moved up a gear, sheer force of numbers allowing them to push all the bins over, letting rancid food and the tell-tale tied up bags of responsible dog owners spill into the street. Cronus and Fenrir gave a few half-hearted barks before realising they were outnumbered and using Polly, and Elizabeth's pushchair, as a human shield.

'Fat lot of good you two are,' she said, stroking their heads. This was new, she had never seen Cronus scared of anything, and while Fenrir was the worst kind of coward before the events of last Wish Weekend he had been a changed dog since.

The little sheds of the Christmas market proved no defence, dogs swarmed over the goods stripping them of anything edible. The shrieks of a woman borne to the ground under the efforts of two Dobermann cross German Shepherds could be heard above the clamour, while she tried to hold a reindeer made from driftwood, seaglass and boiled sweets away from them.

Over by the church gates, Clive and Susan – who were looking after the assorted kids of the Patrick Sumner Trust – had made themselves into a protective wall between dogs and children. Clive waved his prosthetic hand threateningly, safe in the knowledge that it wouldn't hurt if they bit it. The dogs pushed closer, snarling, dripping saliva on the cobbles of the slight rise that led to the moss-covered oak gates. Susan hissed, cat-like, fierce in her defiance, face up against that of Wotan. He snapped, just a warning bite, cold dog snot spattered her face, and she could smell his bin-eating breath, but she held her ground, unflinching.

Clive tried to attract the bigger dog's attention away from her, but couldn't break their delicate fence to swap positions without two poodle-coated mongrels getting past him to the kids. There was nothing he could do but watch helplessly as his wife snapped, hissed and spat at the enormous black dog. He kicked at the dogs on his side, but they just hopped out of range before rejoining the attack. He looked to the rest of the square. Similar scenes were repeated in every corner. There were too many dogs to fight off. Fenrir and Cronus had Polly covered, but their tails were down and their heads back in defensive posture. He hoped that that weird telepathic thing the Dewer pack had would bring a swarm of malamutes to the rescue, but with every second that passed it seemed increasingly unlikely. Hope faded, and just as his resolve began to weaken, a whistle sounded, piercingly bright, above the noise of rampaging dogs. The pack left, leaving the square devastated.

'What was that?' Polly asked Kerry, as Lynn stomped off to begin assessing the damage.

'Don't ask me,' Kerry replied.

'It was that fucking pikey, I told you.' Clive traipsed across with a small train of frightened children clinging to his legs. 'We need to...'

'We need to what honey?' Susan said. 'Complain to the police? Get a lynch mob together and run him out of town?'

'Well, we need to...' Clive began.

'He just paralysed all of us with a few badly-behaved dogs,' his wife said. 'The police didn't bother running a full investigation on the Manor last year, what makes you think they'll bother with this? It's not like anything's even broken.'

'Susan's right,' Jack agreed, putting his hand on her back. She didn't push it away, Polly noted. Susan didn't like people touching her uninvited.

'Thank you Jack.' Susan wiped snot from a toddler's face while trying to make it stop crying. 'We need to figure out what he wants, and who he is, and sort out a plan, yes,' she continued. 'But not right now. We'll get into it tomorrow. I don't think he's coming back.'

'What did you find out in there?' Polly asked Lynn, grabbing her arm as she came back from the Drop of Dew. 'What do we know?'

'Nothing,' she replied. 'Really, not a clue.'

This was bad, Lynn had been the authority on everything since Polly took over as de facto Lady of the Manor. If they had no information about this stranger how could they challenge this?

'Shit, what are we going to do?' Polly asked.

'Clean this mess up, get everything running again and wait for the band to turn up. What else?' Lynn said, looking at Jack's hand on Susan and frowning. He took it away and mouthed an apology.

'Just as I said,' Susan agreed. 'The show must go on, this is Dourstone.'

'Yes it is, and we won't be cowed by a few unruly dogs. Or some shit-stirring outsider.' Lynn gave Polly a very pointed look. 'We're going to have a party, and we're going to have a damn good time. Is your Katie up for baby-sitting Ker?'

'Yep, s'all good, she's taking that lot back with her in an hour or so.' Kerry pointed at the gaggle of kids still glued to Clive and Susan's legs.

'And she doesn't mind?' Jack asked, as his eldest broke off from Susan to grab his knee.

'Not at all, she's champing at the bit to get out of here. All them University visits have put ideas in her head. Dourstone's not happening enough, especially not all the "lame parties and shitty folk bands we put on all the time". She wants to stay in and stream Drag Race all night,' Kerry explained. 'And we're happy she won't be hanging about telling us how uncool we are, so everyone wins.'

'Excellent.' Jack peeled his toddler from his leg, gave it a kiss and sent it running back over to its friends.

'And she'd be happy to take Lizzybet for you Pol.' Kerry bent down and jiggled her fingers in the baby's face. 'I reckon you could do with the night off.'

'I don't know Ker, I was going to take off early and stay home tonight, I haven't finished Stranger Things yet, and Wendy's going to spoiler me any day now.'

'Oh yeah, the new series is excellent,' Clive said. 'You won't be disappointed.'

'New series?' Polly said. 'You mean there's more than one?'

'Jesus, you are behind.' Clive put his face in his hands. 'Maybe you should stay home?'

'No, and don't be a twat Clive. Polly can watch telly any time, we need a good night. Even more so after this. She's worked really hard on planning the Christmas market, and missed every single Saturday night party we've had. She can't miss this last hurrah. These dogs won't stop us, and she needs to start trusting other people with that kid.' Kerry poked Polly in the chest.

'Well whose fault is it that I've got separation issues?' Polly asked.

Katie herself appeared, dragging her brother out from a tipped over shed he'd been trying to salvage as much locally made gin and chocolate as he could from.

'Nobody but yours anymore. It's all in the past,' Dan shouted from the back of the van, where he'd been having a nap before all the commotion. 'Let Katie babysit her this one time, she's got a phone, you can ring her every twenty minutes if you like, she usually rings us more often than that anyway to ask where we've hidden the crisps' – Katie gave her father her best withering look – 'and if you're still worried at the end of the night, well you can pick her up from ours and take her home. Can't say fairer than that can we?'

'No, I suppose not, but…' Polly said.

'Reckon you should leave her to sleep at ours with the rest of them though, it's better than waking them all up in the middle of the night. They're having a sleepover, be nice to include her for once,' Kerry butted in.

'I don't want to leave her over night.'

'Well, you're welcome to change your mind later on. Leave her, take her, no skin off my nose. Offer's there,' Dan said.

'Fine, fine, thank you Katie,' Polly said, reluctantly pushing Elizabeth's chair to the teenager. 'It's not you, it's...'

'You, yeah I get it Pol,' Katie said, poking at the baby and making her giggle uncontrollably. 'We'll be great, little Lizbet loves me. And I don't ring you every twenty minutes Dad, Mum rings me more often than that. Now there's a woman with real trust issues.'

'So, Jack, have you got that stage sorted yet?' Lynn interjected.

'Yes, the Bens are delivering it in… oh,' Jack replied as he set the barbecue back up the right way.

'Oh what?' Polly said.

'Minus half an hour, they're late, sorry.'

'They're always late, what about the band?' Lynn started to work down her mental list, her organisational skills were second to none and Polly knew she needed her around, even if she did sometimes wish that sword thrust had ended her.

'I think that's them now.' Jack pointed to a battered old red Ford Transit, with the Royal Mail insignia still visible despite technically being removed, with a very familiar face waving frantically from behind the wheel.

'Granddad?' Polly shrieked as an elderly black man leaped down from the driver's seat with the energy of a man half his age.

'Polly!' He bounced over on the soles of his hi-top Nikes to envelope her in a bear hug. 'Great to see you.'

'Why are you here?'

'I was in the Beaver when the guys came in asking for a lift. Their van's broken down, their bass player's gone missing, I had nothing else on tonight and I already know their whole set.' He pulled off his knitted hat and scratched at the last of the grey fuzz on his nearly bald head before shoving it back on.

'So you didn't come to see me then?'

'Well, when they said Dourstone, it rang a bell...'

'Funny. I haven't seen you since...' Polly tailed off. She hadn't seen any of her family since Patrick's funeral. She'd been busy, they'd been busy. They weren't the closest of families anyway, not because they didn't like each other, but simply because they always had so much to do. Polly's mother had never had less than three jobs, her sisters and brother had carried on the tradition and Granddad always had some hustle or another he was working on. Usually at the bar of the Beaver Inn in Appledore.

'Yeah, I know. I'm sorry, but you know how it is.' He shrugged. 'You're okay right?'

'I'm fine, yes. And so's your great-granddaughter.' Polly grabbed Elizabeth's chair back from Katie and barked her grandfather's shin with it.

'Oh, there she is, such a pretty girl, she look like her granddad.' He knelt down and stuck his face up close to hers. She giggled as he stuck his tongue out and shook her tiny hand. 'Sorry I haven't been by more often, don't take it personal.' He straightened back up, wincing at the pain in his shin.

'I know you're busy, we're busy too and I'm sorry we never come to visit. It's not all your fault, but my god it's good to see you.' She hugged him again.

'You too, catch up with you in a bit, I've got to do this first.' He pulled away to indicate the band pulling musical equipment from the back of his van. A man with a silver mullet in a brown leather jacket was looking daggers at him as he hefted a keyboard case out.

'I'd wait until the stage turns up,' Polly explained. 'We've got a pretty relaxed way of working round here, you should fit right in.'

'I like that.' He fumbled in his pockets, pulled out a crumpled pack of cigarettes and lit the least bent one.

5

'Are you pleased with yourself?' Father Hearne shouted, crossing the threshold of the stone circle where The Traveller had set up camp, the once-lush grass now churned to mud by dogs, horses and relentless Devon rain.

'I am a bit yes, I think they might have got the message.' He sat at a smoky fire cooking a rabbit. 'But she's still here, and I don't understand how or where.' He stamped his boot in the mud, splashing filth over his camping chair, and causing the priest to take a step back.

'Who?'

'Don't be stupid, you know who. The Dewer woman. I can feel her. But it's been so long I couldn't pick her out of the crowd. Even with this one's help.' He thumped his chest.

'I saw her dead last year. Eaten by her own dogs. Just like I told you,' Father Hearne assured him, moving forward again.

'You know we don't die out like that Arthur,' The Traveller replied, twisting the sad little corpse of the rabbit on his fire. 'It's not that simple. She's somewhere, she's somewhere here. I thought she'd just leave after such a spectacular defeat, but she hasn't.'

'Polly did a real number on her. I don't know how she could come back from that, unless...' Father Hearne indicated a log next to The Traveller's seat, waiting to be invited before sitting down.

'Unless what Arthur? I don't have time to mess around. I want this place back. It's mine.' The Traveller waved the priest into sitting down as he stuck a knife into the roasting rabbit to check the colour of its juices. He looked at the sticky meaty fluid dribbling down the length of the blade before licking it clean from root to tip.

'No, it's not that. Sorry. Anyway, you've got all the time in the world. You've waited long enough, what's a little longer? I'll find her – if she's here.' The priest tapped his foot, spattering his shining black brogues with lumps of red mud. 'You've made your point, now maybe take a break. That was a stupid move, panicking everybody like that. Promise me you won't do anything else just yet.'

'I'm promising nothing Arthur, rabbit?' He lifted the now thoroughly cooked rabbit from the fire and slid it from the spit, leaving a residue of gore along its length.

'No, thank you, but no.' The vicar shook his head with a look of distaste.

'Please yourself,' The Traveller said, opening his mouth wide and biting the rabbit's head off in one.

Later that same night the band were in full swing, Polly's granddad was swaying along with the rhythms he plucked from his ancient Fender Jazz Bass, and most of the town were dancing along (it was the only way to keep warm, the braziers around the square didn't throw off as much heat as the organisers had hoped).

It hadn't taken much effort to right the market sheds and clear up the mess. Most of the damage had been superficial and, with a bit of financial incentive from the Patrick Sumner Trust, the traders had been persuaded to stay on. The elusive Bens turned up at the last minute and made good on their promise of a stage, the band set up and the town relaxed. The good vibes and good times were erasing the memory of The Traveller's disruption. People were happy, drink was flowing and Dourstone felt like its old self.

'Thank you, thank you,' the singer said, in her long black cape and tricorn hat as the chorus of Adam and the Ants 'Stand and Deliver' finally quoi-diddly-quoi-quoied to a standstill. 'The forecast says the weather's set fair all night long, so if you guys are down for it, let's keep this going. Merry Christmas everyone.'

Dan gave a little wheelspin in his chair and whooped excitedly. Kerry skipped away in fear of her feet. Dan was an enthusiastic dancer, but still not quite used to the chair. There had been a few broken toe incidents over the last year but at least dancing in the freezing winter night Kerry didn't mind wearing steel toecaps as much.

Jack was spinning Lynn around by one of the braziers as a queue of single (and a few not-so-single) women looked on, tapping their feet. Clive and Susan were sitting at opposite sides of the square nursing drinks and looking daggers at anybody that came near while

Wendy was prowling the outskirts of the dancers, looking for someone. Polly would bet money on her not knowing which someone she was looking for just yet, but that whoever it was would know very quickly what she was after.

So are you ready to tell me who that was earlier? She said in her head. *Or are you still sulking?*

I think you know what's happened, Mel's voice came loud and clear.

I really don't, please elucidate. Polly fiddled with her coffin nail ring.

I've been telling you ever since you came up with your dumb idea to stop the sacrifices. We did them for a reason, we needed to keep the dogs.

We've still got the dogs. They haven't gone anywhere.

Stupid girl, the malamute pack is not the dogs. Not the ones we need, not the ones I made the deal with. You've seen the pack, they're stupid again. They're just dogs. Normal, no spirit anymore. Nothing inside.

But…

But nothing, you saw those other dogs this afternoon – his pack. Did they remind you of anything?

Polly had to admit, they had taken her back to a year ago, when she had been chased by a pack of dogs, all of one mind, with glowing blue eyes: efficient, ruthless and clever. Those same malamutes she had been taking care of this last year. The same malamutes that have spent the last few weeks bumping into each other with no more grace and co-ordination than any other group of dogs. Howling for food they have already been given, digging up grass they wanted to sit on and howling again that it is no longer there.

But…

I told you he'd be back, and I told you he'd get them. I didn't know he'd be so quick. But I did tell you. He'll want to finish what he started.

I'm sure we can resolve this peacefully. We're being paranoid, that was just a random traveller with some unruly dogs and a grudge against some farmer: probably Clive's dad. It'll blow over Mel.

It won't.

Well, I'm in control now, so we'll see who's wrong.

Silence reigned in Polly's head, and she got back to watching the band, who were battering their way through Shakin' Stevens' 'Merry Christmas Everyone.' Jack had moved on from Lynn and was chatting to a group of wine-drinking mums on the wall.

What do you think all those women see in that Jack? Melissa said. *Is it just the sexy widower thing? Or do you think he's got a massive wang hiding down there?*

I wouldn't know.

Only because you're still too much of a prude to follow up on all those passes he makes at you. Let me take control for a night. It's been too long. We have needs. Let us attend to them.

I'm not shagging Jack. I have standards.

I'm not asking you to, I'm asking you to let me – you don't even have to watch.

I'm not letting you have control, and if you don't drop the subject I'll take it off. Leave you locked in there all on your own.

Fine, at least give me control of your right hand when we go to bed tonight, you do it all wrong.

I'm not having this conversation Melissa. We're done.

Polly took the coffin-nail ring off, zipping it securely in a jacket pocket.

'Fancy a dance?' Wendy wrapped herself over Polly's shoulders. Her hair hung over Polly's face, smelling of roses and cider. Polly could feel Mel's desire rising. Even without the ring she found ways of letting her know what she wanted.

'Nobody out then?' Polly replied. Wendy always forgot her animosity after a few drinks. Polly liked her more then, not enough to do what Mel wanted, but still.

'Not out-out no, but I reckon that one might be a possible.' She pointed at a twenty-something girl with blue hair dancing alone in a long black coat and fending off all male advances. 'She might be out of my league though. You owe me a wife, so you can help me make her jealous. Come on.'

'Okay.' Polly's never-ending guilt meant she was unable to refuse Jack, Wendy or Dan anything they asked. She had widowed two of them and left the other in a wheelchair. She'd also left Lynn for dead, but she had very different regrets over that.

She let herself be taken by the hand to the middle of the square. Wendy spun her, held her close and led her in complicated moves she didn't even know she could do. The nature of the dance brought a good deal of inappropriate touching, but Polly didn't think she could complain. She wasn't sure she wanted to, although that might have been the Melissa inside, desperate for any kind of thrill. Polly had only had one experience with a woman, and that had been under the influence of one of Lady Melissa's herbal drinks. She was pretty sure she was straight.

'Can you slut-drop?' Wendy asked, spinning Polly out to arm's length and letting her go.

'I can try, would it help?' Polly replied, laughing.

'Couldn't hurt, quick, she's looking over.'

Polly dropped to the ground, angling all her best features at the girl in the coat before snapping back up and draping herself over Wendy.

'Any good?'

'A little too good, we don't want her falling for you,' Wendy hissed in her ear.

'Sorry, I'll try and...' Polly's words were cut off as the heavens opened. Snow the like of which they had never seen fell from the sky, quickly piling round them in drifts. The couple of inches the Wish Weekend always brought felt welcome: Winter reminding you that it can bite, but in a gentle non skin-piercing way, like a puppy testing its limits. This felt more like the puppy had grown into an untrained feral beast. Not picturesque Christmas card snow, but a not-so-gentle reminder of Winter's deadly teeth.

'Thank you all for the kind welcome,' a voice boomed from the sky. 'If you do not wish to be part of my new Dourstone then once my storm ends you will have an hour of calm in which to leave. I suggest you take it.'

The wind picked up and snow drifts buried the square. Parents pulled children from ice sheets and carried them away. The band played on, until there was a tinkling of broken glass from amplifier valves and they shared a look of terror before running for their cases. They knew what such quick temperature changes could do to expensive instruments and weren't prepared to risk it for a gig that wasn't even paying.

People ran. A lot of them ran into the Drop of Dew.

6

'That was an over-reaction,' Father Hearne said, lowering himself carefully down thick walls of ice that surrounded The Traveller's camp. The spitting fire underneath the ragged black canopy barely made an impact on the ice, merely giving its sheer faces a more uniform finish.

'It wasn't a reaction at all, just seemed like the right way to start. Weed out the weak, scare off the stupid. Take back my town.' He carried on muttering to the fire as he scattered herbs and powders into the flames.

'But what if...'

'It's fine, the roads will be clear, I shall not hamper anybody leaving.' With a flourish of his wrist, some final piece of sorcery was complete and the last flakes of the blizzard stopped, leaving a waist-high coat of pristine white over the parish of Dourstone.

'What are you going to do?' Father Hearne looked concerned. 'I've watched this place for you for so long. I have grown fond of it, I like its people. It wasn't supposed to be this way, I thought you'd...'

'You thought I'd what?' The Traveller sneered. 'Be all fluffy and nice and kind? Like the Dewer woman?' His hands moved in secret combinations and, with a muttered word, steps appeared in the sheer walls while alleys opened up between caravan and camp.

'She was hardly fluffy and nice and kind. She killed hundreds of them, she killed her own lovers, she...'

The Traveller grabbed the priest's wagging arm. 'I know all that, I know it better than anyone. But she did it for their own good. I am going to finish what I started. Have you not been listening to me at all?'

'You said you loved the place.' Father Hearne pulled himself free of The Traveller's iron grip.

'I say a lot of things, and it's true, I do love the place.' He shook his cloak out before sitting back down.

'Okay, so...'

'Just not the people.' The Traveller stretched his legs out in front of the fire and began to fill his pipe.

'Man, I can't believe they took my van.' Polly's granddad downed his whisky.

'At least they left your bass,' Polly said, swirling the last dregs of her drink about.

'Yes, and now I have to carry it round all night. I'd rather it'd been in the van.' He waved his glass meaningfully at Polly, who tried to get Pete the barman's attention.

Polly's granddad had run to the pub with Polly and the rest of the Sumner Trust when the storm broke. In the panic he had not communicated this to the band, who threw all their gear in the back of his van and drove off. He was regretting leaving his keys with the drummer.

'Don't worry, you can stay with me until the storm passes,' Polly said, pointing to glasses and bottles in the universal sign language of drink ordering.

It's not passing, that niggling voice in the back of her head.

'Thanks, how far is it to that mansion of yours?' He took another whisky from his granddaughter.

'It's less than a mile, but...' Polly counted out change into the barman's hands and thanked him.

'But what?'

'But I don't live there, I'm still in the cottage. You can stay at the Manor if you want, but I thought you'd like it at mine. It's cosy, easier to keep warm. It's...'

'Impossible to get to in this, even on foot.' Clive stamped snow from his boots as he, Jack and Susan came in. They had ventured out as the weather calmed to try and work out how bad it was.

'Yeah,' Susan agreed. 'We got back to ours okay, but when we tried to head further up the hill towards your place it started again, the ground turned to ice and we couldn't do it.'

'Laid off once we turned round and headed for mine though,' Jack said. 'Weird.'

'Yeah, weird.' Susan grabbed Polly's drink from the bar.

'Thanks,' she added.

'Anyway, I don't fancy your chances getting up that slope without one of you falling over,' Clive said. 'I'll get you another drink Pol, sorry.' He gave Susan a hard stare.

'So not much good for a pensioner carrying a priceless 1959 Fender Jazz Bass that used to belong to none other than John Paul Jones then?' Polly's granddad said, stroking his instrument case.

'Not a good idea at all,' Clive agreed, waving to get Pete the barman's attention. 'I think we should stay here until we get a handle on the situation. Pete! How do you feel about an all-nighter?'

'Are you paying cash? The card machine's down again,' Pete the barman shouted back, hands full of glasses and frantically pulling pumps.

'Yes.'

'Well then, I will be needing to hear a lot of "and one for yourself barman" to make sure I don't suddenly have to close.'

'And one for yourself barman,' Clive said, handing over two twenties as Pete passed him a pint of his usual.

'That'll do nicely. Shall I keep the change?'

Clive nodded with gritted teeth.

'Hi, I'm Neville, we didn't get introduced earlier, you want to buy a bass?' Polly's Granddad said to Clive as he sat back down.

'Not really.' Clive grinned, waving his prosthetic hand by way of explanation.

'Fine, I'll find someone else, previously used by Led Zeppelin, worth a fortune, I'll take...'

'Stop it Granddad.' Polly shut him down. 'You're not going to swindle these people. They're my friends.'

'But it...'

'Came from Jimmy the fake-maker in Bideford. You told me all about it when he built it for you five years ago. Stop hustling for a minute, we've got a real problem here.' She pushed the instrument aside.

He grudgingly gave in and went back to his drink.

You do. I told you it was him. Melissa would not be ignored.

Okay, you were right. I thought he was like you, you always said he was like you. Polly found it hard to form words in her head, rather than out loud, but here was not the place to be speaking to unseen voices.

No, I said he was much worse. That you wouldn't like him.

So all this, you could do all this? Polly made a firm picture of the whirling snows that had forced them to take shelter.

I could do a lot of things if I wanted to. I don't. I told you I was the nice one.

'So what we doing now?' Dan asked. 'Leaving town?'

'We ain't going nowhere Daniel,' Kerry confirmed. 'This is Dourstone, we are Dourstone. I don't care what he is, he's a fucking blowin and we're fighting back. Right?'

There was a conspicuous silence.

'I said, right?'

'Well, okay, go on then,' Susan drawled, feet up on a table. 'Let's get out there and fuck him up.'

'That's a bit more like it, thanks Susan,' Kerry said.

'Not right now though,' Jack said. 'It'll all look better in the morning Kerry.' He waved her objections down. 'We'll wait 'til the sun comes up. I'm not going out in that, but I'm not running either. This is my home.'

'Okay, Jack. Lock-in it is.' Susan nodded, a grin spreading across her face.

Clive shot a look from his wife to his friend, then wiped his forehead. 'All in favour of Jack's idea?' he said.

Everyone raised their arms, nodding and grunting in agreement.

'I'm going now. I need to get my baby. I can't sit here and do nothing,' Polly said, banging her empty glass down. 'It's not far to yours Kerry, I'll pick her up and take her home, where she'll be safe.'

'Don't be stupid, you're not getting through that ice in the dark,' Dan said. 'Stay here, Jack's right, she'll be fine 'til the morning.'

'I know, but I don't care, I can't leave her. I'm going.' Polly shoved the door open and was greeted with a blast of freezing wind. She stepped out and slid on the pavement, landing painfully on her bum.

'You won't make it,' Jack said, pulling her up. 'It's too dangerous. There's something behind this weather, believe me, every turn I made earlier brought me back here. It'll be the same for you.'

'But he wanted us to leave, he said it would be safe.' Polly pulled herself up Jack's arm.

'I'm not sure he's entirely trustworthy. And you're not trying to leave town any more than we were.' He pulled her all the way back to her feet.

'I need to try, I can't do nothing.' Polly began to cry into Jack's shoulder.

'You have to,' he said. 'You're no good to her dead in a ditch.'

7

'It doesn't look that bad,' Polly said, opening the pub door and surveying the square the next morning. 'Maybe that magical snow was just snow.' The drifts on the pavements didn't even reach above her ankle boots. Looking over the icy road to the thick crust of snow on top of the church gates she could almost fool herself it had all been a dream. Dourstone looked like a Christmas card, gleaming white and picture perfect.

Yeah, and that voice was just the wind, you're perfectly safe. Melissa's voice might well have been entirely in her head, but it told the truth about the events of the night before being anything but.

'Brilliant! Can one of you give me a lift back to Appledore?' Neville said.

'Sure Granddad, I left the Land Rover at the Manor, come back with us, I'll drive you home,' Polly said. She wanted to pick up Elizabeth, go back to the cottage, light the fire and pretend nothing had happened over a Netflix Christmas special. But she knew that wasn't really an option.

'Okay then, shall we go?' Wendy said. 'The Manor's closer than your place Kerry, can you drive Alexander over when you get back?'

'Fuck home. Katie can hold the fort a bit longer, and I don't think I can deal with her just yet. We're coming with you,' Kerry replied.

'Yeah, she threatened to do Sunday lunch when we said we were staying out all night, and I know what that means if we're back too quick,' Dan added. 'She's already sent a million messages asking where the pans are, where the peeler is, what a swede looks like.'

'Okay, makes sense. I'll pick up Alexander and Lizbet when I take Granddad home,' Polly said, clapping a hand on Wendy's shoulder.

They set out into the crisp cold morning, boots crunching on unbroken snow and wheels sliding on ice. While Dan was in complete control of his chair on the gentle slopes of the town, he did keep trying to do tricks. It felt like a nice morning, a good day. The winter sun shone down on pure white ground that reflected what little heat it had straight back into the atmosphere at the speed of light.

'Is it always this quiet?' Polly's granddad said. 'I like it.'

'It's Sunday morning, of course it's quiet,' Lynn snapped, her words caught in frozen water droplets that fell from her mouth.

'Yeah, but...' Wendy pointed at the usually car-lined streets, unencumbered by poorly parked vehicles. 'I think everyone else ran.'

'Oh,' Polly said. 'You're sure Katie's still at home? Looking after the kids I mean? You don't think she's run away as well?'

'Unless that thing announced everyone had to leave on Tik-Tok and she learned how to drive while we were out, I think we're fine,' Kerry said. 'Also I sent her a lot of texts last night and she hadn't even noticed it was snowing.'

PING – Dan's phone made its notification sound and he span back towards them in a figure of eight past the fish and chip shop. 'Also, she wants to know if there are any more Coco Pops. She's definitely home.'

'Was she okay with the babies? Does she know what to do? Is she up? Did I leave her enough feed?' Polly asked.

'Don't sweat it Pol,' Wendy intervened. 'I've left Alexander with Katie loads of times, even before she got sensible. She knows what she's doing, more than I do most of the time.'

'That isn't as comforting as you think it is Wend.' Susan slid between Polly and Wendy.

They walked on in silence.

'Helloooo,' Lynn called down the length of the Manor's kitchens. 'Anybody here?'

They made it back without incident (unless you count Wendy's undignified slide through the courtyard onto her backside) but had returned to an empty house. None of the residents or employees of the Patrick Sumner Trust could be found. It may have been an ungodly hour on a Sunday morning, but there were never fewer than four people hanging around the big kitchen, drinking coffee and bitching about something. The Manor was fast becoming its own little community aside from the town. But not today. A lot of the residents were outsiders, not from Dourstone, so they didn't come to every single little event in town like the locals. Having not lived there for a whole year, a lot of them didn't even feel welcome, despite Susan, Jack, Polly and Wendy explaining how they weren't local either, and yet the town still took them in. It was a good place to be an outsider.

'Must have all gone out to play in the snow,' Polly said. 'Tenner says you'll find them up in the big field, by the cairn, sledging.'

You tell yourself whatever you need to hear, Melissa said. *They've run, they know what's good for them.*

'No. No they haven't,' Polly said.

'You just said they had!' Clive laughed. 'Make your mind up.'

'Sorry, no, unrelated. They are, they have, they're fine.'

'They're fucking scared, same as the rest of us,' Susan said as she stoked the rayburn back into life. 'Same as the rest of the town, they've gone.'

'Maybe they're gone? Maybe they're sledging? We'll find out sooner or later, right now I need a cuppa.' Jack stretched his legs out under the kitchen table. 'Get on with it.'

'Get on with it yourself, you lazy shit,' Susan said, clipping him over the back of his head and laughing.

'Ah, come on, you do it so much better than me.' He looked up from under his fringe, big puppy eyes doing their thing.

'I'll do it,' Lynn said, pushing past Susan and filling the kettle. 'Else we'll be here all day.'

'Right Granddad, let's go.' Polly grabbed a set of keys from the rack by the door.

'Can I not get a cuppa tea first?' He looked longingly at Lynn as she put the old kettle on the rayburn. 'I'm an old man, I need certain things.'

'I need to go and get my daughter, I can't sit around here waiting for Dan to get out of having to cook his own lunch.' She jingled her keys and shoved Neville out of the door. 'You can have a cuppa at Kerry's once I know Lizbet's safe.'

'It'll be quicker,' Jack muttered under his breath. 'They've got a proper kettle there.'

'You worry too much girl.' Neville grinned.

'And you never worry enough, remember how I got this scar?'

She pointed at a long-healed burn on her forearm.

'Why yes, you were fighting the fire-breathing dragon that had flown over from Wales. That was a good day, you saved my life with that crossbow,' he said.

'No, not that day, and it was a nerf gun,' Polly corrected him. 'I got this when you were too busy trying to figure out how to get free Sky Sports on your telly to notice me dicking about with your ancient three bar heater.'

'Ah, you were okay, never in any serious danger.'

'No, never.' Polly shook her head. 'Come on.'

'Nice to meet you all, and I hope to see you again.' Neville waved as they left the kitchen and stamped across the frozen cobbles of the courtyard.

'Are you staying at Mum's still?' Polly asked as he clambered up the passenger side of Lady Melissa's ancient rusting red Land Rover, parked by the main gates in what would have been – in any other manor house – a public car park. Polly had grown attached to it and sold off her and Patrick's shiny, but ineffective, 4x4. The Land Rover held the road better, as long as it felt like working, and more importantly cost a lot less in parts when it did go wrong, as Chris at the garage could bodge it back together with spit and bailer twine.

'No, got my own place back again.' Polly's granddad had a difficult relationship with his landlady. Usually he could live there rent-free for certain favours, but every now and then her jealous streak surfaced if he'd been out and about with other women and he'd have to find a new place to live. It never lasted longer than a month and Polly couldn't understand why he didn't just commit to her. They'd been together for as long as Polly could remember.

'Good, how is Auntie anyway?' She'd had the nickname for so long nobody could remember her real name. She was an only child.

'Ah, she's fine, same old Auntie, wouldn't be without her.' He grinned, doing up his seatbelt.

'Well, let's get you back to her before she kicks you out again yeah?' They turned out of the courtyard and down the driveway, the Land Rover kicking snow, mud and ice in a filthy spray behind it.

After only a couple of turns on the twisting road they slid over the old bridge and screeched to a stop. Where the roundabout onto the bypass should have been was a wall, an impossibly high barrier of snow and ice where there should have been three bollards and a banner advertising the special Midnight Mass. Not even Lady Melissa's Land Rover was going to get over the top of that.

'Shit, we're not getting back this way,' Polly said. She did a three point turn and they sped into town, skidding round corners and spitting gravel at the windows of the Drop of Dew. Once they had passed the square the snow was a blank canvas to tear apart under thick black tyres.

'Look, there's the cottage,' Polly said as they passed it, wishing she had kept Elizabeth with her last night. She was an easy baby to entertain on a night out, happy enough to sleep in her ear defenders, oblivious to noise, crowds and weather. Polly shouldn't have let her out of her sight. What if she couldn't get to Dan and Kerry's?

They only got so far up the hill before the road vanished into deep snow and all four wheels lost traction. The stone circle came into view, glimmering in morning sunlight, a point of hope on a horizon that slipped away as the car slid back down the hill. Nothing could grip those steep frozen slopes.

'Shit,' Neville said. 'You got room for me in there?' He pointed at the cottage as they coasted past in reverse.

'I have, but we're not beaten yet.' Despair turned to determination as she spun the car round on the ice and gunned the engine.

The Land Rover tore off downhill, heading for the western road out.

'Okay, no need to panic anybody, but we're...'

'Cut off?' Wendy said, doing exactly that to Polly as she and Neville came into the great hall of Dourstone Manor. The western road had proven no better, nor the east. She had always joked that you could check out of Dourstone any time you liked, but you could never leave. It suddenly seemed a lot less funny.

'Yes, how did you know?' Polly asked.

Wendy just shrugged and beckoned her into the drawing room where a big plasma screen TV was broadcasting the local news. Even the BBC couldn't cross the frozen walls around the town and were reporting from outside in the usual brown Dartmoor mud.

'There's no way we can get through, look at that! I'm so sorry Pol, I should never have talked you into it,' Kerry said. 'What are we going to do?'

'Anything and everything we can. We can't give in, they're our children.' Polly started rummaging through cupboards. Not that she would find anything to help, but she had to be doing something.

'They're okay, and there's nothing we can do until there's at least a bit of a thaw,' Clive said. 'Have a cup of tea, get some food inside you. You can't think straight on an empty stomach.'

'Alright, thank you my man,' Neville said, taking a mug from Clive and breathing in the smell of not-quite-burned toast floating from the kitchen.

'But Elizabeth. I can't leave her, not again,' Polly stammered.

'She's with Katie, she'll be right and we'll get back through soon. It's only snow Polly, it melts.' Dan wheeled in from the kitchen with two full toast racks, a coffee pot and a selection of jams worthy of a hotel breakfast buffet. Polly's granddad pounced on it.

'It's alright for you two, yours are big enough to look after themselves, but my Lizzybet's only a baby, she needs her mum.' Polly carried on hunting through drawers.

'Look. Isn't that Katie?' Jack grabbed Polly's wrist and pointed at the TV.

'It is.' Kerry's jaw dropped. She turned up the volume. Her daughter was being interviewed on the local news, baby Elizabeth in her arms.

They were filming on the other side of the bridge Polly had skidded to a halt by, where the town boundary proper was. Polly remembered walking the line of it (though they had gone through the river 500 yards further up where there no longer was a bridge) with Patrick – beating the bounds. It felt like a lifetime ago, not a mere eighteen months. A sheer drift of snow and ice went higher than the cameras could, hiding the bridge from view, and Katie stood in front, explaining to the grinning presenter that her parents, and the parents of all the children she was babysitting, were on the other side.

What she didn't tell the reporter, or the other tutting families there, was that she hadn't realised anything was wrong until her phone started pinging with messages that her estate was on the telly. She'd then very quickly done her face, dressed up nice and headed out, borrowed baby in arms, to get on camera.

The camera panned round to show the estate where Dan and Kerry lived. Polly had offered them rooms in the Manor, along with the rest of the Trust, but, despite there being a lot more space there,

Dan and Kerry were staying put in their rented shoe-box. They didn't want charity, and whatever the shortcomings of the house, it was their home and filled with the attendant memories. Nobody was allowed to mention it to Katie or her brother Alfie, as they had no such sentimentality and would much rather have the big suite in the massive house.

Since Katie and Alfie hadn't wanted to stay out anyway they had happily accepted a bribe to look after all the Sumner Trust kids. The other residents of the estate were all too visible in the wide shot, and the story became about how they were all going to make sure these kids were okay until they could be reunited with their parents. Polly could hear the undertone in the commentators' voices – they should not have left their kids alone. They should not have stayed out all night. They were bad parents.

But they had not seen Jack having to force Polly to stay in the pub. They hadn't been there when that weather kicked in, when that voice came from nowhere. Some of the faces on screen had been, and ran for safety the same as everyone else. It's just their safety had been on the other side of that massive wall of ice. Polly and the Trust members had a responsibility to the whole town. According to Melissa this was all their fault, so they'd had to stay in town and plan their next move. Had she known she'd be trapped on the wrong side of this wall, away from Elizabeth, she would gladly have ignored Jack to crawl across treacherous ice from pub to estate.

'I'm getting out.' Polly strode to the front door.

'How?' her granddad interrupted through a mouthful of jam-smeared toast. 'You tried every way out, there's no way through – if that Land Rover couldn't do it nothing can.'

'Who says I'm going through?' Polly grinned.

'What other way is there?' Jack asked, supremely relaxed now he knew his children were happy, being taken care of by somebody else, and there was no way he could possibly help.

'Over.' Polly ran to the front door and slid into the courtyard, giving a well practised whistle.

Fenrir and Cronus led the swarm of dogs that came running to meet her.

8

It's a death-trap, I'm not even sure it's ever been used. Melissa was worried. After half an hour of ransacking the furthest reaches of the huge barn the malamutes called home, Polly had uncovered what she was looking for and dragged it out to the yard.

'Oh come off it,' Polly shouted, not caring if anybody heard her talking to herself while she readied the ancient dusty sled. 'You must have.'

Okay, yes. I did, a few times, but it wasn't at all safe out there, on the moor. There's too many buried rocks, you can't see them coming. And what makes you think you can get over the top where even a BBC reporter can't? They have helicopters.

'Not for the Spotlight team they don't. And if it doesn't work, then at least I'll have tried.' Polly finished untangling reins and ropes as the malamutes circled. Most of them couldn't keep their excitement in at finally being able to do what they were bred for and were giving little woos and huffs at regular intervals. They hustled against each other, worried they might not be placed on the team, convinced that rubbing right up against the ancient wood of the thing gave automatic inclusion.

You don't have to. Everyone's okay on the other side. She's with some mums, some kids that are friends of hers, well-fed, warm. There's a whole community over that side of the river to look after her, a lot better than a lot of the stuck up bastards over this side. This isn't like last time you were parted, not like when I stole her away.

'I never said it was. But I can't do nothing. I've already made that mistake once.'

It wasn't a mistake. Jack was right, you wouldn't have made it there and back again. I know that spell, you might have got out, but not back in. And you'd have killed yourself – and the child – trying to. It's a stronger charm this morning, and it works both ways. So

47

don't blame me when they find you dead in the melted snow. And it will melt, that's what snow does. Wait it out.

'Oh you'll be fine without me, you can have Lizbet all to yourself, like you wanted in the first place,' Polly spat.

I needed my old body for that to work, if you remember.

'Well I'm sure you can just grab another one from somewhere.'

I don't do that.

'And yet here you are, in my head.'

You knew what you were doing when you took that ring.

'Hardly. Anyway, I'm not going to die, I do know what I'm doing now, and even if not, the dogs will.'

They're not the same dogs they were. You have lost the protection of the pack. You now just have a lot of dogs.

'They're still Alaskan malamutes, they were born for this, look at their little faces!' Polly whooped and started harnessing them on. 'Sorry boy,' she said to Fenrir as he pushed in front. 'You can't come, you're not built for this.' She pointed to his paws, all clogged up with bobbles of snow in direct contrast to the snow dogs who were sleek, warm and clean.

'You can't do this alone,' Wendy said, walking across the cobbles with an armful of blankets. 'I'm coming, no arguments.'

'You?'

'Yes me, I'm more use in a crisis than any of those lot. Besides, my Alexander's not that much older than Lizbet.' She threw her bundles into the sled and stepped up.

'Fine,' Polly agreed, tying Cronus in place at the front. He may have been old and grizzled, but he knew how to lead.

Good choice, Melissa said. *My Cronus never steered me wrong, he's a good boy. He'll get you there if there's a there to get to.*

'You remember he ate you right?' Polly laughed.

'What did you say?' Wendy asked.

'Oh nothing, just talking to the dogs, come on that's the last one on. Let's go.' She climbed into the sled and swished the reins. The dogs pulled them out of the yard with a howl and a rush.

'It's a bit much isn't it?' Wendy said, waving around at ornate carvings of hound heads, green men and winter trees that covered the big sled. It had two bench seats at the front, and a large storage space at the back, though it didn't look like it would ever have a sack of toys stored there, unless they had been stolen. 'I feel like the ice queen of Narnia, where on earth did you find it?'

'Back of the barn,' Polly explained. 'There's loads of weird old stuff stashed around the Manor. The Dewers were prepared for anything.'

'I bet.' Wendy nodded, staring out over the white tundra. 'You know most of those dogs aren't pulling us right?'

'Yeah, there weren't enough harnesses for the whole pack but nobody wants to be left out.' Polly waved at a huddle of dogs running alongside with their tongues hanging out. 'I don't think I've ever seen them this happy.'

That's because you never really looked at them making a kill.

'I saw it a lot closer than I ever wanted to thanks,' Polly muttered, the wind whipping loud enough to hide her voice from Wendy.

Neither of them saw the black and white collie-ish mongrel watching from behind the tree. Nobody saw it run off over the moor. The malamutes were all too excited to be out running to remember their duties as guard dogs and Fenrir had gone back inside to sulk.

'Again!' Polly cried, cracking the reins. The dogs pulled, but even they foundered on the powdery ground. The sledge went awry, collapsed on one side, half buried in snow. The wind battered at them, colder, faster and stronger up here at the top of the drift. The snow kept building up, threatening to engulf the sled. It no longer fell from the sky, but the wind ensured it hit as hard as any blizzard, blowing from the Dourstone side of the wall to the front, where it piled higher, rather than further.

'They can't do it Polly. We're not going to make it.' Wendy gently took the reins from Polly's hands, her own sheathed in thick black leather gauntlets that peeped out of Lady Melissa's old fur coat. She had borrowed it from the store room in the Manor's hall for warmth and it matched the dogs' fur closely enough to make her worry about Melissa's reuse, restore, recycle mantra. 'They're snow dogs, and even they didn't want to come up here. They know what they can get through and what they can't. That's why they're so stubborn remember? Trust them, we have to turn round.' She brushed snow from her knees, and pulled on the reins to stop the dogs. They didn't need much encouragement.

'I'm not giving up. You stay here, keep your phone on. I'll ring you from the other side.' Polly jumped down. 'Cronus, to me.' The dog slunk obediently to her side with a whimper and she unharnessed him.

'Listen to the dog Polly. Come back, we can find another way.' Wendy almost stepped out of the sled, before thinking better of it and pulling her PVC go-go-booted leg back in. She could see Polly starting to sink through the snow that the dogs so easily danced across.

They had been going up and down the slope at the bridge for half an hour now, each attempt more futile than the last. The snow was too steep and powdery. The nearer they got to the top the more they sank. The dogs were thoroughly spooked and burrowed themselves into the ground, preparing to make camp. Wendy was not so defeated and stood up in the sled to shove away the worst of the snow that threatened to bury it. She looked across at the hollow the dogs had dug, filled with warm furry bodies sharing their heat. It might prove a useful last resort.

'No.' Polly crawled across the snow, spreading her weight out as far as possible. 'It'll be okay, as long as I keep my whole body flat I don't sink. I can stay above. Don't worry, I'm not going to drown. There will be a way. We'll find it, Cronus is unstoppable.'

'I don't care about you dying.' Wendy shoved the last of the snow off the side, sat back on the front bench, and wrapped herself in another blanket. 'I just don't want a fucking orphan hanging about the place looking for a new mum. It's Lizbet I'm worried about. And you proved how unstoppable Cronus isn't last year, when you and Fenrir quite literally stopped him.'

Polly didn't say a word, just carried pulling her belly across snow, Cronus padding along next to her. When the ground caved in, as she always knew it would, she found herself under the white, inside the drift. Blinded. It was all enveloping, she lost all sense of up and down and began to panic. But then the dog dug down and found her. He tried to pull her out, but she pushed him back, refusing his help. He might not believe in them, but she did. They could make it, she just had to persuade him to help, show him it was possible. Her determination paid off and he let go, but would not leave her.

She clawed with her mittens at the snow, pulling herself towards the other side. To the estate, where the BBC reporters were. Where Lizbet was. The reassuring weight of the malamute grounded her, centred her and showed her which direction to go. Forwards, onwards, clawing, pulling, hauling desperately through endless, formless white. She was too slow, so Cronus pushed her to one side, frantically scrabbling through with his massive paws, far better equipped for this kind of work than Polly's gloves. He was genetically equipped to get them out of here, the malamute mind reacts instinctively to the perils of snow and his was acutely aware of the growing weight of it above. He had no intention of letting either of them die and so they dug together, woman and dog in perfect harmony. They started to make good ground and kept their tunnel true and straight for what seemed an eternity of blank, white nothing, before finally, light, real, pure daylight, unobscured by the icy roof of their prison. Cronus pulled his massive head out first, howling with delight as his paws hit air instead of snow, with Polly right behind, 'Lizbet!' she screamed, 'I'm coming.'

'I don't think this is going to work you know.' Wendy smirked, lying in the midst of a warm huddle of dogs – almost invisible because of her coat, and scrolling her phone right where Polly had left her. Somehow she and Cronus had gone around in a circle, however straight they had dug their tunnel. She could see the hole they had gone in through slowly refilling with drifting snow. 'And I've got no signal now, phone's completely useless. Thank God you're back, let's go home.'

'FUCK! FUCK FUCK FUCK FUCK FUCK FUCK FUCK!' Polly screamed, throwing herself back into the snow, hammering her limbs against it in frustration. Some of the malamutes came out of their huddle to push gently against her. They could tell she was upset, and wanted to help but all they did was cover her in yet more snow that fell from their thick, warm, double coats.

'Come on, let's get this thing the right way up again.' Wendy climbed out of the dogpile and started digging out the sled's buried runner. The wind died down and the ground seemed a good deal firmer than before. In fact, things started to go a whole lot more smoothly once they spun the sled back towards the Dourstone side.

The Traveller looked into the depths of his fire and chuckled. He made a few complicated swiping motions and the flames changed from red, to green, to blue, then back to red again. He stared more closely before leaning back and nodding.

'Good, exactly as I hoped. Thanks for the tip off.' He stroked the head of the black and white dog by his side. 'You know what to do.'

His dogs formed up in front of him, they did not salute, as they were dogs, but gave the impression that they would if they could.

'I will do what I must.' Father Hearne raised himself from his log by the fireside. 'I only hope you've listened to what I said.'

'Leave it to the dogs. They will know. Do as I ask and all will be well,' The Traveller replied.

'Are we not going back to the Manor?' Wendy said, aghast as the dogs ran full tilt past the turning.

'No.' Polly didn't even turn her head, just kept her hands firm on the reins.

'Are we going back to your place?'

'No.' The dogs sped up even more on the straight past the newsagents.

'Then where the fuck are we going?' Wendy grabbed hold of Polly's arm to stop her falling from the sled as they took the corner into the square.

'Up to the moors.' Polly took one arm from the reins to put it round Wendy's shoulders.

'The moors?' Wendy leaned in to Polly, looking up through her furry hood at implacable, unreadable features.

'Yes, we either get out the long way round, or find out some answers, that's where he's camped isn't it? Either way, we have to get up there. I can drop you off if you're scared?'

'Scared? Me? Don't be ridiculous. I'm coming, let's do this, just...'

'What?'

'If it's too hard to get to the other side, can we be chickens and go back?' She huddled into Polly's anorak. 'Don't try and tunnel again, I really meant it about not wanting to have to look after your kid.'

'Sure.' Polly gave a grim laugh. 'There's something working against us though, some kind of magic. This isn't ordinary weather.'

'No shit Sherlock, I heard that voice. It's definitely magick, with a capital K. We should have made the sacrifice shouldn't we?' She wriggled in her seat as the sled cruised through the square.

'No...' Polly shuddered. Her eyes rolled back in her head and came back steely grey. Wendy could feel vibrations through her body, it wasn't just a physical shaking, the palpitations came from Polly's very soul. Wendy didn't know how she knew this, but she felt it in her bones. Polly's voice changed timbre and she continued. 'Yes, of course it is. Stupid girl, never doing what I tell you. We have to end this…' Her eyes changed back as she shook her head and shouted, 'NO! You do not have the right to...' She fought to pull her glove off – throwing it from the sled before taking the coffin nail ring from her finger and stashing it safely in a zip pocket.

'What. The. Fuck?' Wendy's eyes went wide as she pulled herself free of their embrace. 'You need to tell me everything.'

'Haven't you guessed?' Polly said, reeling as she regained control of her body. 'She's inside me, Lady Melissa. She's not dead, I don't think she can die.'

'Can she do that whenever… whenever she wants?' Wendy trembled, reaching across to touch Polly, glad of the malamutes. If they'd been doing this in a car they'd have undoubtedly crashed by now. The dogs had had free rein to run all over Dourstone their whole lives and could anticipate every turn.

'No, it's the ring. That's how she does it, that's how she kept the real Lady Melissa suppressed all those years. It's her connection to the real world, I think without it she's just a disembodied spirit.'

'So why would you wear it?' Wendy had both arms round Polly now, holding her in place at the reins, stroking her back, calming her.

'It's addictive, having her to talk to. It's not dangerous, I'm in control, you saw that. I can give her up any time I like. I defeated her and she knows it. She can't take me over completely. I've not been bred to it like a Dewer woman.'

'So, is your little girl..?'

'Never ever putting that fucking ring on? Damn right she's not.' Polly patted her pocket. 'That's why I need to keep Melissa close, keep in contact. Make sure I know what she's up to, so I can keep her away from Lizbet.'

'So that's how you know how to run this town.' Wendy slapped her own forehead. 'I knew you couldn't be that clever.'

'Hey!' Polly grinned. 'I am that clever, but yeah. Having Melissa about helps. She's not keen on my changes – as you heard – but she's useful, there's no way I could run the Manor without her, no way I could have won the locals round.'

'I knew it. Well, I didn't, couldn't have ever guessed that, but both of you, in there...' Wendy tapped Polly's forehead with a leather-clad finger. 'That's interesting.' She winked.

'What do you mean?' The dogs had slowed to a halt and started sniffing at the snow outside the pub, possibly in hopes of this being their destination.

'I mean,' Wendy said, hopping off the sled and walking back to where Polly's glove lay in the snow. 'That I blame both of you for the death of my wife, and now you're the same person.'

'We're not the same person, it's complicated.' Polly jumped down as well, explaining to Cronus in a series of gestures which way she wanted the dogs to take them.

'I know that, but you kind of are, and it's kind of...' Wendy took Polly's hand and slid her glove back over her fingers. 'Kind of, I don't know. Like two wrongs making a right?'

'A right?' Polly finished pulling her glove on herself, snatching her hand away.

'It's the only explanation for why I don't hate you as much as I should.' Wendy smiled back and helped Polly up on to the sled.

With a quick whistle and a few incomprehensible shouts, the dogs moved off again, taking them up past the cottage to the moors.

Polly didn't want to tell Wendy how scared she was. That had never happened before. Melissa had always stayed a passenger, prodding and advising, but never taking control. She hadn't thought she could. Not without a pure blood Dewer girl. That was why she had gone to all that trouble to get Lizbet, because nothing but a Dewer female would do. Why, if she could take control of anybody with that ring? It couldn't be that hard to trick someone into putting it on. Polly knew she probably hadn't put it on of her own free will, but knowing where Mel was and what she was doing, being able to put herself between her child and its potential abductor, was worth the risk.

Fighting her off had taken almost every ounce of mental strength she had. It was probably because she was weak from the struggle through the snow bank, but for those few seconds she had been helpless, a guest in her own body: watching through her own eyes while Melissa controlled everything. She hadn't even felt the cold, cut off completely from her nervous system. She had read about locked in syndrome, after seeing it on an episode of *House,* and it terrified her. To be inside yourself, unable to control anything, just watch as all your decisions are taken away. Unable to even request an end. This felt like that, but far far worse, fully functioning, but against your will, the imperius curse made real.

'Mush! Mush! Hyaaah!' Polly shouted, as the dogs reached the point where the Land Rover had failed. Their paws proved more sturdy, claws finding purchase in the ice. No car can compete against centuries of selective breeding. The malamutes were in their element. They reached the brow of the hill, flying across snow towards freedom before stopping abruptly at the stone circle. The sled slid around, nearly tipping its passengers out over the motley group of dogs that had caused the halt.

'Are you looking for me?' The Traveller said, standing up from his fireside, his camp now a neatly arranged series of covered areas and walkways around the imposing black caravan.

'No, we're trying to get past this wall, what are you doing...' Polly began to answer before recognising his deadman's hat and long black cape. 'Wait, it's you isn't it? You're the one doing this.'

'Yes, at your service. Your new keeper.' He bowed flamboyantly, his cape billowing in the breeze.

'Can we have the pleasure of your name at least?' Wendy asked, with a suspicious look at the dogs.

'If I could remember it you'd be welcome to it, but as it is I'm afraid it's slipped my mind.'

'How unfortunate for you,' Wendy mumbled, rearranging her coats and blankets as she pulled herself back up in her seat.

'It is, most assuredly it is.' He sat back down and filled his pipe.

'So why are you keeping me from my daughter?' Polly said. 'I can't get through your walls and she's on the other side. Please, where's your humanity?'

'Ha, humanity!' He blew a plume of smoke from his mouth as he coaxed the tobacco into a deep red glow. 'And I'm not keeping you from anything. I gave you all a choice and you chose not to leave. I think that says more about you than me.' He poked at his campfire, his big silver sunglasses glinting in the winter sun.

'I chose nothing, let me through,' Polly screamed, standing up in the sled.

'You are free to go, any time you like. You just have to ask.' He stroked his long silver and black beard.

'Fine, can I go and get my daughter please,' Polly asked. 'I won't be long.'

'Oh you will. You can't come back you know. If you leave.' He sucked at his pipe again. 'This land is mine and I don't like sharing.'

'And what of the rest of Dourstone? Can they go?' Wendy asked. 'Have they gone?'

'Plenty have left already. Those who remain, remain under my protection. Everybody is free to leave, as long as they don't mind never coming back. The decision is yours.'

'Sounds okay to me, how about you Wendy?' Polly said, tidying the reins. The dogs remained lying in the snow, having established a rapport with The Traveller's dogs that involved ignoring them completely. 'I'm sick of this town anyway, it's taken everything from me.'

'We might have to discuss it with the others first, we can't just disappear, but in theory...' Wendy fiddled with her boot zips.

'What's to discuss?' Polly countered. 'You've got nothing left here, we can start again, somewhere else, I've got...'

'What, what have you got?' Wendy asked, slapping her hand against the PVC of her boot.

'Shit, nothing. Everything I have is tied up in the Manor, if we go I'm leaving everything aren't I?'

'Oh, you're the pretender living at the Manor are you? Well that changes everything. As Lord of Dourstone, the Manor is now mine my dear, you already have nothing.' The Traveller stood up and waved his hands at the fire. It fizzed angry green sparks as he turned to face them, drawing himself up to his full height and snapping his fingers. 'If you leave then at least you'll be with your daughter. And alive.'

His dogs closed up the perimeter they had created while they were talking. The malamutes jumped to attention, shaking snow from their coats; outnumbered but alert and guarding. Cronus padded up to Wotan, and lowered his head with a growl, as if to say, I could take you, but I'd rather not have to. Wotan nodded back in precarious truce.

'What do you mean?' Polly said, pulling at the reins and preparing to leave.

'I have no need of those who are no use to me. Especially if they oppose my rule.'

'Well how can we be of use?' Wendy asked, stopping Polly's hands with her own. Polly eased back the reins and sat down.

'Hand over the Dewer woman,' he said. 'I can feel her. She's here somewhere, like she's always been. Keeping this place from me, laughing at me. Well, she's not laughing now is she?'

'No, she's dead,' Polly insisted, worried now she knew she had the right bargaining chip. 'Has been for a year, you're too late.'

'Your dead isn't the same as ours. She's here, somewhere, somehow weakened. I would like to help her understand exactly what our dead is.'

'Is that why you're here?' Wendy asked, not contradicting Polly. 'For this… Dewer woman?'

'Don't play dumb with me,' he snapped. 'You know her, you certainly have known her, I can smell her on you. If you're the one at the Manor then maybe you know something more. Maybe you are some use to me after all. Perhaps I won't let you leave. And no, this isn't all I'm here for, she means nothing to me. This is just a side perk. I want this place, it is mine. She had no right. Took my dogs from me, took my land from me...'

'Okay, well we'll just go and find where she's hiding, and then we'll be back, we'll let you know. Maybe we can come to some kind of arrangement on the Manor, but bye for now, right Pol?' Wendy grabbed the reins and pulled the dogs into line.

'I can feel her again, she's stirring.' The Traveller moved closer to the sled, stepping impossibly lightly over the snow, almost floating towards them. 'I don't think you've been telling me the whole truth. Maybe you should stay here.' He held his hand out and his dogs formed up in ranks behind him.

'No, we're going, lovely to meet you.' Wendy snapped the malamutes into action and they ran in the opposite direction to The Traveller's dogs who blocked the moorside exit that led to the most direct route back.

'Wait,' The Traveller shouted. 'I can make you a deal, you will want for nothing.'

They sped off down the hill, leaving the stranger standing on the horizon, his hand on Wotan's head as he watched them go.

'Why aren't we leaving town?' Polly said once they were past the cottage. 'This is the wrong way.'

'Because he's clearly not going to let anybody go. He wants Mel, and anybody connected to her, dead.' Wendy pulled the dogs back to slow them down on the hill, the slick ice was making everything a lot faster than felt safe.

'But we can help with that,' Polly said. 'We could give him the ring then bounce on out of here back to our kids, don't you want to see Alexander again?'

'Of course I do, with all my heart, but I'm not abandoning my friends. You said nobody else needs to die and, just for once, I agree with you. We're going back to the Manor, you're going to put that ring on, we're going to talk to Melissa – all of us – and then we can make a new plan. One where that dickshit leaves and we get our town back. Who the fuck does he think he is?'

Cronus gave a howl of agreement as he led the dogs back through town.

9

'Oh, thank God, I was starting to worry nobody else was here!'
Father Hearne said, lifting his bicycle onto the sled. 'The place is
like a ghost town.'

'You're welcome Father,' Polly said. 'What made you think you
could get through this on that thing?'

They had found him fiddling with his chain at the car park
entrance after a terrifying slide from the top of the hill. Had his bike
not been such an ancient solid thing it probably wouldn't have been
in one piece. As it was, the iron sit-up-and-beg just had a few
scratches and a loose chain.

'It's the only transportation I have,' he explained. 'The weather's
never stopped me, or it, before. I suppose this is a little extreme
though. Not seen anything like it since...'

'Since when?' Wendy interrupted, pulling the bike the last bit of
the way onto the back of the sled.

'Well, since ever, I suppose, truly unprecedented.'

'How did you get into town in the first place?' Polly asked,
pulling him up. 'I thought all the roads were blocked?'

'I was here when all this began,' he explained, foot slipping as he
tried to climb aboard.

'I didn't see you at the market,' Polly remarked. 'Didn't see you
all day.'

'Yeah, I distinctly remember you explaining you couldn't help us
due to other commitments out in Exbourne.' Wendy shuffled across
to let the vicar sit down.

'I did, I was there all day, sorting out Christmas support packages
for poor families, all day, but I snuck back last night to put the
finishing touches to my Christmas spectacular in the church. I was
up a ladder over by the altar giving Jesus a cheery tinsel scarf when
the snow came,' he explained.

'So how come you didn't jump off it and leave like everybody else did?' Wendy asked.

'Why would I leave because of a bit of bad weather?' He raised an eyebrow as he made it on to the bench seat. 'I mean I get it now I can't get home again, but it made more sense to take shelter in the bell tower. I put the halogen heater on and made a little bed out of old kneelers. It was quite cosy.'

'Did you not hear the voice?' Polly said.

'What voice?' The vicar raised his eyebrow.

'The big booming one that drowned out the band and told everybody to leave?' Wendy all but screamed. 'It was pretty unmissable, like the panic that kicked off afterwards.'

'Noise-cancelling bluetooth headphones.' He pulled them out of his pocket. 'Best you can get, I was listening to Radio Four I'm afraid, so I had no idea.'

'You daft broom,' Polly said, laughing. 'I hope it was worth it.'

'I'm sorry I haven't a clue,' he replied.

'Well, if you don't know, then there's no way we will,' Wendy said.

'No, that was what I was listening to, the gameshow, I'm Sorry I Haven't a Clue, it's always worth it. Tim Brooke-Taylor is a national treasure,' he explained. 'I don't suppose either of you have a biscuit or something on you? I haven't had any breakfast, and I skipped dinner last night. I was expecting to get home for a late supper and I'm starving.'

'Well, you're with us now so we'll get you back to the Manor and fed.' Polly whistled to the dogs, who yipped excitedly as they pulled away.

'Thank you, thank you so much. I'm sorry to be such an old fool.'

'You're no fool father,' Wendy said, eyeing him sideways.

'Did you get out? Did you get to the kids? How are they? We lost phone signal almost as soon as you left, have you still got signal? Can you get hold of Katie? Should we all come out, or will we bring them here?' Words fell from Kerry's mouth faster than she could articulate as she ran from the Manor.

'No,' Polly said, her face dark as she unharnessed the dogs. Cronus padded over to Fenrir, once the wolfhound was done leaping at Polly, and nuzzled up against him while the others ran back out into the snow, unperturbed by their adventure and no more tired than when they set out. The last stragglers (who hadn't been harnessed to the sled and just went along for the run) appeared through the gates, thoroughly pleased with themselves despite having done absolutely nothing to help. 'I'm afraid we have something of a situation.'

'Yes, Polly's got a few things to tell you before we make any decisions,' Wendy explained, sweeping across the courtyard with a swoosh of her coat. 'Now can somebody get Father Hearne some bacon and eggs before he starves to death.'

'I'm sure we're got more than enough to spare,' Jack said, putting an arm around the vicar and leading him inside. 'Clive and I have been cooking up a storm while you've been out playing in the snow. And if we don't then I daresay you can do that loaves and fishes trick.'

An hour later everybody was up to speed and Neville was having an after breakfast snooze by the rayburn.

'We ain't handing the town over to some arrogant incomer. Not happening, we might have to live out on that estate, but that's because of fucking blowins like him buying up all the houses in town. Just because we can't afford to live here don't mean we don't belong here. I ain't going without a fight.' Kerry banged her fist on the kitchen table. Like all the most important decisions, it was being discussed over a pot of tea.

'But the kids...' Susan began.

'Are all perfectly safe,' Dan finished. 'Because me and Kerry can't afford to live in town, and you lot wanted a night out on the piss without them.'

'He's only interested in Dourstone proper, for now,' Lynn clarified. 'And I don't know if the magic extends out to the estate. Lady Melissa always said this place was a thin place, where the worlds come together and fall apart at the same time. Maybe that's why he's here?'

'We need to talk to her, put it on Polly.' Wendy took Polly's hands. 'I won't let anything bad happen. I'll make sure you come back.'

'What are you talking about? Come back from what?' Lynn said. 'What don't I know Polly?'

'Fuck's sake Wendy, didn't I ask you to keep it to yourself?'

Polly said, searching the room for a friendly face and finding none.

'This is no time for anybody to be keeping secrets Pol,' Wendy said. 'That's a powerful weapon you've got inside you, it may be the only thing that can get us out of here.'

'What? What is it?' Kerry joined the demand.

The men seemed much more relaxed about withheld information, they were used to women not telling them more than they needed to know, and glad of it, more often than not.

'Polly, tell them.' Wendy took her hand. 'They need to know. We need to speak to her.'

'Fine, okay, Lady Melissa is alive and well. Are you happy now?' Polly said, spilling tea as her hands shook.

'Lady Melissa is what?' Lynn said, face going white.

'You heard me, this ring' – Polly rummaged around in her pockets and pulled the coffin-nail ring out – 'lets me communicate with her. She's in my head. She isn't dead.'

'So...' Kerry encouraged.

'So all those times you thought I was talking to myself when nobody was around I've been talking to her. She knows everything that goes on around here,' Polly explained. 'I didn't want to tell you as you'd probably all think I was mad, or justifying my right to make unilateral decisions. Trust me, everything I've done for this town has gone through her.'

'So if you put that ring on,' Lynn said. 'You can talk to her, and she can hear everything we're saying. Like she's riding in your head.'

'Sort of yeah,' Polly said. 'Honestly I really don't know enough about how it works to say anything with confidence. I know it's all about this ring, and that it's real. But she's still as secretive as ever.'

'Okay, but Wendy's right,' Kerry said. 'She might have been a stone-cold psychopath, but she was our stone-cold psychopath. She'll know how to get us out of this and get our kids back better than anyone. No offence Pol.'

'None taken,' Polly replied.

'So what's your problem?' Lynn asked.

'She took me over earlier, without my consent. It's never happened before. That's why I took the ring off. If we do this I need you all to promise you'll make her bring me back.'

'I thought we were a team,' Lynn said. 'Surely you can trust us not to stab you in the back – or even the front.' She rubbed at the scar Polly had left her.

'Well, no. That's why I can't, you've all got reasons to want me gone. You were Melissa's puppets last year. Why should I do this?' Polly replied.

'Because you want the same thing we do. Our children back by our sides.' Wendy squeezed her hands tighter. Polly hadn't realised she'd been holding them throughout the confrontation. 'You want your Lizzybet. You said yourself, Melissa can't take her without you.'

'Father Hearne,' Polly pleaded. 'Don't let her take me. You're a man of God.' She trusted Father Hearne. He was an outsider, not from the town. Not one of Lady Melissa's minions. If anybody in this room could be on her side it was him.

'Of course. I'll make sure,' he said, feeding a malamute a treat from his pocket. 'You've got nothing to worry about. Lady Melissa and I have always had an understanding. Now do whatever it is you need to do.'

'Okay.' Polly took a deep breath, picked the ring up and very slowly slid it onto her finger.

About fucking time too. You went to meet him without me. Are you insane?

'Sorry Mel, but you...'

I know, I lost my temper. I didn't mean to. We're a team, I won't do it again without permission.

'But how? I thought you could only talk inside? I certainly didn't think you could do anything I didn't want you to.' Polly needed to know, the unwanted audience no longer mattered. 'You...'

Took you over, yes, sorry. I had to do something.

'Am I in control at all? Are you calling all the shots?'

I may have been underplaying my abilities, but I'm on your side.

'We'll talk about this later, right now there are more important things, and I'm sorry for blanking you off.'

Apology accepted, get me up to speed.

'Is she here?' Jack asked. 'Oh what a lark, talking with the dead.'

'It's okay Melissa.' Polly steeled herself. 'Just let me take back control when I ask, please?' She couldn't shake the memory of being captive inside her own head.

You have my word. Melissa could feel Polly's dread fear of that awful isolation.

Polly's eyes rolled into her head and came back silver.

'Well hello all, how lovely to see you,' Melissa spoke, Polly's whole demeanour changing as she slouched in her chair and waved an arm languidly.

'Holy crap.' Kerry's jaw dropped in time with her teacup.

'Nothing holy about it my dear, I've missed you. Can somebody pour me a glass of the Cheval Blanc 1947?'

'Good idea, it's been a hell of a morning, we could all use a drink, I'll go to the cellar.' Jack headed off in search of booze, unfazed by this strange turn of events. Kerry shook her head and picked up her mug, while Dan mopped spilled tea from the table.

'It is you, isn't it. Good Lord!' Father Hearne said, eyes aglow.

'As I said, it's got nothing to do with him, nice to see you again Arthur.' Melissa gave him an odd look, weighing him up and tapping Polly's fingers on the table. 'Why are you here?'

'My flock need me,' he said, 'and I got trapped in the church last night.' He gave the malamute he'd been petting a last stroke before it headed off out to the courtyard, eyes flickering an electric blue as it looked back.

'Yes well, it seems "my flock" have got in the shit without me, well done.' She stood up, walked to the head of the table, sat down and stretched out in what had been Lynn's chair, pushing paperwork and clutter out of her way. 'Now what do you propose to do to get yourselves, and me, out of it?'

'I vote we cut Polly open, yank you out, hand you over to this freak show and get the fuck out of dodge,' Susan said, with a smile.

'Won't work.' Mel waved a hand. 'I'm not a tumour.'

'Might be fun to try though?' Wendy agreed, toying with a carving knife.

The eyes rolled again and came back brown.

'Nobody is cutting me open, you're not funny. Sorry, back to her.' Polly felt a huge rush of relief at regaining control.

Eyeroll.

'Cutting Polly open won't get me out.' Melissa gripped the arms of her chair, turning Polly's knuckles white.

'What will then?' Wendy asked, easing the knife back into its block.

'I'm not explaining the nature of my existence to you.'

'Why not?' Clive asked.

'Because we don't have time, it's difficult to explain to mortals and you lot aren't the brightest.'

'Charming, thanks.' Jack came back in and poured two glasses of deep red wine from a very dusty bottle. 'Anybody else?'

'I will thanks,' Susan said, slurping back the last of her tea and holding the chipped mug out.

Nobody else wanted a drink, though Father Hearne asked if he could have a small sherry instead, sending Jack back off to search for it.

'Give us the short version then, the relevant bits,' Dan asked shaking his head as he refilled his mug of tea.

'Fine, we are not corporeal, I exist as a spirit, uncontainable. Brought forth from land and trees and wildlife. He and I are older and more complex than you could possibly imagine. Handing me over won't help you, even if it were possible. You don't understand him. I do.' She swirled the dark St-Emilion in her glass before sipping it.

'So what can we do?'

'You need to finish him. Knock him out of the picture, fight for this place.' She watched the wine slosh round the glass in the light from the window, moving it slowly and smiling at the results.

'But what is he? How do we fight him?' Kerry said, slurping her fresh tea.

'As I said, he is like me. I'm not entirely unique, obviously. We are many, but mostly solitary.' She looked sideways at the priest with a raised eyebrow, but said nothing. 'I explained this to Polly last year, it's why we have the rituals, the sacrifice. To keep him away. I told Polly she couldn't afford not to do it, but she didn't listen. Her claims to have run decisions through me is only a half truth, she may have told me, but she did not listen to my reply and you have all fucked everything up with your useless compassion.'

'So how do we kill you?' Wendy grinned, sliding the knife in and out of its block.

'I'd rather you didn't, but there is a certain artefact that will do the job. You would, however, have to be certain that all of me was contained in just the one body.'

'You can be in more than one person?' Susan asked.

'Can, I prefer not to, but you know, sometimes a spirit's gotta do what a spirit's gotta do.' She raised her glass. 'He always used to be a one body kind of guy anyway, too arrogant to think it would matter, or too stupid to realise it was an option.' She leaned back in her chair, spreading her legs out. 'If we can find the thing – and that'll be hard enough – then I'll need to get up close to him. Find out if it's worth him finding out we've got it.'

'Where is it.' Lynn stood up. 'No time to waste right?'

'Well, that's the tricky thing,' Mel explained. 'It got lost.'

'Lost?' Lynn said.

'Yes, I'm afraid it was taken from me,' Mel apologised. 'I know this might surprise you but sometimes I upset people.'

'No, really?' Wendy laughed.

'Yes, really.' Mel drank the last of her wine down in one. 'Oh God that's good. Anyway, the Bellever Hagstone was hidden from me by a jealous lover a long time ago.'

'How long ago?' Lynn asked.

'Sometime in the late nineteenth century I think. There was a clue, she wanted me to play along and find it, I wanted her to leave me alone. In hindsight I may have underestimated her hiding skills.'

'You mean a treasure hunt?' Clive clapped his hands. 'I'm the best at treasure hunts, this will be easy.'

'Yes, I think it probably will be a treasure hunt. The clue she gave me led to the cellars. I never bothered to follow it. We can only hope the hagstone is there. But that wasn't how Sophia worked, there's bound to be more. Her constant clamour for attention became a dreadful annoyance. I lost the first clue years ago, but I never forgot what it said: *Search in the dark, beneath our love, Where you store the things you will never possess*". I got as far as the cellar, but everything I've got down there I clearly already possessed. I didn't need the hagstone at the time, so I told her I wasn't playing her stupid game and took the dogs out. Didn't really think about it again until now, so fuck knows. Anyway, we'll need one of you to be as clever as you think you are to get started.' She eyeballed Clive, with a suggestive wink.

'Plenty clever here thanks,' Clive said. 'Now what does it look like?'

'It's a granite hagstone, a piece of rock with a hole in the middle. Very old, and worn smooth with centuries of fondling, with five horseshoe nails driven through and pentagrams wound round in copper wire on either side.' Mel held out Polly's hand with fingers outstretched.

'Okay, cool, I think I've got it, does it look like this?' Lynn held up a picture she had drawn in her notebook.

'No, not really, but if it makes you happy, you'll know it when you see it.' She poured herself another very large glass of red and drank it down in one.

'Fine, okay. That's long enough now, give Polly her body back.' Father Hearne tapped his watch as Jack returned with the sherry. 'We've got enough to be getting on with, and you gave your word.'

'You have, and I did. Now find the Bellever Hagstone and we can finish this.' She slammed her glass on the table, her eyes rolled back and there was Polly.

'So, to the cellars?' She stood up. 'Oh, fucking hell. She's got me pissed hasn't she?' She sat back down with a thud as her head bounced off the table.

A barking from outside was the first they knew that anything was wrong.

10

'What is it?' Wendy said, first to her feet, running out the front door.

Fenrir and Cronus were in the courtyard, barking at a swarm of mongrel dogs coming down the driveway. Wendy acted instinctively, running to the tall, spiked gates, but they were too heavy to move on her own. She pushed fruitlessly at them, having pulled up the long rods that slid deep in the ground pinning them open, but nothing. 'Help me!' she shouted. Lynn tutted her way past Wendy to the gatepost, where she turned a crank handle, moving both gates in unison to a firm close.

'Thanks very much,' Wendy said, pushing her hair out of her face before dropping the gate's heavy bar. 'Just you then?'

'Looks that way, just the two of us, against all that,' Lynn replied.

They shared a look before running back inside.

'Did nobody else hear me? Does nobody else want to come out and maybe have a little look at what all that barking's about?' Wendy shouted, slamming the front door before stomping into the kitchen.

'You looked to have it in hand, and anyway, Lynn was right behind you,' Clive said, sipping coffee and opening a bag of ginger nuts.

'For fuck's sake. He's coming. There is a horde of dogs on the driveway and they're not ours. Get up and get on it,' Lynn said.

'Shush!' Susan said. 'You'll wake Neville up.' She stroked the old man's head as he wriggled in his sleep.

'Good! This is no time to sleep. Now are there any back doors?' Wendy slammed her hands on the table. 'We need to lock down, now, plug any gaps.' Neville remained oblivious, decades of standing next to drum-kits having ruined his hearing.

'Ummm... there's...' Polly slurred, trying to will her brain back up to full power. She could never hold her drink as well as Melissa.

'Fine, I'll do it then, same as everything else round here,' Lynn said, jumping into action. Her years of working closely with Lady Melissa gave her an unrivalled knowledge of the ins and outs of the building. 'We can defend the immediate house if the grounds are lost.'

'The grounds are lost, forget them. Bar anything we can.' Wendy ran to the window, peering out at malamutes howling aimlessly in the courtyard.

'Hello!' The big amplified voice on the winds again. 'Give me the Dewer woman and I'll allow you all to leave and live. There's no reason for anybody to die today.'

Polly span the coffin-nail ring idly behind her knuckle.

Don't fall for it. He's trying to split you up. Make you argue, even if you did find a way to hand me over without you he wouldn't leave you unharmed.

'So you don't want me to hand over this ring and be shot of you forever then?'

Obviously not. But it takes more than just that ring. I can't stop you giving yourself to him if that's what you want.

Polly had no idea who to believe, but erring on the side of caution seemed prudent. If Mel was right then they could hand her over and still end up dead. If Mel was lying they could always trade her later on if this hagstone gave them a way to separate her from Polly. Staying put and defending the Manor seemed the best option, and her head was in no state for making a big decision after all that wine.

'Everybody grab a weapon, it looks like we're at war,' she called, before picking a bow and arrow from the wall of the great hall and heading for the courtyard.

She walked carefully up the steps onto the walkway that followed the inner walls of the Manor over barns and stables. Looking out she could see dogs, black against pure white snow, surrounding them. The Traveller's caravan was on the driveway. He sat on top, in the driver's seat, leaning against ancient cracked leather. His horses stamped restlessly, tossing their heads.

'Why are you doing this?' she shouted – making her head spin even more. The light hurt her eyes, even if she shut them against the glare of sun on snow, the inside of her eyelids burned red and amplified the unstoppable throb in her brain.

'You should ask your friend. She'll tell you, we've got history.

Now hand her over.' The Traveller turned his gaze on Polly, stuffing his pipe, and dangling a leg from the roof of the caravan.

'I don't know what you mean, Lady Melissa Dewer is dead and gone, eaten by her own dogs. Leave us in peace, we have nothing for you.' She grabbed at the battlements to try and keep her footing as dizziness took over.

'I told you, this is my place, and I am keeping it. Those who have chosen to stay are mine. And since you have chosen to be mine, you will do as I say, now hand her over.' He jumped from his seat, landing heavily on the snow, pipe clamped in his mouth as he chocked his wheels and unharnessed the horses.

Polly looked around at the dogs, assessing her chances of getting away. They wouldn't be good if she were stone cold sober, and even if she could, where would she go? Back into town? Hole up at the pub forever? There was no better place than here, the Manor was defensible. Besides, she had her own canine army, and the malamutes were bigger, stronger and better cared for than these mongrels. All they had to do was find the Bellever Hagstone, hope Mel could remember how to use it, and rid themselves of this troublesome stranger.

'I can't, she's not here. Your spidey-sense is barking up the wrong tree.' Polly raised the bow, trying to pull its string taught and only succeeding in bouncing it off her knee in agonising recoil.

'It is not, now stop this before I have to really hurt you.' He tied the last horse up to one of the trees lining the driveway.

Polly hopped on her good leg, wishing she could go home to her cottage and forget all about this. 'I'd like to see you try,' she replied, in empty threat.

You wouldn't, Melissa said. *You'd come off worse, even if you were sober. Anyway, he can't take a hint and you can't take your drink, do you mind if I take a turn?*

'No, no, I suppose this is more your arena than mine, if you're sure you want to be exposed there's nothing I can do to stop you,' Polly muttered.

Her eyes rolled back in her head again. 'Why are you back? Why do you want this place still? Can you even remember?' Lady Melissa spat as they flew back silver.

'Ah, there you are. It's been too long, have you missed me?' The Traveller doffed his hat and gave a mock bow. 'How do you like this body?' He gave a shake and laughed as he rammed the hat back on his head.

'I'm sure it's very nice.' Melissa strung the bow first try and nocked an arrow. 'Now answer my questions please.'

'I am back because I can be, because you got sloppy.' He filled the horses' feed bags and looped them over their heads one by one. 'I always wanted this place, and I want it even more now for all the centuries you have denied it me.'

'So that's all it is? Because I wouldn't let you have it? Like a petulant child?' Melissa flexed the bow, not aiming it anywhere, just testing the strength of the string.

'You know what this place is, what it can do, that's why you've protected it, kept it to yourself all these years. Made sure nobody else can get through.' He waved his hand, clearing a wide circle in the snow without touching it.

'Not none, there have been others,' Melissa replied. 'Just not you.'

'Yes, I know.' He made a small pile of sticks in the middle of the cleared circle, carefully piling them up in a wigwam shape and stuffing the centre with dry hay. 'Oh how I know.'

Cronus loped along the walkway to his former mistress and nuzzled his head into her hand.

'I'm sure you know everything, you always had your spies, I've never denied entry to those without evil intent.' She loosened the arrow, letting the bowstring hang slack.

'And I have evil intent do I?' He clicked his fingers and his little fire burst into flame.

'Always. Nothing but.' Melissa waved the arrow dismissively.

'So you're not coming out?' He pulled a chair from the back of the caravan to place by the fireside.

'No, you wouldn't let these people go even if I did.' The arrow was back in the bow, sharp, dangerous and ready to loose.

'You underestimate me.' He sat down, pulled his pipe from his mouth and knocked the bowl out into the flames.

'Never have, never will. If anything I've over-estimated you, this is pathetic.' Lady Melissa lowered the arrow.

The Traveller fired a projectile from deep within his sleeve.

With lightning fast reflexes, she whipped the bow back up and shot his missile from the skies.

'Same old tricks, my god, I thought you might have learned some new ones. Pathetic, like I said.'

'It's just a friendly test, to see if you've still got it.' He spread his arms wide and sat back down, relighting his pipe.

'And have I?' Melissa gave a twirl.

'Always, I've almost missed you,' he replied.

'The feeling's not mutual. Good luck with the siege, I'll be back to check on you later.' She walked off back down the steps, Cronus padding behind her like she had never been away.

'So how are you getting me home girl?' Polly's granddad said, waiting for her by the barn, cigarette and coffee in hand. 'This is my last smoke. How'm I going to get more if we can't break through this ice?'

'All in good time my good man,' Melissa said, handing him the bow and leftover arrows before pushing past to search the barn.

'Polly?' He recoiled.

'Nope, not Polly.' She turned her head and gave him a wicked grin. 'Lady Melissa Dewer, very pleased to make your acquaintance.'

'I thought you were dead, Polly said…'

'Polly lied. She does that.'

'Yeah, I don't know where she gets it from.' Neville tugged at his beard.

'You know, I never noticed just how handsome you were.' Melissa loomed over him. 'Maybe I need to find another body, unless…?'

'Heck no lady, that's my granddaughter, I ain't like that, not one bit. You stop thinking that way.' Neville pulled back as far as he could as she leaned in.

'I don't mind if you don't, she'll never need to know.' She breathed down his neck.

I will know, I will fucking know, please stop Melissa, you're not funny, Polly screamed inside her own head.

Oh, come on, he's a good-looking guy, you can't blame me, Melissa replied.

'Please, Lady Dewer, can I have Polly back?'

'Not just yet. Let me know if you want me to find another body honey, you're well-preserved, and believe me, I know well-preserved. Now help me.' She turned back to the barn and began pulling boxes one by one from a stack of jumble.

'Help you what?' Neville replied, glad to be out of the headlights.

'Help me look for this...' She kicked the pile of boxes over, swirling the contents out across the muddy floor with her foot. 'No, don't bother yourself. Sophia wasn't bluffing, it's not here...' Melissa turned back round and swooped into the yard, only to find her way blocked by a wall of fur. 'Get out of the way you great oafs.' Her malamutes were keen to get reacquainted, they knew her in any form and weren't going to let her past without a cuddle.

11

'Will the dogs hold if he breaks the gate?' Clive asked, pacing between counter and table, fiddling with anything he could grab. 'Christ, it's like Helm's Deep! Bagsy be Aragorn.'

'I'm Eomer then,' Jack said, sticking his hand in the air.

'I think I'd rather be Merry and Pippin and dick about with the Ents thanks,' Dan muttered.

'The dogs are just dogs now. They won't hold anything.' Lady Melissa was still in full control of Polly, standing at the head of the table unmoving. 'We need the hagstone.'

'So cellars still?' Wendy said.

'Yes, if nothing else then it's the usual place for a final showdown if they get in the house. We're saving time,' Lynn said, rubbing her side. 'Skip to the finale.'

'Great, and I'm the only one here old enough to be Theoden King, brilliant.' Neville grumbled as they made their way to the cellar.

'Oh my dear,' Melissa said, snaking an arm round him. 'I could make Gandalf feel young. Stick with me kid.'

'Please remember that's my granddaughter you're using like a fancy dress costume ma'am.' He pulled away.

'Sorry.' Melissa pinched his bottom and carried on past.

'So what are we looking for?' Wendy asked, keen for any distraction from the memory of her last trip to the cellars. She had avoided coming down all this last year, since she found her wife, Delia, underneath an unconscious Clive with the snapped off end of Polly's pike through her chin. The image still haunted her dreams, and yet through all her wanting to blame Polly, she couldn't help but like the woman. Couldn't help understanding that she would have done the same had it been Alexander in that room. She wished, and not for the first time, that Delia had stood aside and abandoned Lady

Melissa's orders. But what was done was done, and this melding of the two people she blamed most for Delia's death dangled in front of her like the most delicious forbidden fruit. She wished it wasn't, but lust is lust.

'I told you, it's an ancient hagstone with five iron horseshoe nails driven through and copper pentangles wound round either side,' Melissa reiterated.

'A what?' Jack asked. 'Sorry, we're looking for a rock?'

'Weren't you listening at all?' Susan said, with a condescending look.

'I had to hunt out the sherry,' Jack said. 'Do you know how many old green bottles there are in this place?'

'More than ten?' Kerry laughed. 'Get it, I said...'

'Yes, we heard you, very good,' Lynn said, before filling Jack in on what he'd missed.

'Piece of piss then,' Jack said, once she'd finished. 'Must be a hundred of those down here.'

'Well, yes, in all honesty there might be,' Melissa said. 'But it needs to be that specific one.'

'What did the clue say?' Lynn interrupted. 'We're in kind of a hurry aren't we?'

'It said: "*Search in the dark, beneath our love*", so cellar. I got that bit myself, after I'd checked under the bed.'

'And?' Lynn was getting impatient.

'And: "*Where you store the things you will never possess*."'

'How can you store them if you'll never possess them?' Clive kicked a stone that rattled down the spiral staircase. 'That's just stupid.'

'I know right?' Melissa said. 'That's why I've never found it.'

I know where it is.

'Do you?'

'Who are you talking to?' Wendy asked.

'Polly's got an idea.'

'This is going to take some getting used to, we might need a signal.' Clive scratched his head with a shiny metal finger.

'Shut up boy, there's no need for any of that, it's perfectly simple and obvious. Now pipe down and let me listen.' Melissa grabbed Clive's arm and moved him out of her way.

Give me my body back and I'll help you.

'You're too drunk to drive.' Melissa grinned.

'Give her back her body,' Wendy said. 'She's the best at crosswords, doesn't get out enough.'

'She's not the best,' Lynn interjected. 'She's maybe third best at best.'

'Really?' Wendy put her hand on her hip.

'Really, I still hold the record for the Times Cryptic, Kerry's after me and Polly just got lucky a few times. She isn't consistent.' Lynn grabbed at the handrail as Cronus and Fenrir barrelled down the stairs, determined not to be left out.

'Is this really the time?' Jack asked. 'And anyway, I've seen the board, Polly's on top of your stupid crossword league, so she's the best.'

'She is not, she just caught a couple of days where we weren't on form, a few lucky breaks. Just because she knows all that London financial mumbo-jumbo. It wasn't our fault and we're still the best.' Lynn folded her arms, stopping in the middle of the narrow stairway.

'That's as maybe Lynn,' Kerry piped up, nearly falling as she came to an unexpected stop. 'But we've got no idea about this clue, and if she can get it, she should have a go. You're a damn sore loser Lynn.'

'Yes Kerry, I am very sore.' Lynn poked herself meaningfully where Polly had stabbed her.

'Okay, okay, I know, we've all got reasons Lynn.' Kerry looked down at her husband as she carefully lowered his wheelchair down the winding steps. 'But haven't we managed to forget all that, forgive her, get along over the last year?'

'Yes, I've forgiven all that, but she's not as good at crosswords.' Lynn sulked.

'Anyway,' Wendy said. 'If we could have Polly back now Melissa? She might be able to help.'

'Fine, but don't blame me if she holds you back,' Melissa said, sinking to the back of Polly's mind.

'It's the jars, the cabinet with the jars in, that's where it is.' Polly shouted as she regained control of her body, grabbing the rusting handrail to stop herself falling down the last few steps. 'Shit, still pissed then.'

'What cabinet?' Clive asked, helping Kerry get Dan's wheelchair to firmer ground.

'Didn't she ever tell you what you were guarding?' Polly turned to him, hand on hip. 'The cabinet in the final room. The room I knocked you out in front of. Where she keeps the hearts – the thing she will never possess!'

'Ooooh, major burn,' Kerry said as they headed to the deepest room in the cellar.

It was a long way, past gaping arches filled with darkness and tiny corridors that could lead anywhere, the barrels and bottles of the Dewers' extensive and expensive wine collection and rooms and rooms of long-forgotten dust-covered crates. They trudged on in silence each pondering the riddle, hoping to find the prize themselves and prove Polly wrong. Cronus and Fenrir ran on ahead, and then back again, and then ahead again, and then back again, and then ahead again...

Wendy was first to the door, trying not to look at the dark stain on the ground where Delia's life had spilled out. Clive took her arm and helped her open the door, doubtless remembering his time lying beneath Wendy's wife's corpse, soaking in their mingled blood.

Once past the ancient, cracked-leather and brass-studded door, the room lay before them, unchanged since the previous Wish Weekend. Polly had fully intended the room remain unused for the rest of time. A raised dais stood in the middle, a throne of bones atop it, not yet finished, but no less threatening. To its left was another patch of darkness that Lynn tried her hardest not to look at. To the right, a small pile of bones and dust marked all that remained of the mortal Lady Melissa Dewer once time and her dogs had caught up with her. A sad memorial to a pillar of the community – the urn in the family vault was empty, as were all its predecessors.

Why are those bones not part of the chair? Melissa's disembodied voice screamed in Polly's head. *The Dewers must be joined.*

'That's not important right now, where would your ex think to put your heart?' Polly asked.

The chair is important. We'll talk about this later.

'What does she say?' Lynn asked, keen to leave this place.

'Nothing useful. Start opening drawers,' Polly said, pointing to an ancient cabinet that took up a whole wall. Its top was like a mediaeval altarpiece, all gilt and gaudy colours, though the pictures were not really for the religious and it was probably best not to examine them too closely.

Clive and Susan pulled at the top half with little regard for its age or value, while Wendy and Lynn hunted through the lower portion with something closer to reverence. Each section of the cupboard – and there were a lot of sections – held a selection of jars and bowls, not dissimilar to those found in the pyramids of Egypt. Lynn very carefully removed the top of a clay pot before sniffing it, cautiously tipping its dusty innards into her hand and then carefully pouring them back in. The glass jars were easier, you could see the organs of Dourstone's yearly sacrifice floating inside, standing as a promise to the dogs. Knowing what they were didn't make them any more palatable.

'Got something,' Wendy cried out, wielding an object the size of a fist, pierced through the centre and shining with jewels.

'Give it here,' Lynn said, snatching it from Wendy's hand. 'Obviously this isn't it. That's silver wire, wound in a hexagram on only one side round steel nails. Not even close. It should be copper, both sides and wound round iron horseshoe nails. And I'm pretty sure that's limestone, not granite.'

'Well then get back down here and let's keep hunting,' Wendy cheerfully replied, pulling out a bowl of what looked to be knucklebones.

'Wait, there's something in here,' Lynn said, pulling out a note tucked behind the wire hexagram. 'Oh you must be joking.'

'What is it?' Polly said.

'It's another clue, this is ridiculous, it really is a treasure hunt.' Lynn laughed.

'Well, spit it out then, what does it say?' Clive leaned in.

'It says: *"My darling Elias, if you really must have the Bellever Hagstone, then recall our triple-backed chimaera by the light of the triple goddess: where blood ran free and we raised the earth's bones. I think it foolish you would keep such a weapon in the house, as you know. None but you or Nathaniel may solve these clues and since you murdered him it is safe from those who would use it against you. I hope you never need find this note – all my love, Sophia."* Who are Elias, Nathaniel and Sophia?' Lynn folded the note up and put it in her pocket, patting it twice to make sure it was there.

'May as well give up, hand Polly over to that chap out there and start house-hunting,' Jack said, picking up a silver knife from the cabinet. 'Any room at yours while we get ourselves together Dan? At least you and Kerry had the foresight to live outside the bounds.'

'No, and why are you giving up so easily?' Dan said.

'Only this Elias can solve the clues, I assume he's long dead and there's no way out of here that doesn't go past those dogs. Fuck it, I'm done. Let's surrender.' Jack sat on the bone chair, swept his ankle up over the opposite knee in a languorous slouch and picked at his nails with the knife.

'The Lady Sophia Dewer was Melissa's wife when Melissa called herself Lord Elias, and Nathaniel was her lover. We're a long way from beaten,' Polly said. 'Tell me what she meant?'

'Well you should know, you're the one that's got her inside you,' Lynn said.

'I know, I wasn't talking to you, shut up so I can hear myself think.' Polly grinned.

It's our stone circle, obviously. That's where we need to go. Melissa explained. *Where we raised the bones of the earth.*

'Oh.' Polly shuffled her feet, downcast. 'Maybe we are beaten, anyone got a way to get to the stone circle?'

'The stone circle?' Dan said, face downcast. 'Is she sure?'

'Told you, we're fucked,' Jack chimed in, sliding further down the chair.

'Can't we smash our way through the dogs on that sled of yours?' her granddad said. 'It looked pretty sturdy.'

'I don't fancy our chances,' Wendy disagreed. 'It was hard enough going with only two of us.'

'We could sneak out the back, through the kitchen gardens and the orangery?' Father Hearne suggested.

'We're surrounded, dogs all the way round, we'd never make it.' Polly shook her head.

'But there's more of us, and we've got your malamutes, why the fuck are we hiding?' Susan ranted. 'We can take them. Time to take back control.'

'The malamutes are just normal dogs now. And he's got magic.' Polly explained. 'Being scared is a better option than being dead.'

'We've got Mel, she's the same as him isn't she? Can't she re-magic the dogs?' Susan continued.

'It doesn't work like that,' Polly said. 'Mel says she's too depleted to work any serious magic – yes that's my fault, I know, don't keep on – and the dogs are their own. You have to pay them their price. And we're not paying it again.' She held up a glass jar of hearts and looked through it to the winter sunlight pouring from the lightwell high above. 'Unless you'd like to volunteer?'

'No, fair point, what's your plan?' Susan folded her arms.

'There is a way – according to Melissa – a secret passageway.'

'Of course!' Lynn shouted, slapping her forehead. 'I'd forgotten. We can go that way.'

'How do you know about it?' Clive sputtered.

'I did a lot of things for Lady Melissa, some of them a little less than honest. She showed me the secrets of the Manor. Follow me.' She led them to a tiny door by the altar, stepping carefully around her own bloodstains, and opened it. 'See?'

'No. Not really.' Behind it was a small, dark, damp-smelling room.

'Back in the fourteenth century, the black death was becoming something of an irritant. The Dewers kept the Manor house as sanctuary for anyone healthy. Quarantining them here kept people safe. Not all, but as many as could be saved.'

'That's very interesting Lynn,' Wendy said. 'But is this really the time for a history lesson?'

'I'm getting to that. The rituals still needed to be obeyed, the dogs and the magic and the sacrifices that kept them from ending up locked in a cellar trying to find a way to stop a maniac knocking down their doors and killing them all in revenge for some undisclosed grievance.' Lynn poked about the walls.

'Yes, thank you, I know, I'm sorry,' Polly said, trying to tune out the exact same story monologuing in her head.

'Nobody wanted to risk infection by walking through the town, and they couldn't risk fobbing the dogs off with plague victims. So they dug this tunnel to facilitate the ritual. Come on.' Lynn pushed in a loose stone, causing the back wall to swing wide without the expected ominous creak. 'I oiled the hinges last time I used it, didn't want anything giving me away.' She gave Polly a wink, turning on her phone torch to illuminate a narrow tunnel.

'Wait up, wait up,' Dan said, looking at the rough stones and pot holes that made up the path. 'Couple of things: one, I am not going to get through there without a lot of help.'

'Come off it love, we're not leaving you,' Kerry said. 'No more deaths, remember? All for one and one for all, we're a team aren't we?' She looked to Polly, who nodded.

'No, it's not that. Thanks though honey, means a lot,' Dan explained. 'But the Manor's not lost yet and there's no point me slowing you down.'

'He's right,' Father Hearne said. 'Some of us need to hold the line.' He moved back from the tunnel and leaned on the wall of the throne room.

'Fine,' Lynn said, assuming control. 'You and Dan stay here then, who else?'

'Maybe you should stay Granddad?' Polly suggested. 'After all...'

'No, I'm not getting any younger, you're right, and no, I'm not staying here. I go where you go girl. No matter what.' He gave a reassuring smile. 'Your mother would kill me if I left you alone.'

'Thank you for pretending she cares,' Polly replied.

'Okay, so that's three of us for team explorer.' Lynn scribbled in her notebook, ignoring the family tiff. 'You, me and Polly, who else?'

'I'm coming with you,' Jack said. 'Can't stand it down here.' He shivered, the memory of his wife dying on the steps still all too fresh.

'Understood.' Polly touched his arm in what she hoped was a gesture of apology.

'Same,' Wendy added, snaking an arm around Polly's waist.

'Yeah,' Jack said, his arm sliding over Wendy's to ensnare Polly between them.

'Okay, so I suggest we split up like this,' Lynn said, looking up from her list. 'Polly, Jack, Neville, Wendy and I shall continue the quest, while Dan, Kerry, Clive, Susan and Father Hearne hold down the Manor.'

'What makes you think you'd be better than me out there?' Susan put her hands on her hips and stood between Lynn and Jack.

'I don't, we can swap if you want?' Lynn backed down. 'What do you think Arthur?'

'I'd be glad of your help here Lynn, we've need of a good

organiser.' Father Hearne nodded.

Polly had never been quite sure whether Lynn and the vicar were a thing or not. It had certainly looked that way a year ago, the two of them were never far from each other: always out on secret bike rides, and Lynn helping out with church business that needed no help. Patrick had thought they were, but then Patrick had thought a lot of things, and Lynn had revealed herself to be an excellent actor right before Polly ran her through with Neville's old sword.

Whatever the truth, Susan had just carefully excised Lynn from Jack, and herself from her husband. Polly was absolutely certain she knew what was going on between them.

'Fine, you go Susan, I'll stay. Okay?'

'Very thanks.' Susan grinned and leaned against Jack's thigh to fiddle with her boot laces.

'And we'll need these two,' Polly added, pulling herself out of Wendy and Jack's awkward clutches to stroke Cronus and Fenrir's heads. 'The other dogs should be enough for you. They listen to Saxon number three when these two aren't here, then Sky seven.' The pack hierarchy wasn't made any less confusing by so many dogs sharing names.

'Okay, let's do it.' Susan sprang into the passage.

'Wait, you need supplies, you need tools, you need...' Lynn interrupted, counting off a mental checklist on her fingers.

'At least to put a coat on honey.' Clive slapped his forehead.

12

The tunnel was long, damp, uneven and dark: its connection to the plague no comfort.

'How much longer does this go on?' Wendy said, pulling cobwebs from her hair with a grimace. 'It never seems this far above ground, we should have been there hours ago.'

'It's a good mile over land, and there's a river in the way, who knows how deep this thing goes, or how they decided to get round it 600 years ago. Keep crawling, it hasn't even been ten minutes Wendy,' Polly said.

'I've seen worse, back when I was a desert rat in WWI, I tunnelled my way from...'

'This is no time for one of your stories Granddad,' Polly scolded. 'They were fun when I was a kid, but I've made a lot of money out of being very good at maths since then, and you're not old enough for any of them to be true.'

'Yeah, but I did work in the last days of the Bideford paint mines, it was pretty grim down there.'

'Worked?' Polly stopped in her tracks, causing him to bump into her and the whole line to come to a stop.

'Fine, me and Mickey used to break in there after school, it was a good place for a quiet smoke out of the rain where his ma wouldn't catch us.'

They carried on in silence a while longer before the narrow space opened out and a barking and scrabbling announced that the dogs had found the end.

'Any ideas how this opens?' Susan said, first on her feet.

'There's a key hole,' Polly said, squinting at the handle of a mildewed wooden door with no window. Polly would have expected at least a peephole, to check whether or not anyone exiting was being observed, but no. Just gnarled wood. The old, deep scratches running down it brought a chill. She hoped they'd been made by impatient dogs.

'But we don't have a key,' Polly's granddad pointed out.

'I bet Lynn had the key, she's always got everything organised,' Jack said, patting his pockets as if it might have turned up there.

'Oh yes, perfect bloody Lynn, I'm so sorry for taking her place, do you want me to go back and switch? See if she has the key, beg her to come instead?' Susan growled.

'No, no, don't worry, it was just a thought.' Jack put his hands up in self-defence. 'If she'd had it she'd have given it to us, it's not the sort of thing she'd forget.'

'True,' Polly said. 'There may well not be a key for it anymore. Lynn might never have had to come all the way to the end, I know she talks a good talk, but a lot of it's bullshit. It might not even be locked?'

'It fucking well is.' Susan pushed and pulled at the handle in every combination of rattling moves there was. 'What if we have to go back? I don't want to go all the way through there again, with those farting dogs. It smells disgusting.'

Cronus and Fenrir gave a quizzical look before letting off a squelching harmony.

'Seriously?' Wendy stepped forward, standing up to full height now the passageway was tall enough to allow it. 'Stand back.'

She drew her leg back and kicked at the door as hard as she could. The centuries-old hinges fell apart instantly, allowing six foot deep snow to flow over them.

'Fuck's sake Wendy, why can't you think before you do things,' Susan muttered, spitting snow from the corner of her mouth.

'I think the phrase you are looking for is "thank you Wendy for getting us out of the hole,"' she replied, shaking snow from her coat before stepping into the cold light of day.

'Where are we?' Neville asked, jumping aside as the two massive dogs broke for daylight. They ran off over the snow, glad to be out of the tunnel and chasing each other like puppies.

'Woods,' Polly noted. 'Just down from the circle. I recognise this spot.' She leaned over to pet Fenrir as he avalanched to a halt, remembering how he had saved her from Cronus here last year.

Outside the Manor something was up.

'Why are the dogs looking at us? Shouldn't they be facing outwards? Keeping the other dogs out?' Kerry said, trying to sidestep malamutes in the courtyard as one after another ambled into her way.

'I'm sure the dogs know what they're doing,' Father Hearne shouted from his perch at the front door, filling his pipe as he leaned against a pillar.

Kerry finally got through the dogs to the gate and patted the top of the bar, making sure it was all the way down.

'He's cooking out there. Making himself some lunch on that fire of his,' Clive yelled down from the wall. Sure enough, The Traveller was sitting by his fire with a spitted badger over the flames.

'Not long now, get ready.' He looked over at Clive with a smile and a wave.

'Does he think he can just wait us out?' Clive said, walking back along the wall.

'He doesn't think it,' the vicar replied, straightening up as he sucked his pipe ablaze. 'He knows it.'

'What do you mean?' Kerry asked, trying, and failing, to get back to the house through a huddle of dogs.

'He's good at waiting, he's been waiting a long time.' Father Hearne slotted himself in front of the door, covering the entrance.

'How do you know so much about it?' Clive had a bad feeling about this.

'I didn't want to, you know. I'm still on your side, but...' The vicar shrugged. 'I want everyone to win really.' Five enormous dogs sauntered over to surround the entrance, he fiddled with his pipe, trying to knock out ash without losing the cherry. 'The thing is, I already had commitments, now if the two of you could give me a hand with the gate, I'd be most awfully grateful.'

'Ah, come on, you're meant to be a man of God.' Clive stopped halfway down the steps. 'Why would you do this?'

'He's a double-crossing shitbag is what he is. Don't do this father, give it up and you won't get hurt. It can't work. Doggies, to me, get away from him,' Kerry called to the animals guarding the entrance, rubbing her fingers together in the universal gesture for treats.

They didn't move.

'Hey, who wants a biscuit?' Clive called, stepping carefully down the last few steps into the yard. All he got in reply was a hard stare.

'I see, you've changed.'

'Yeah, fuck this Clive, let's go round the back.' Kerry turned round to see the narrow passage that led round the house blocked by a wall of tooth and fur. 'Oh.'

'Oh,' Clive echoed. 'Maybe let's try something else.'

'Get out of the way, you stupid dogs,' Lynn said, on the other side of the kitchen garden, brushing a malamute away as she had a thousand times before. The dog growled, snapping at her hand as two more appeared to back it up.

'What the fuck Lynn?' Dan shoved himself back towards the house. 'What's with the dogs?'

'I don't know Dan,' Lynn answered, rubbing her hand. 'They're never like this, they're always so friendly, so docile.'

'What's happened to their eyes?' Dan leaned down out of his chair, not daring to get as close to the dogs as he normally would. Hot breath hit his face as one of them snapped off a warning bark. He backed off further. The dogs' eyes, normally a dirty amber, were glowing bright blue. 'It's like they are – or at least were, before, when we did it the old way, on the… you know… Wish Weekend.' He didn't want to give full voice to his fear.

'They're dogs Daniel, just ordinary mutts, I've been looking after these lot for years. Something's spooked them, probably them other dogs, but I'm sure they'll be fine. They're Dewer dogs, their allegiance is to Elizabeth, and we're on her side. Even if they have gone peculiar.' Lynn clapped her hands. 'You're supposed to be keeping them out, not us in, you stupid animals.'

They didn't flinch, just carried on circling, slowly, carefully.

'I don't think they're listening to you Lynn,' Dan whispered.

'At least we know they're some use as guard dogs though.' Lynn shrugged. 'Not gone totally useless like Polly thought.'

'Yes, but who are they guarding?' Dan wheeled round, looking for a gap. 'I really don't think they're on our side any more.'

The only gap was back to the house, so that was where they had to go, herded by dogs.

'Read the clue again would you Wendy?' Jack said, sitting on one of the stones of the circle, blowing on his fingers and wishing he had brought gloves. 'I'm still not even sure how it got us here, let alone what we have to do.'

'"*Recall our triple-backed chimaera by the light of the triple goddess: where blood ran free and we raised the earth's bones*",' Wendy read. 'Not a great deal of help is it?'

'Well, it's got us this far,' Neville reasoned. 'I'm sure we can work out the rest with the right help.'

'Granddad!' Polly said. 'Surely you're not on her side, not with the way she keeps on with you when she's... you know... inside me?'

'Oh no, not like that, no, never,' Neville insisted. 'You mean you can hear her, feel what she feels? When she's all up in my business?'

'Enough, yes, so can you cut out the polite flirting please.' Polly folded her arms.

'I will do, I will – though I seen pictures of her in her old body. Not too shabby for her age...' Neville looked off to the tops of the distant tors.

'Not a difficult thing to achieve at her age,' Polly said, turning red in recollection of what she had done with that body. 'Don't fall for her tricks.'

'I know girl, I'm sorry.' He hugged her. 'And I promise, strictly hands off.'

'So are we going to get Mel back again? Do we trust her?' Wendy asked, washing the tunnel from her hands in the snow for a fourth time. 'To let Polly back I mean.'

'Who gives a fuck?' Susan countered. 'Mel knows the answers, Polly doesn't. Let her out Pol.'

'Thanks for your concern Susan,' Polly said. 'I'm sure Melissa is of more use than me, yes. But I need you guys to promise you won't let her keep me. I can't be a prisoner in my own head, I just can't.'

'I'll hold her to it, and no funny business.' Neville tightened his hug until she almost couldn't breathe. 'You're coming back.'

'Thanks Granddad.' She kissed him on the cheek, then fumbled in her pocket for the ring. Anytime she wore it she could feel Melissa, subtly directing her, changing her mood, not in control but always lurking at the back of her mind. Knowing Melissa needed a Dewer female to fully come back into her own, she had supposed Melissa could only communicate with her through the ring because she had carried a Dewer baby inside for nine long, painful, months. She had feared Melissa might be able to exert more power over her ever since she started hearing her voice, but now it was confirmed she was taking no chances and kept ring and finger separated. The idea of never being able to come back was too terrible to contemplate.

Her mind went fuzzy and she lost the feeling in her body, *Thanks, I promise to take care of your grandfather*, she heard, as she fell to the deepest corner of her own mind.

'It's underneath that one. Somebody needs to dig.' Melissa pointed at the stone Jack was sitting on. 'You're a young fit chap, you do it.'

'How do you know it's that one?' Susan said, sidling over and taking her arm.

'Because that's the one we took the longest to get up,' Melissa returned Susan's embrace, catching the underside of her breasts as she slid her hand round her waist.

'I didn't get that from the clue,' Jack said.

'No, you wouldn't, but the reason we took so long to get it erect, was that it reminded us of a vulva.' She traced her fingers over the gnarled cavities of the rock, tickling its zenith with a laugh.

'So?' Susan said, pulling away.

'So it got us all hot and bothered and we had to go home and get it out of our system, if you know what I mean.' Melissa winked Polly's eye.

'Nice story,' Jack said.

'It got better, we came back up that night, when nobody was around, went two more rounds in the hole we'd dug, Sophia fair bent me over that rock backwards, then Nathaniel bent me forwards, and then I forget, but dear God we had a night, a triple-backed chimaera indeed.'

'Eeeeeewwww!' Jack said, hopping up from the stone.

'Fucking prude,' Melissa said, laughing. 'Now dig it up, obviously Sophia wanted to commemorate the best fucking of her entire life. Don't blame her, I was very good.'

'Jesus, give it a rest,' Jack said, bending at the waist to hide the proof he didn't mind this story as much as he claimed. Anyway, I haven't got a spade have I? Why can't the dogs do it?'

'You try telling them what to do.' Wendy laughed at his discomfort, pushing him in the chest to try and force him to straighten up. 'They only do what they want.'

'Okay, a challenge is a challenge. Cronus seems to recognise me, let's see if he's got any more obedient since I died.' Melissa bent down and whispered softly in the craggy old malamute's ear.

He was still her dog at heart, the once fearless leader of her pack. The Nymet hunt, as were. Something deep inside his doggy brain recognised his old mistress, separating her from her new shell and he gave a little woo of happiness and licked her hand before starting to burrow at the base of the rock.

'See, good dog,' Jack ruffled the fur on Cronus' head.

'Impressive,' Susan said, glad to be out of Melissa's grip. 'Good to have you back your ladyship.'

'Don't try and cosy up to me now, I've heard everything you've said for the last year,' Melissa explained. 'You may not have known I was riding around in Polly's head. In fact you can't have, or you wouldn't have said all those things to suck up to her.' She advanced on Susan, stalking through the snow, her silver eyes, so unlike Polly's deep brown pools, drilling tiny icicles into Susan's heart.

'I didn't... I wasn't... I...' Susan stammered, stepping backwards faster and faster until she fell over a stone and her whole body crunched through the top layer of snow into freezing depths.

'Oh it's fine, you incomers are all the same when we let you in the inner circle.' Melissa chuckled. 'Do anything to keep your seat at the top table. Such climbers, so vain, so self-important.' She reached down to pull her up. 'I love it. You wouldn't be so easy to exploit if you didn't. Don't go changing Susan.'

'Thank you.' Susan tensed up, flinching from the offered hand by instinct before realising she had to accept it. Polly's arms pulled her up. She brushed snow from her anorak then wiped at the top of her boots to try and stop any more forcing its way inside.

'I love you just the way you are.' Melissa grabbed her in another awkward hug and kissed her on the lips before walking away.

'Can we have Polly back now?' Wendy said.

'No, not yet, I don't think,' Jack said. 'We'll need Melissa for the next clue, once the dogs have dug it up.'

'Dog.' Polly's granddad gave Fenrir a rub behind the ears while they sat together watching Cronus work.

'Fair point.' Jack laughed.

'Malamute doing what it's told while the wolfhound refuses to please,' Melissa said. 'And I thought I'd seen everything.'

'I think he's got something.' Susan ran towards the dog, glad of getting away from the Melissa/Polly hybrid. It was creeping her out. Susan knew Polly didn't really like her, after her part in setting up Patrick the year before. In fairness, she hadn't really liked Polly before the fight at the Manor. Somewhere between running at her with a pike and getting 200mcg of Fentanyl injected into her neck, Susan had found a grudging respect for her.

In the year since, she had watched Polly eschew the easy life she could have had, taking all the wealth and power the Dewer legacy gave, and ploughing it into doing good for the town; for its womenfolk, for its children, for its less advantaged, and been taken aback. She had come to like her more than the terrifying old woman she replaced, though now regretted saying anything on the subject in their presence. Things would have been much easier if Lady Melissa Dewer had just stayed dead.

'What is it?' Jack said as Cronus howled excitedly before digging faster and pulling something from beneath the stone. Jack tried to grab it from his great jaws but the dog took it away, sauntering obediently back to his mistress to drop it at her feet.

'It's not the hagstone,' Melissa said. 'Just the strap-on cock we used that night.'

'Bollocks,' Susan said.

'No, they weren't really that realistic back then, see, it's more of a smooth shaft.' Melissa held the sex toy up, running Polly's fingers along its length. 'Ones with bollocks didn't come along until much much later, we never knew we'd like the feel of them slapping against us until we did.'

'So, another clue then?' Neville said, trying not to watch his granddaughter's hands fondle the enormous wooden phallus.

'I expect so,' Melissa replied, pulling sharply at the tip and making the men wince. 'Oh don't be such babies, it comes apart, there's a hollow bit in the middle, she's probably...'

'Well?' Jack picked impatiently at his fingernails, looking anywhere but at the intimidating substitute.

'Yes, another one,' Melissa said, pulling it in two and removing a scroll of paper. She unrolled it and scanned its content. 'Come on we need to go.'

'Hang on, what does it say? We're all part of this.' Susan put her foot down a little too hard and was rewarded with the boot she had only just tipped the snow from refilling with icy cold.

'Does it matter? Only I can solve them – with my memories from my time as Lord Elias – how are you lot going to know what Sophia was thinking 150 years ago? We go this way.' She stamped off towards the road.

'No, we're a team now.' Wendy grabbed Melissa's arm and span her round, Polly kept moving, dragging Wendy along with her. 'We spent years blindly following you, doing what we were told and never questioning why. We kept the secrets, and a fat lot of good it did us. My wife's dead and Susan's had to spend years cheating on her husband just because you told us we had to keep on sacrificing people who turned out not to have done anything wrong – not that she wouldn't have cheated on him anyway.' Susan glared at Wendy as she hopped behind, pulling her boot back on. Wendy just shrugged. 'No more death, no more secrets. What does it say?'

'Fuck's sake,' Mel muttered. 'It won't make any difference.' She backed down, removing Wendy's arm from hers but not stopping.

'Maybe not, but you know. Baby steps. I lost my wife as well.' Jack stopped in front of her, bringing them all to a grinding halt. The dogs ran round them in circles, not wanting to slow down.

'Fine, let's waste time. It says *"Where I did mourn my murdered love, your murdered love did pine. While both lives weighed upon my heart, the murders both were thine."'*

'What?' Polly's granddad asked.

'Exactly,' Mel huffed. 'We're going to the pub because Sophia couldn't get over her dead girlfriend.'

'Pub?' Jack perked up and backed off. 'Excellent, I could do with a drink.'

13

'Come off it Arthur, we're mates aren't we?' Clive said, stepping carefully towards the priest. 'Let's go back inside, have a chat about this and maybe come to some arrangement?' The dogs moved closer, hackles up and teeth bared.

'I'd very much like to do that,' Father Hearne replied, 'but it's not me you need to persuade.'

'You mean?' Kerry asked, eyes darting from dog to dog, looking for a gap.

'Yes, the only way we're getting out of this alive is to work with him.' The priest pointed to the smoke of The Traveller's fire rising through the trees. 'If you want to finish this, then you're going to have to open the gates and listen to his side. The Dewers are not blameless.'

'Yeah, we're not going to do that,' Clive said, edging closer to the door.

'Well it seems we're at a stand-off then. We need the Manor. We don't need you two, I'm sorry.' Father Hearne took Clive's arm and led him down the steps, surrounded by malamutes.

'Where are we going?' Kerry asked, herded along by the press of dogs.

'I believe Lady Melissa's old dog-grooming parlour still has the strongest lock of any outbuilding,' Father Hearne explained as the dogs pushed them towards it.

'So locking us up?' Clive nodded.

'Only choice I'm afraid,' the priest apologised. 'The others will be joining you soon, if all goes to plan, and it will.'

'What if we said we'd like to join you?' Kerry suggested, pushing up against the priest and fluttering her eyelashes.

'At this point I'm afraid I wouldn't believe you.' Father Hearne shook his head and opened the shabby, weather-beaten door of the stables onto a gleaming salon where Lady Melissa's dog grooming equipment remained in perfectly organised rows, hidden behind crumbling walls. 'You'll have to wait in here until you can convince him of your allegiance. But even I can tell you're lying.' He turned back to face them – ushering them towards the door. 'And I don't think you're any more his type than mine Kerry, sorry.'

'Fair enough,' Kerry replied, giving the priest a little shove against the granite mounting block behind his knees, sending him sprawling onto the cobbles. 'Go, Clive, for the doors now!'

They ran through the gap in the dogs his floundering body created, slipping on the ice for precious seconds, but rallying in time to get ahead of most of the pack.

Though not all.

They were knocked to the ground by a huge fluffy malamute that had been skulking underneath the wheelchair ramp. It only took a paw on each of their chests to immobilise them.

'Don't do this, it'll be easier if you co-operate,' Father Hearne said as he pulled the bar from the gate and the pack surrounded them. They weren't going to get a second chance. 'I'm sorry, but there's no other way. I've tried everything else.' He beckoned them towards the stables and they had no choice but to let the dogs herd them back.

Dan's face appeared at the front door, 'Guys, get back in, the dogs have changed, we need to lock up!' he shouted.

'So has this double-crossing shitrag of a priest. Get in, quick, we're done for, save yourself!' Kerry shouted as Father Hearne pushed her through the stable door.

'And Lynn, save Lynn!' Clive added, fighting against the dogs.

'Yeah, I suppose, save Lynn as well,' Kerry said, aiming a kick at the priest, who muttered a few words under his breath. Clive and Kerry found themselves unable to resist any longer and were pushed into the stable.

'I can't just leave you,' Dan shouted. He looked down the ramp, saw the dogs swirling round, weighed up the odds of getting down and back to help, and was about to push himself off when an enormous black bear of a dog swaggered through the gates with a roar. Wotan's master could not be far behind.

'Yes you can, you have to,' Kerry screamed, no longer visible. The door was locked and the priest was striding towards him at the head of the pack.

'Yep, yep, you're right. Sorry.' Dan span back round into the house and shoved the door closed, slamming bolts and turning keys. 'Lynn!' he shouted. 'We're in even deeper shit than we thought.'

'You're not kidding,' Lynn shouted as dogs poured from the kitchen. 'The back door won't hold. Cellar, now, we've got no choice.'

Dan rolled as fast as he could to the cellar door, expertly bouncing down the first steps and managing to stop at the top of the long winding slabs that led underground. 'Yep, you're not wrong, get a wriggle on!' he shouted.

Lynn ran full tilt across animal skin rugs, slipping at just the right time to avoid snapping teeth and slide to the cellar door. A malamute, Grey Wind Four, she thought, was right on her heels and pushed her over the threshold, where she rolled over Dan to scream all the way down the steep cellar stairway.

Dan punched the dog in the nose, knocking it back into the house. The last thing he saw before he forced the cellar door closed was bolts sliding themselves back across the front door, locks clicking open, before Father Hearne carefully came in and wiped the snow from his brogues.

'Can you give me a hand?' Dan shouted, jamming a long bar up behind the cellar door. 'If you're okay, these stairs are a bit tricky.'

'I'm alright, thank you for asking, give me a second and I'll be up.' Lynn pulled herself back to her feet, wiping dust and grit from her clothes and glad of all the yoga that kept her supple.

'Shit. Why though?' Dan said. 'What possible reason can Father Hearne have for doing this?'

'I don't know.' Lynn said, climbing the steps. 'But we've lost the house.'

'Yeah, and you might be able to escape the same way as the others. But I'm stuck here.' Dan indicated his wheelchair as Lynn started carefully lowering it down the steps.

'I won't leave you behind. We can both hide down here, it's massive. Anyway, I'll carry you through myself if it comes to it,' Lynn said. 'You know, we should really look at getting a lift put into this old place, if we're going to have to keep getting you up and down.' She grinned.

'I know I should be grateful, but that feels kind of like an attack. I don't really like coming down here you know, I'd rather not do it at all when we don't have to hide from sneaky bastard priests and packs of wolves.' Dan shrugged as Lynn levelled his chair out at the bottom. 'Not that I'm not grateful for the help. Thanks.'

'You're welcome,' Lynn said, hands on knees and panting. It didn't matter how fit she was, getting Dan all the way down the worn old spiral staircase was not easy. 'But it would definitely be more for me than you. I'm putting it to the trust at the next meeting.'

'Cool, now give me a hand blocking the bottom of these stairs off?' Dan grabbed at a huge iron gate, hidden in the dark.

'Whoa! How come I've never seen this before?' Lynn said, stepping back in surprise.

'Don't know,' Dan replied. 'It's always been there, thought it might be a good idea. You probably just missed it. Try looking back once in a while.' He grinned.

'Fine, does it work?' She grabbed one side as Dan pulled the other.

'Yeah, sure,' Dan confirmed. 'Gate goes right over, big key, bolts, the works. Nothing's getting through that. Nothing that isn't magic anyway.'

'So why didn't we use it last year?' Lynn put her hands on her hips and rubbed her side where the scar still hadn't quite healed. A scar she might not have had to endure.

'No idea, I was lying in the hall upstairs with a broken spine. Down here was all you wasn't it?' He slammed the gates together and pulled the bolts across.

'Fine.' Lynn turned the big key in the lock and stuck it in her pocket. She seethed at Lady Melissa for not using the gates. They could easily have kept Polly out, so she could do whatever she'd needed to do with the baby and kept Dourstone life the same as it ever had been. It wasn't like Lady Dewer to trust people over big locks and spells. Could somebody down here have been rooting for Polly?

'So what are we going to do?' Dan said. 'Are we going to try and get through the tunnel?'

'Not unless we have to,' Lynn said, rubbing her chin.

'We're trapped if we don't though,' Dan said. 'Like rats in a sack. And it won't just be that vicar, it'll be the guy. The guy with the horses and the big hat from the Hammer Horror movie. He'll know we're here, he can get us, we're not safe.' Dan's eyes darted around, looking for hiding places among pillars, alcoves and tunnels.

'He doesn't want us. He's got what he wants.' Lynn calmly pulled down a bottle of wine and cast her eye over the label. 'This should do.'

'Do for what? What's the plan?' Dan said.

'Do for an aperitif, open that bag.' She pointed to a gym bag lying innocuously next to the wine racks.

Dan hefted the bag onto his lap and unzipped it to reveal a feast of sandwiches, crisps, potato salad and every kind of picnic food neatly packed in tupperware boxes. 'Well, I can't say I'm not pleased, but how does this help?'

'Well,' Lynn said, pulling a second bottle from the rack. 'After the aperitifs, this sancerre should go very nicely with the tuna sandwiches, and after lunch we'll have a bit of a think about what to do next. I'd say we're safe enough down here for now. Drink?' She pulled the cork from the bottle, took a swig, then grabbed the bag and started laying food out on a barrel top.

'Really? We're going to get pissed and have a snack? That's your crisis plan?' Dan said, eyeing the food.

'Not pissed, no, just a couple to take the edge off,' Lynn explained. 'I had an idea we might end up having to hide out and did a bit of preparation this morning while Polly was off messing around in that sledge. There's supplies up in the tower as well, and any other easily defensible room.'

'Well, never let me take the piss out of you for being too organised ever again.' Dan bellied up to the table and grabbed a mini pasty. 'This is just what I needed, thanks.'

'You're welcome, I think Lady Mel used to keep the tasting glasses in...' Lynn rummaged through storage boxes beside the wine racks. 'Yes, here they are – oh! I've had an idea already, told you this was a good plan.' She rinsed off two glasses under the tap.

'It is. Fuck it, when in Dourstone, do as the Dourstonians do,' Dan said, reaching out for a glass.

'You are a Dourstonian Dan. The blowins are all in the raiding party.' Lynn handed him a brimming glass of Domaine Leflaive Montrachet Grand Cru. 'And we need to figure out a way to rescue Clive and Kerry from the stables. Aren't you worried about your wife?'

'Yeah, but she can take care of herself. Probably already on her way back.' Dan took a swig of the wine. 'Fuck me this is good. I knew those bloody Dewers had been holding the good stuff back. Tight bastards.'

'I'd believe that of Lady Melissa,' Lynn explained. 'But in Polly's case I think she just doesn't know good wine from vinegar.'

'Ooh, jealous much,' Dan laughed.

The others made their way into town. Ever conscious there could be eyes everywhere.

'I can't see any of his dogs,' Susan complained. 'There's nobody watching. We don't need to do this.'

They were behind the treeline, travelling through the woods, rather than keeping to the road. Admittedly, the road wouldn't have been a lot easier, being knee deep in snow, and at least under the trees the ground was a little closer to their feet. But what lurked under snow in the woods was more treacherous than tarmac.

The dogs were making short work of it, Cronus being built for this, and Fenrir having learned all he needed of trees under snow last year. One or other of them would double back every couple of minutes and bark at the humans to keep up. It was slow going on two legs, picking over hidden boulders, logs and rabbit holes.

'It's not just the dogs, he can use the birds and the badgers and the mice and the...'

'Okay Melissa, you don't need to list all the animals on the ark,' Jack interrupted, pulling up short as his boot caught another unseen obstacle. 'We understood you the first time. Why can't you do that?'

'I can.' Melissa puffed Polly's chest out, leaning one hand against a tree as she waited for Jack to free himself.

'Well, can you borrow a sparrow to go and check on the Manor then?' Wendy suggested. 'See how they're holding up back there.'

'I can't at the moment. I'm in a bit of a...' Melissa let go the tree and began walking again.

'Bit of a what? Why are we stuck with the weak one? Maybe we should go back and work with the other guy,' Susan quipped, bouncing through snow to catch up.

'Maybe you should. He'll certainly make you a wonderful offer, too good to be true no doubt.' She turned her head and grinned. 'You can take the gamble if you like, but if he can't think of a good use for something, or someone, he tends to destroy them.'

'Why can't you do any magic?' Susan stood her ground.

'Because...'

'Actually,' Wendy butted in. 'We never saw you do any real magic when you had your own body. Nothing Derren Brown couldn't do, a bit of suggestion here, a knowing wink there. It was all just swagger, right?'

'I kept that body alive for 250 years, do you think Derren fucking Brown could do that?' Melissa scowled, kicking a branch up from under the snow. It flew much further than you'd expect before crashing back through white waves. 'I don't do magic for fun. Nor just for show. It isn't a toy. I only do it when it's needed.'

'We need it now,' Jack muttered.

'Yes, I am aware of that, and I am sorry. But thanks to this one' – she pointed at Polly's chest – 'killing me off last year and leaving me having to borrow any old passing piece of second-class flesh, I'm not exactly my old self.'

'Then why are we putting up with your moaning?' Susan said.

'Only I can solve these riddles, remember?' Melissa reminded her. 'And I know more about our adversary than any of you. I've faced him before, this town is everything it is because of the history between us. You need me.'

'Fine, but we need Polly back. You promised,' Wendy said, grabbing at her elbow as she slid on a patch of ice.

'You'll get her back, don't panic, but I've still got a few tricks up my sleeve.' Melissa smiled as they burst from the trees into town. 'Here we are then. Come on, pub time.'

They slid downhill to the Drop of Dew, wide-eyed and looking out for birds in the roofline or rats on the ground. Jack reached the door first and was surprised to hear the sound of lunchtime drinkers spilling out over the street. They marched in to find a perfectly normal Sunday afternoon. A table by the window were just finishing up their roast dinner, a group at the bar were drinking, chatting and laughing like nothing had happened, and Anna was sitting in the window, reading a book and checking her watch every time she glanced nervously out.

'Hello all,' Pete the barman greeted them. 'Usuals?'

'Ummm... not for me,' Wendy replied, temporarily taken aback. 'I'll just have a double shot latte if you don't mind. Polly?' She raised her eyebrow. 'Do you want tea?'

'God no, I'll need a Sherry Cobbler first, then a whisky, on the rocks, to chase,' Melissa replied.

'Okay, one of each of those, to start with Pete, thanks very much,' Wendy confirmed.

'Well, I'll see if I can remember how to make a cobbler, haven't had to make one of those since...' Pete tailed off.

'Hi Jack,' Anna said, appearing behind him without a sound. 'I was beginning to think you'd forgotten our date.'

'Shit, sorry. I had.' He checked himself in the mirror behind the bar. 'Given the circumstances, I assumed it was off.'

'A bit of snow never stopped anybody round here before Jack, and you're here now.' She slid an arm around him.

'Um, yeah, of course, sorry – excuse me ladies, Neville, I'll catch you later.' Jack allowed Anna to steer him away to her window seat.

'Fuck's sake.' Susan exhaled loudly. 'Fucking men, it never ends. What are we looking for Mel?' She spun on her heel and folded her arms.

'Difficult to explain until I find it. Do you have a cigarette?' she asked, looking over to the back door.

'No,' Susan answered, a little too quickly.

'Do you?' Melissa stared into her eyes with those silver gimlets that bored into the soul, stripping away any pretence. Melissa had lost none of her mental agility since losing her body and Susan found her resolve slipping.

'Okay, yes I do, would you like one?' She pulled a pack of cigarettes from her inside pocket.

'Yes please, let's pop out the back.' Melissa led the way to the beer garden.

'Can I?' Neville butted in, grabbing a cigarette. 'I've run out and my spares were in the van. I'll get some more later, pay you back, I'm not a cig-moocher, promise.'

'No worries Nev,' Susan said. 'Nice of you to ask nicely.'

'Sorry I didn't offer you one earlier, didn't know,' he explained as they headed down the corridor.

'No, I kind of wanted to keep it that way,' she explained.

The beer garden was dominated by an elaborate construction of decking, shining hand rails, wicker guards and anti-slip strips topped with a proper thatched roof. It had cost the pub a fortune to put in over the summer to replace the old smoking shelter – a bit of crumbling galvanised and wood leaning against the wall – that flew off over the roof in the previous winter's storms taking the chimney with it. The new one had just enough wall to keep the wind out, and just little enough to allow people to legally smoke inside. So that was where they went, the two dogs scattering to the far corners of the garden to write their names in the snow.

'Have you got a light?' Melissa asked.

'Shit, no,' Susan admitted, patting her pockets in search of a lighter she rarely used and had left in a different coat.

'Here,' Neville said, tossing a battered old zippo across. 'Use mine.'

'Thank you handsome,' Melissa lit her cigarette and winked before exhaling a long plume of smoke from Polly's lungs and watching it float off.

Polly's granddad spun the cigarette between his fingers as his lighter skipped across to Susan, who seemed to take an age to get hers lit, before coming back to him. He lit his own and sucked gratefully at the smoke – too old now to see any reason to give up.

'Doesn't this strike anybody else as odd?' Wendy said, fiddling at her rings.

'What?' Susan answered, slouching into the bench, more relaxed now her secret was out and nobody seemed to care.

'This place, carrying on as if nothing's happened? Like it's just an ordinary snowy Sunday?' Wendy leaned forward.

'They're probably just making the best of it,' Susan replied, flicking ash to the floor. 'You know, don't let the bastards grind you down. Blitz spirit, Dourstone style.'

'Yeah, you're probably right.' Wendy nodded. 'Keep on keeping on, keep your chin up and keep drinking.'

'Good advice,' Polly's granddad said, swigging on his half of Guinness.

'Heh, yeah. I should listen to myself.' Wendy wiped coffee froth from her lip. 'Might have a real one. Anyone for seconds?'

'Yes, yes and yes,' Melissa answered for all. 'We need a break. Time to think, rally our thoughts and figure out what to do when we have the Bellever Hagstone.' She stubbed out her cigarette, watching the smoke trails thoughtfully.

'Not for me,' Neville said. 'I've still got plenty thanks. But I could do with some crisps if you don't mind. Breakfast feels like a long time ago.'

'Okay, I'll get them in.' Wendy headed inside. 'Talking of breaks, can we have Polly back now?'

'Fine, fine,' Melissa said. 'I need to do a bit of thinking without you lot constantly interrupting, here you go.' Her eyes faded back to brown and she started to cough uncontrollably.

'Fuck's sake, I can't believe she smoked that. Cow,' Polly spluttered on her return.

'I didn't realise you'd given up love,' Neville said.

'I never smoked Granddad, never have, never will. You're thinking of Ruth.'

'Your sister, yes, so I am, sorry, must be the alzheimers beginning.' He grinned and looked imploringly at Susan who handed over another cigarette.

Sorry Polly, it wasn't without good reason though. Melissa reassured her.

'It better not be,' Polly said, standing up and stumbling. 'Can somebody stop her putting alcohol in me?' She sat back down again.

'What do you reckon for the rest of the day then Wendy?' Jack asked, feet up by the fire in a comfy armchair. 'Stay here, have a few drinks, maybe get some food before we get the kids from Katie? I'm starving.'

'Are you on crack?' she replied, stopping in her tracks as she headed for the bar. 'We're up against forces we cannot comprehend, we're trapped, our friends are – hopefully – holding the Manor against an unholy pack of dogs, we can't get out of town to get anywhere near our kids. And you're just going to sit here and get pissed?'

'I... I...' Jack shook his head, never once taking his eyes from Anna's cleavage opposite.

'I see what you're doing,' Anna said. 'Making up some drama just because you're jealous he's with me. You're like all those other posh mums, trying to get a piece of Jack now he's single. Well it won't work, he's going to be with me now, and only me, no more philandering with other people's wives. Isn't that right Jack?' She tensed her biceps against her boobs to maintain his attention.

'I... I...' Jack said again.

'Fuck's sake Anna, I'm gay. I'd be more likely trying to get him out of the way so I could have a go on those hypnotic funbags of yours.' She was having trouble not staring, she couldn't remember if hers had defied gravity like that when she was younger and childless, she'd like to think so, but Anna looked like some comic book artist's fantasy made flesh. 'But I'm not, you're young enough to be my – and his – daughter. Haven't you noticed what's happening here?'

'Yes, you're trying to ruin my fun, that's what.' Anna pouted, fluttering her eyes at Wendy.

'Okay, if that's the way you want it, yes I am.' Wendy dragged Jack to his feet and pulled him out to the garden. 'Come on Jack, you've had enough fun for one afternoon. See you later Anna, call me if you're feeling a little bi.'

'What's going on?' he said, as he was lowered onto a bench.

'You seem to have been brainwashed by Anna's tits, that's what.' Wendy stood over him, back to the sun, and folded her arms.

'Where are the drinks?' Susan asked. 'I'm thirsty and you went in to get the next round.'

'Sorry, Jack and his little tart knocked it clear out of my mind,' Wendy replied, spinning on her heel.

'Did they now?' Susan grabbed Jack's leg and stared him in the eye.

'I'll get the drinks then,' Polly croaked, glad of the opportunity to be alone.

'And food, can you get a menu please Pol, I'm starving,' Jack said.

'Yeah, custard tart maybe?' Susan said.

'It's just Anna. She's harmless, nice girl, I feel sorry for her,' Jack said.

'Yes, I'm sure you do a lot of feeling,' Susan replied with arched eyebrow.

Jack turned a deep red and shrugged.

'Do you remember what we're doing now then?' Wendy was well aware of what was going on between Jack and Susan. She was aware of what had been going on with Jack and most of the women in town since Edwina died, she'd shared a few. Not at the same time of course, but once you dug your fingers underneath, as it were, this town was a hot bed of secrets, lies and infidelity. A combination of the widowed life and Tinder had really opened her eyes.

'Yes,' Jack replied. 'That was a bit weird. I genuinely didn't remember, it felt like a normal Sunday afternoon. Total amnesia. Maybe there's something in the Guinness?'

'No,' Wendy confirmed. 'Neville's been on the black stuff as well and he can remember what we're doing can't you Neville?' she asked Polly's granddad.

'Looking for a hagstone to stop the weird monster guy with the dogs.' He saluted. 'And dying of hunger, what happened to my crisps?'

'Yes, I've said I'm sorry Neville, but something's going on. Polly'll get them, and she won't get waylaid.' She smiled before turning back to Jack. 'See, it's not the drinks. It's probably those tits,' Wendy theorised. Seeing them in her mind's eye she was pretty sure they could brainwash anyone. If she'd learned one thing from her hookup app adventures it was that even the most hetero of housewives can turn out to be a little bit gay.

'I don't think it's Anna's tits.' Jack sulked.

'They're pretty decent though.' Susan swirled what was left of her drink around and nodded.

'Maybe I should go in and check?' Neville added. 'I'm getting to be a pretty good judge of the occult.'

'No, I think you're safe for now.' Jack grinned. 'Don't let me stop you if you want to though.' Both women started to admonish him for this everyday sexism. 'Joke, joke, sorry. Anyway, it's more complicated than that. The longer I was in there, the warmer and fuzzier I felt. Like nothing's gone wrong, like...'

'Like what?' Susan asked, rubbing her head. 'And what do you mean? What's wrong?'

'I'm not sure, are we getting more drinks?' Jack asked.

'I could take another half, yes,' Neville said. 'I'm glad I came down here, you guys are okay.'

'Yes, I can't believe we've not met before Neville. You'll stay a few more days? Help us out running the Manor, see what your clever granddaughter has created?' Wendy said as Susan offered her cigarettes across.

'Of course, of course.' Neville took the proffered smoke, lighting hers and his with one deft motion. 'Maybe I'll nip back and bring the rest of the family over for Christmas, help Polly remember where she comes from.'

'Yeah, that would be nice. We all need more family. But for now we'll get some drinks in. We'll make an afternoon of it, the kids are with Katie all day,' Wendy said. 'It'll be nice. It's my round right?' She got up, heading for the door. 'Maybe we can plan a Christmas party when I come back.'

'Sorry Jack, they've stopped doing proper food now, so I got you and Granddad some Scampi Fries and Doritos…' Polly nearly spilled the tray of drinks she was carrying outside as she bumped into Wendy. 'What are you doing?'

'I'm… I'm… I'm not sure Polly.' Wendy rubbed her forehead. 'Something very weird is happening. I don't think it's the boobs.'

14

'Do you think he's in the house now?' Dan asked, clearing plates and glasses.

'Yes,' Lynn said. 'And I don't think there's anything we can do to change that.'

'So we should leave then? There's no point staying here. I'm sure I could wheel that tunnel if I gave it a go.' Dan put the pile of dishes on his lap in the sink.

'Well yes, we could run and hide and wait for him to win,' Lynn muttered. 'But I've been thinking, like I said, I have the beginnings of a plan: we should stay here. Be eyes and ears, find out exactly what he's doing. It'll speed things up when the others get back with the hagstone.'

'If they get back with the hagstone,' Dan said. 'If they don't then we're sitting ducks. He'll flush us out like a shitty drainpipe.'

'But if they do then information is vital.' Lynn banged her hand on the barrel. 'Pinpointing where he is and the quickest route there without being caught could be the difference between finishing him off and being stuck here forever, doing his bidding. We're more use to the cause doing something than nothing.'

'Been doing Lady fucking Melissa's bidding for years, hasn't done me any good,' Dan muttered. 'Now we do Polly's bidding and we're locked in a cellar. Maybe he wouldn't be so bad.'

'Ha, you saw what he did to the town, you heard what Mel said. I know what she's like, but I'd believe her over that maniac any day.' Lynn rubbed her hand, the barrel was harder than she thought. 'No, we stay with her until we have no choice. We fight.'

'But we're in the cellar Lynn,' Dan pointed out. 'We can't hear or see anything. And even if we could, who are we telling? How are we helping?'

'We have this.' Lynn grabbed a large wooden wheel and gave it a twist. A box, just about the right size for a person to squeeze inside, appeared in the little window at the bottom of its shaft. 'One of us could fit in. Perfect for spying.'

'The dumb waiter? I reckon I could give it a go if you give me a bunk up, yeah.' Dan's eyes lit up at the chance to do something useful.

'And we've got the speaking tubes.' Lynn waved her arm towards the old servant's waiting room where a series of what looked like antique telephone mouthpieces hung from the ceiling. 'They're two-way, don't ask me how I know. Lady Melissa used to give me some very weird jobs.'

'You and me both Lynn,' Dan answered. 'What if he comes down here though? I don't think that gate'll hold very long against his magic, the front door didn't.'

'Well then, we'll just have to put a few more things in his way won't we?' Lynn grinned. 'Melissa had a lot of tricks set up down here, if we can remember how to re-arm them it's very defensible.'

'So why do we keep forgetting?' Susan asked, lighting another cigarette.

'It's a kind of magic,' Polly's granddad said. 'Don't let me forget to buy some more of those before we leave. I don't want to smoke your whole stash.'

'It is,' Polly agreed, coughing again. 'Mel says he's making everyone forget what happened last night, forget that they're trapped here. As long as they feel content, and like it's another normal day it leaves him free to concentrate on whatever he's doing, rather than fire-fighting the whole town. This is buying him time.'

'So why isn't it working on us?' Wendy said, brushing a stray piece of ash from her sleeve.

'It is, sort of, just not all the time. I think that's probably my fault, well, Mel's. She thinks being in proximity to her is what's keeping us unaffected.' Polly held her arms out in a 'not-my-fault-if-it's-bullshit' gesture.

'That makes sense.' Susan nodded.

'Yeah, or it could be something entirely different. Anyway, you're not going to like this next bit,' Polly said, getting back to her feet. 'We've got to take this whole thing down.'

'What whole thing?' her granddad said.

'This shelter, Mel says the Bellever Hagstone – or probably the next stupid treasure hunting clue – is underneath it. She thinks the clue leads to some old shell grotto that used to be here when people had things like shell grottos and the public could be trusted not to fuck them up.' Polly explained. 'But it got buried sometime in the middle of last century when it became apparent that the general public could no longer be trusted not to fuck them up, and that stupid fucking landlord has built this right over the top with – and I quote – "no regard whatsoever for local history".' Melissa always got a bit ranty when the Drop of Dew's owner came up. He bought it as a handy tax write-off and lived on a tropical island for similar reasons. He never visited his investment and rarely threw any money at it, so the extravagant smoking shelter had been quite the shock. There had been talk that he was handing the place over to his useless layabout son to try and teach him the value of hard work, but the shelter was the only sign of this new intervention. Other than that, Pete the barman (who was the de facto manager, but refused to take any title higher than barman without the accompanying salary) ran the place from day-to-day, rarely being questioned over any expense he ran up, as long as it ensured the place ran at the right level for the owner's tax bill.

'How?' Jack said, getting down on his knees next to the shelter and looking underneath. 'It's concreted in down here. There are steel supports, they look deep.'

'Just get the floor up, we should be able to get to it if we can hit the actual ground, right Polly?' Wendy said, kicking at the wooden decking.

Polly shrugged, 'I guess, I mean I can't say for certain what's going to work. I'm not even sure Melissa's got the right end of this riddle.'

'Won't know if we don't try, I've got this,' Polly's granddad pulled a cheap multi-tool he used for on the fly guitar repairs from his pocket. 'It's got a slot-head driver. Should help.'

'Great, I'll make a start then,' Jack said, taking it from him and jabbing it into the first screw head he came to. 'In the middle you reckon then Polly?'

'That's what Mel says, yeah, try there first.'

'Ow, fuck it.' The head slipped from the screw, causing Jack to stab his finger. 'This might take some time, can somebody get me another drink?'

'I'll go,' Polly said.

'No, anybody else.' He jerked his head up, eyes wide. 'If you get caught up in there I'll forget what I'm doing.'

'I'll do it, I can grab some cigarettes while I'm in there,' Polly's granddad said. 'Besides, I'm not from round here, I'm less likely to get waylaid by a bunch of people I don't know distracting me.'

'Really?' Polly tilted her head. 'Hasn't that basically been the story of your whole life?'

'Maybe sometimes, but I know I've come here to see you, so I'll come right back out, won't I?'

'No, but you'll be back out as soon as you need another fag, so you're still our lowest flight-risk. Your round Granddad.'

'Fair point, fair point.' His grin widened.

'Mine's an orange juice and lemonade, anybody else?' Polly shouted.

'Coffee!' Wendy said.

'Tribute,' Jack.

'Any decent red, large please,' Susan added.

'And I need a cuppa tea,' Neville finished.

'Good, remember that, at least, and get us some more snacks.' Polly patted him on the shoulder and sent him in.

Enough of all this distraction, we've already taken too long. Has anybody else got a screwdriver? Melissa's voice battered the edge of Polly's brain.

'I wouldn't have thought so,' Polly answered out loud.

'What's she on about now?' Susan asked, crawling about the decking to hunt out loose boards.

'Wants to know if anybody else has a screwdriver.'

'Does she think I'd be scrabbling around down here trying to do it with a five pence piece if I had a fucking screwdriver?' Susan's head jerked up, eyes livid.

'No, I suppose not.'

'Ow, there goes a nail, I hate this,' Susan cried as another screw failed to move.

'These heads are all shot to shit,' Wendy confirmed, getting up from her own laboured attempts to remove screws with loose change and bending over to watch Jack's lack of progress. 'We need a drill, at the very least.'

Fuck's sake, this is taking too long.

'Well, what do you suggest Melissa?' Polly shouted. 'Devon and Cornwall Farm Stores closed down months ago. Nowhere in town to buy tools, no time to go and rustle them up from our homes. Probably can't get back into the Manor now, even if we had time.'

Jesus, if you want something doing… Polly felt a tightness in her head, her limbs getting heavy.

'No, not again, please, I don't…' she said, stumbling against the wall to try and keep her balance.

Yes you do, stop fighting it.

She didn't stop fighting, she pushed back against the bubble expanding through her head, but Melissa was strong, the bubble's influence got thicker and she felt herself being forced out.

'Here you all go,' Polly's granddad said, carefully laying a tray of drinks and crisps down before opening a fresh packet of cigarettes.

'Thank you,' Melissa said, pulling Polly's body upright, taking a cigarette and lighting it with a snap of her fingers. 'Everybody stand back, we don't have time for this.'

Nobody needed to be told twice, they jumped from the decking and grabbed their drinks as a loud screeching sound – as of rusting iron grinding against ancient oak – filled their ears. Melissa stared intently at the shelter's decking, sucking on the cigarette and blowing smoke in intricate patterns. She swooped the cigarette through the air, typing on an imaginary keyboard with her other hand as screws popped from boards, walls, roof and handrails before the whole structure crumpled like ten year old flat pack furniture and piled itself up neatly behind its previous position.

'I thought you couldn't do…' Jack said.

'Can't really, probably shouldn't have, sorry Polly, you're really going to feel this.' Melissa's eyes rolled back in Polly's head before she collapsed on the gravel. The wreckage fell back to the ground it had so recently been an integral part of.

'Shit, little help here,' Jack said reaching out too late to catch her.

'What happened?' Wendy said, her face dropping. 'We need both of them, not just Melissa, we need Polly. Polly! Polly!' she screamed as she shook her on the ground.

'I'm not sure that's going to help, that looked painful.' Susan gently pulled Wendy away. 'Maybe a little restraint?' She carefully checked Polly's vitals. 'She's alive, give her a minute.'

'I'm no expert,' Neville said. 'But it looks like Melissa did something to Polly to pull that off. Like she's been drained by the magic.'

'Yeah, no shit Granddad,' Wendy said.

'Hey, I'm her granddad, not yours,' he replied.

'I'm sorry, I'm just worried about her. I... I...' Wendy tailed off.

'I guessed that, apology accepted.' He smiled and put a comforting hand on her back. 'Now make sure she's not like this for nothing and go see what's under that floor.'

Wendy and Susan clambered into the wreckage to try and find the hagstone.

'This is just a mess, I can't find anything,' Wendy said, kicking at bits of wood.

'No, there's a clear spot right here, that must have been deliberate.' Susan stared at the arrangement of debris. 'It wouldn't randomly fall like this. I wonder...' She lit a cigarette and dropped to her knees.

'What are you doing?' Wendy said.

'Melissa didn't take that first cigarette just for a smoke. She never smoked before, not unless she'd had a skinful. And she grabbed that other one right before she started doing whatever she did. There must have been a reason... there, see that?' Susan's smoke was being sucked down into the ground rather than floating off to the sky. 'Smoke doesn't do that. There's something there, pass me that bit of handrail.'

Wendy pulled a length of shining steel from the heaped rubbish and passed it over. Susan hacked at ground that fell away.

'See, there's a passage down here, or something. The air's pulling down anyway, give us a hand.' Wendy and Jack both grabbed bits of wrecked shelter and began beating at the ground until it revealed an opening.

'There's a cave, it's like she said, there's some kind of grotto down here,' Jack said, lighting his phone torch. 'How did this get lost?'

'I don't think it was lost, I think it was hidden,' Wendy said, noting the careful boundary stones that ensured it was only filled in as far as the door. Inside it was clear of rubble, lined by a stone bench with a table-height rectangular stone structure in the middle. 'Look, the top comes off, anybody want to take a guess at what's in there?'

'Not really,' Jack said. 'It looks a bit like a tomb. Look, it's even got a name on it.'

They peered at the monolith and found the name Caroline Louisa Linton-Dunsdon engraved on top in gothic lettering.

'Who the fuck is Caroline Louisa Linton-Dunsdon?' Susan said. 'And what's she got to do with Melissa and this Sophia and Nathaniel?'

'Search me, we'll have to wait for Polissa out there to wake up. But this thing didn't get filled in for nothing… Will you look at that?'

The dust cleared and Jack's phone illuminated the cave, it was intricately inlaid with all kinds of shells, interweaved with lacquered bird feathers, animal bones and hagstones – though none big enough to be the one they sought.

'What do you suppose they did with this?' Wendy asked, running her hands carefully over sharp-edged cockleshells.

'No idea,' Susan replied, sitting on the bench and finishing her cigarette. 'Looks like some weird witchy shit again. Honestly, this fucking town. Some days I wish I'd never met Clive.'

'Is that so?' Jack grinned, pushing his hip against her shoulder.

'Get a room you two, we don't have time for this.' Wendy stormed past them and tested the weight of the stone lid. 'One corner each, come on, if this Caroline Louisa's a vampire, then at least we'll catch her in daylight.'

They took a corner each and manhandled the top off.

Susan ground out the end of her cigarette in the dust of the tomb-like hole. Inside was a mother-of-pearl-engraved jewellery box and an old-fashioned pewter tankard with a wooden lid. At least it wasn't ancient bones, or worse, new ones. She picked up the box and rooted through it. The only contents were a silver necklace in the form of a hare and a pale green garter. 'Well, this is no fucking help. What about that thing? Is that the..?'

'No,' Polly said, limping up behind them. 'It's not, but...' She picked up the tankard and read the inscription on the front: '*For Nathaniel Harker, the city gent who won our country hearts, from Lord and Lady Dewer.*' She opened it and found a piece of rolled up paper. 'Yep, another clue.'

'You're okay!' Wendy could not disguise her grin as she threw her arms round Polly. 'Thank God, I thought maybe you were...'

'I was what, dead? In a coma? Out of the game?' Polly pulled herself free before accepting similar hugs from Susan and Jack. 'Takes more than a bit of ill-advised magic to break me.'

'Thank the lord for that, girl,' Neville said, enveloping her in a bone-crushing hug that she thought he might never release. She didn't mind.

'So what is this place? What does it mean and where do we go next?' Wendy asked.

'Well, Mel's not going to be much use for a while. That took more from her than it did me.' Polly leant against her granddad as she unrolled the ancient paper.

'Read the clue,' Susan said, scowling.

'Okay,' Polly began. 'It says: *In the heart and the hearth your trust betrayed, love dragged apart and never saved.*"'

'What the hell does that mean?' Jack said, swigging his drink to clear the dust from his throat.

'It means,' Polly said. 'We're off to my ex-not-quite-in-laws' place. Lucky I've got these isn't it?' She reached deep into her anorak pockets and pulled out an enormous bunch of keys.

'How on earth did you figure that out?' her granddad asked as they clambered from the grotto to make their way back across the wreckage of the beer garden.

'The Sumners are how I got dragged into this mess in the first place. All this ties into them, Nathaniel Harker, and the madness that led to Patrick's great-grandfather being given to the Sumner family, who still own the house. I can do this bit, I read Nathaniel's diaries, and he seems to be the key to these clues. Melissa has a bit of a blind spot where Nathaniel's concerned, especially when it comes to his relationship with Thomas Sumner.' Polly knocked back the last of her orange juice and lemonade, slammed the glass on a picnic table, and opened the gate. 'Come on then.'

15

'Any more bright ideas?' Kerry said, lying on a high dog-washing table with a soft top, knees in the air.

'I'm out, or rather, we're in.' Clive slid down the wall to sit on the floor. 'There's no way out.'

Since being locked in the stables, Clive and Kerry had tried all the doors, windows and skylights, but to no avail. Inside the weathered, crumbling old stable block, Lady Melissa had fitted modern locks, heavyweight doors, and thick, strong walls. No matter how hard the captives kicked at doors, picked at locks or hammered blunt objects against windows there was no way through.

'So what do we do?' Kerry asked. 'We can't just give up.'

'I can,' Clive said, reaching into a cupboard where he had spotted a tell-tale glint from behind the shampoo. 'Especially with this.' He pulled a bottle of gin and two glasses from Melissa's secret stash.

'Fine, pour us a drink then,' Kerry sat up on the table. 'Any mixers?'

'Not just mixers, there's a whole cocktail cabinet.' Clive shook his head. 'I'm not knocking it, but why on earth did she keep this out here?'

'Probably so she could seduce any sexy dog owners, you know what she was like,' Kerry said, taking a gin and tonic.

'Yeah, like a female Jack.' Clive laughed. 'Do you think she'll get hold of Polly and let Jack take her for a ride?'

'Poor Jack, she'd eat him alive.' Kerry laughed.

'I expect he'd give her a run for her money these days,' Clive replied. 'He's been getting enough practice since Edwina died, and I doubt Polly's been letting Melissa keep her hand in.'

'Yeah, much as I like a bit of a flirt, even I'm getting bored of Jack's endless innuendo.' Kerry sipped her drink. 'Dunno why all them girls are falling for it.'

'You know Sue's banging him too?'

'Well, yes, I had figured it out. I didn't like to say, but they're not very subtle.' Kerry said. 'Are you okay?'

'Yeah, it's just a sex thing for her, I know what she's like. I don't ask, she doesn't tell, and sadly I'm too clever for my own good.' Clive finished his drink and went to pour another.

'And you're okay with that, I mean Jack's your friend.'

'Yeah, he's my best mate, and he's shagging my wife, I should be livid. But that kind of makes it easier. I know him, I know what he's like, and I know he won't take her away from me. He's just fucking about. It's kind of better this way, if I'm honest.'

'Really?'

'It's better than not knowing who she's with, or what she's doing. She could be out there hooking up with all kinds of rapists and murderers on please-fuck-me.net. At least with this she's just banging my mate in the shed when she doesn't think I'm home.'

'Yeah, but your best friend is shagging your wife,' Kerry pointed out.

'I know, but then I'm not,' Clive explained. 'So I can't really complain. She's a very sexual woman. I can't let her waste that while I'm sitting around watching repeats of Top Gear. And that's about as exciting as I am now, no libido whatsoever. Doesn't mean I don't still love her and want to be with her.'

'Whatever gets you through your life I suppose.' Kerry shook her head. 'Christ, who isn't he fucking?'

'Polly,' Clive confirmed. 'But not for want of trying.'

'Welcome to Casa Sumner,' Polly announced, throwing back a pair of unremarkable gates on the square.

'Fucking hell,' Wendy said. 'You wouldn't think it from the outside would you?'

'You would not,' Polly agreed. Behind the frontage of a small terraced house lay an enormous courtyard leading to three large outbuildings and a very decent sized house and gardens.

'No wonder none of the houses on Market Street have got gardens,' Susan remarked. 'This place must go all the way to the top and all the way out to the sides.'

'Coopers need space to coop, right?' Neville joked.

'Right Granddad,' Polly laughed. 'And overpaid wankers from London need a big country pad to impress their rich country friends.'

'When were they last down?' Jack asked.

'Funeral.' Polly shrugged.

'Oh yeah, course, sorry.' He wheeled about aimlessly on one foot, unsure of what to say.

'You're alright, they didn't come down once in the year Patrick and I were here together. They've had this place ever since Patrick's gran died – she was the last Sumner to live in Dourstone full time, even if she was only a Sumner by marriage. By rights they should have sold it off, or at least rented it out, but no. They kept it, they still keep it, and deny good local people the chance of a home in town. I tried to talk them into finding a new community use for it after Patrick died, or selling it off to somebody local. I thought they might see reason, want to do some good after losing him, but no. They never come down, they don't want to use it, they won't sign it over to the Trust. Seems like his dad got all the shitty bits of the Dewer blood and none of the good.'

'Never met them,' Susan said. 'Sounds like I don't want to.'

'They didn't even want to have the funeral here. Said he should go back to Chelsea with them, have a service with all their fabulous friends and his mum's family up there. It took all I had to persuade them he'd want to stay here, with me and Elizabeth.' Polly knelt down to pick up a storm-damaged flower pot.

'That's awful, is it because...' Susan began.

'Because we weren't married, yeah,' Polly finished. 'Then I had to do it all over again with the ashes. They wanted him on the mantelpiece, I wanted him in the garden at the cottage, where he could see the moors, where some of him could blow over the fence and be out there on a phantom bicycle.'

'Wankers, they don't deserve you, or this.' Wendy put her arm round Polly to help her back up.

'They don't even come out when they are here, they bring their fancy friends down, shut the gates and enjoy their fabulous wealth in private. Pricks.' Polly leaned in to Wendy's shoulder and walked her over to the front door. 'Come on, we need to get to the bedroom. That's where it will be.'

'Bedroom it is.' Wendy grinned.

'Oh, how fun. Nosing around the rich people's house while

they're out!' Susan clapped her hands together. 'Do they have a wine fridge?'

'Forget wine, please let them have food,' Jack said, Neville nodding along.

'Yes, hopefully to both,' Polly said.

They walked down a cobbled passageway – being a barrelworks there had to be a way through from one side of the property to the other in order to roll the big ones in and out – and then through another locked door to the side which opened into a huge kitchen. Polly opened a wine fridge that loomed like an alcoholic altarpiece. 'Ta dah! Knock yourselves out.'

'Oh my,' Wendy gasped, running her fingers over bottles and pulling out a chilled Chateau d'Esclans Rosé. 'Do you have any idea what this is worth?'

'Have we not drunk enough yet?' Jack asked. 'Food Polly, food?'

'No, not today we haven't.' Susan snatched the bottle from Wendy. 'All that work in the beer garden fair sobered me back up. I need this.'

'Far be it from me to disagree with a lady,' Neville said, pulling glasses from a welsh dresser and setting them up on an oak island that dominated the kitchen. 'But Jack does have a point, breakfast was a long time ago, and those crisps did nothing.'

'Here, I don't think you'll find anything else.' Polly threw 3 bags of kettle chips, half a pack of chocolate hob-nobs and a four-pack of baked beans across to Jack, who managed to catch all but the hob-nobs, that made a crunching sound against the cupboard door.

'Who's drinking this then?' Susan opened the bottle of Rosé.

'None for me,' Neville said. 'I don't drink perfume, I'll put the kettle on.'

'Lovely, I'll have a cup of tea as well please Neville,' Wendy said.

'Me too,' Polly agreed, noting that the kitchen surfaces looked too pristine for actual food preparation to have ever sullied them. She'd hazard a guess that the closest this kitchen had ever come to it was unloading takeaway cartons, despite it being both large and well-equipped enough to cope with even the most demanding of chefs.

'Am I drinking this alone then?' Susan gaped, pouring herself a large glass.

'Never.' Jack came up behind her and slid another glass next to hers.

'Thank you, at least I can rely on you.' She filled it up. 'Okay then you lot, here's to a successful mission and a proper Christmas.'

'Proper Christmas,' they all chanted as her and Jack clinked glasses. Wendy ripped open the crisp packets, spreading them out flat as makeshift sharing plates.

'Oh thank God,' Neville said, putting the shattered hob-nob from the top of the open packet into his mouth and eating it fast enough not to notice how soggy it was. 'I thought I might pass out if I didn't get some food soon.'

'Same here, thank fuck for posh crisps. Can't ever afford them myself, yum,' Jack agreed, ramming a handful into his mouth and having to take a drink to counteract the dehydrating salt. 'Jesus, this is vile.' He spat the priceless wine into the sink, tipped the rest of his glass out and refilled it with water before drinking it down in one. 'That's better.'

'Told you it was perfume.' Neville grinned as he made three cups of tea. 'You want one of these?'

'No thanks, I'm alright with water,' Jack said.

Susan glared at him.

'Right, you lot stay here, I'll go and get the Bellever Hagstone,' Polly said, before taking a big mouthful of tea.

'You seem very sure of yourself. Are you that confident you know where it is?' Susan asked.

'Yes, the clue was very specific. It's where love was betrayed, where Nathaniel was dragged away from Thomas Sumner, thinking he'd been abandoned by everyone who loved him.' She swung on the kitchen door.

'Sounds pretty desolate,' Wendy said.

'It is,' Polly replied as she headed out of the room. 'It's my mother-in-law's bedroom. Wish me luck.'

'Luck,' Neville shouted, rummaging through drawers for a tin opener. 'How long have these been here? Tins have ring pulls now.'

Polly went carefully through the hall, automatically picking up the post from the mat and placing it on the credenza in the hall as she had done ever since she moved to Dourstone. Whatever her station now she was still the Sumners' housekeeper, and always would be. She somehow owed them a debt for not being able to save their son from being knocked off his bicycle by a bus, despite giving them the granddaughter they doted on from afar. (They would never have believed the truth, even if Polly had wanted to tell them. They had enough trouble believing there was a bus going near Dourstone.) A debt they insisted on continuing to collect with no word of thanks.

She tiptoed up the stairs, although her heavy snow boots wouldn't make a sound on the thick, expensive carpets even if she stomped. She had never dared enter the master bedroom – she may be their unofficial housekeeper, but never their cleaner – and was a little hesitant to go through the door. She knew from Nathaniel Harker's diaries that he had been taken from Thomas Sumner's bedroom, the one he had described so romantically with its window facing the church, back when the church had still had a roof. The clue was – if you knew how to read it – very specific. The hearth was not a metaphor, Sophia had hidden the hagstone in the fireplace.

The room bore no resemblance to Nathaniel's cosy love nest, aside from the window facing the ruined church. The loft had been knocked into a mezzanine level where two comfortable leather chairs faced shining new velux windows cut into the thatch for watching the sunset. Thomas and his wife would never have used the space so wastefully. It was needed for storage, or to keep the livestock inside in winter. The last of the living Sumners to keep the name, however, needed no such compromise. The house had been extended into old workspaces, giving more than enough space for two people who were never there.

'Bugger,' Polly said curling her lip in distaste at the chintz, doilies and china ornaments that spilled over every flat surface. Her in-laws had blocked up the fireplace, an open fire in a bedroom was just asking for trouble after all, and the central heating was more than adequate. She could see the chimney breast with its marble surround (almost certainly not original) but where there should be a gaping mouth of fire were decorative British racing green tiles. 'Can one of you get a hammer?' she shouted down the stairs.

16

'Have they all left?' The Traveller said, striding triumphantly through the gates.

'They took the old plague tunnels,' Father Hearne replied. 'Just as you predicted. The Manor is yours, will you have the dogs track them down?'

'I only want Lord Elias. He will pay for what he did.' The Traveller stopped up short in the cobbled yard, looking up at the magnificent stone frontage of the house he had coveted so long. The gargoyles and big empty windows stared down to appraise their new master. He liked it, he loved it. It unlocked memories in his host's mind that he had never before had access to.

'The Lord Elias has been dead over a century sir, let bygones be bygones.' Father Hearne opened the front door and ushered The Traveller in. A wave of dogs followed hard behind and swarmed through the house, alert for any traps. They met up with the malamutes already inside who quickly deferred to Wotan as their new alpha. All one pack again, all together. Except the two that had got away, the pack wanted their former masters to bow to the new top dog.

'Bygones are never gone,' The Traveller replied. 'And they are no more dead than you or I. As you well know. We just need to find where they're hiding.'

'Very well. How many dogs shall we send?' Father Hearne beckoned a malamute to his side, it checked with Wotan before sauntering over.

'Not many, just a few. Send the Dewer dogs, they might not have worked out they're ours now. They may even welcome them.' He laughed, throwing his coat over a huge carved oak armchair. 'Now, fetch me a drink. Where's the ale?' He stomped to the first of the kitchens and stopped short. His eyes faded to a pale green as he looked at the old ovens in the wall. He shook his head and they darkened back to black.

'Are you sure your ex-in-laws will be okay with this?' Susan said, hefting a sledgehammer onto the Van Gogh Iris print duvet.

'They'll have to be,' Polly said, giving the fireplace an experimental kick. 'There's no other way. We need to get behind this wall.'

'Okay, on your head be it,' Susan said, and swung the hammer back. 'Last chance.'

'It's not like they'll find out any time soon is it?' Polly pointed out, running to safety on the other side of the bed. 'They never come here. Do it.'

Susan swung back, smashing tiles and a chunk of plaster from the fireplace. 'Oh, that feels good, who wants a try?'

'Oh God yes, I really do.' Wendy grabbed the hammer and slammed three bricks into the back of the original fireplace. 'Jack?'

'No, far be it from me to deny you ladies the pleasure,' Jack said, climbing the steep ladder to the mezzanine. 'Hey look, I found the scotch.' He pulled a bottle from a bookcase of vintage penguins and diamond-cut glasses.

'Neville?' Wendy turned to Polly's granddad.

'No no, my wall-breaking days are long behind me, I think Polly should give it a go.' He put a foot on the ladder. 'Room for another up there Jack?'

'Sure, sure, there's room, and there's plenty of… hey, another one, not even been opened. We've got a Macallan M, or a Dalmore 64 Trin… Trini, no idea, can't read it which do you fancy?' Jack waved two bottles from the platform.

'I'll have a small drop of Trinitas you philistine,' Neville said, hopping up to the mezzanine. 'Be very rude not to.'

'Your go then Pol,' Wendy said, stroking the handle of the sledgehammer as she offered it.

'I don't think I...'

'Just take it.' Wendy pushed the hammer into Polly's hands and closed them over the shaft. 'Trust me, you need this.'

Polly tapped gently at the bricks, knocking one more in. The contact shuddered all the way up her arms, with a small thrill at the destruction. She took another underarm swing, smashing the lower rows of bricks through. This was wonderful, she shouldn't be here, in the bedroom of two of the worst people she knew. She should be at home, in the cottage, with her Lizbet and Fenrir, curled up by the fire watching her tatty old VHS of *The Box of Delights* for the five-millionth time. It was Christmas God damn it.

She raised the hammer over her head and put it right through the wall with a primal scream of fury, halving the marble top of the mantelpiece. Then she swung again. The standard lamp got in her way, but she didn't care, taking a short diversion to knock it into splinters. She swung once more, removing another row of bricks, and a pair of Spanish gentlemen with lightbulbs protruding from their heads. All the worry, all the frustration, flowed down her arms, across the wooden shaft of the sledgehammer and out from its head to leave her calmer than she believed possible inside. She swung again, and again, and again.

'Polly, stop, stop stop!' Wendy grabbed for her arms. She carried on, screaming louder with each and every swing, smashing cute china dogs, tearing through doilies and scattering horse brasses until every country cottage cliché was lying in plain sight of the ancient stone fireplace.

'Fuck you, and you and you and you and...' Polly wound herself to a halt and stopped. She had taken out the whole wall. Even the old chimney would be no use now. This was going to be expensive to fix.

Jack stopped mid-pour and put the whisky bottle back down. He and Neville shared a look of fear before he picked it up again. Neville held out his empty glass and nodded.

'Feeling better?' Susan took the hammer from her with a grin.

'Yes, much, thank you.' Polly grinned back. 'I had no idea I needed that.'

'You're surprised you have issues?' Wendy laughed. 'The woman who killed the father of your child lives in your head, you've either killed the loved one of, or seriously injured, every single one of your closest friends, and now you've been cut off from the only person you really trust. And she's only a year old.' She put her arms round Polly.

'Well, when you put it like that... I think I might need some of that whisky.' Polly snuggled into the hug.

'You should try and keep a clear head. We still don't know how to stop this. How to stop him,' Jack said, holding the whisky bottle as he clambered back down the ladder.

'Yes, so should you.' Neville clapped him on the shoulder as he came down behind, pockets brimming with Hugo Sumner's collectable whiskys. 'So should we all. Them beans down there should be alright, I'll heat us all up a bowl, get something in to soak it all up.'

'You might be right, but frankly all this has kept me a good three drinks below sober all day,' Susan argued. 'I need this to stop me being completely fucking terrified all the time.' She snatched the whisky from Jack.

'True that,' Neville agreed. 'We did the same when we rode into the valley of death, cannon to the left of us, cannon to the right...'

'You were not in the charge of the light brigade Granddad, give it a rest.' Polly left Wendy's arms to help Neville down.

'Okay, so you're with me Neville,' Susan summarised. 'Now get the fucking thing Polly, you know where it is.' She took a gulp of whisky that would probably have paid the balance of her mortgage.

Polly nodded and walked into what was left of the chimney. She switched on her phone torch, aware that Sophia would have hidden it somewhere the fire couldn't damage it. This was still a fully functional fireplace when the Bellever Hagstone was hidden. Peering around the widest part she saw a patch of bricks that didn't quite match. She grabbed at it, pulling away brick, cob, mortar, ancient coal dust and tar until the hatch came away and she pulled out its contents.

'Bollocks.' She spat dust from her mouth and shook cobwebs from her hair.

'Not the hagstone then?' Wendy asked.

'No. Different bit of granite.' Polly waved the offending piece of rock. 'Probably just another fucking bread oven.'

'It's engraved, look,' Susan said, pointing excitedly.

'Oh yay! Another clue, thank you so much Lady too-much-time-on-your-fucking-hands Sophia Dewer,' Polly droned. 'I'm not surprised Melissa got bored waiting around for her to die.'

'What does it say then?' Jack asked.

'"*In the heart of the moors, where true love began, the bones of the earth hold your most dreadful weapon*",' Polly read, sitting back down on the bed.

'So, any ideas? Or do we need Mel?' Wendy asked.

'I know exactly where those two first got it on, just as well as Lady Mel herself. But it's no good. It's all over, it was up on Nymet Tor, in the rocks at the top, outside the town boundaries. If she's hidden it there we're not getting it today.' Polly fiddled with the pocket the ring was in, but didn't unzip it.

'But it might not actually be there?' Neville said. 'There's still a chance.'

'Not really, even if it's just another clue there we're still fucked. Susan's right, let's have a drink, maybe the Sumners have got a number for a builder.' Polly wandered downstairs in a haze. That was it. Their one chance was gone.

Cronus barked from the yard as Fenrir hurried in to meet them.

17

'Are you sure these things still work?' Dan asked.

'Move back about a metre,' Lynn replied, leading by example.

'Okay.' Dan followed her.

'Right, now watch this.' Lynn rolled an empty barrel along the ground, when it reached the point where Dan had been just a few seconds ago, there was a loud grinding sound and the passageway was suddenly impassable.

'Owch, that's sharp!' Dan said, tapping one of the long iron spikes protruding from the wall.

'It was built to last, and as far as I know nobody's made it this far through the gauntlet,' Lynn replied, cranking a handle to wind it back into its hiding place in the open mouth of a Green Man: along with its fellows that had sprung out of both sides along a two metre stretch.

'Well, lets hope they never do.' Dan rolled forward and carefully turned over the loose stone in the floor that re-armed the trigger.

After heading back through the cellar to check the gate was secured, Lynn had shown Dan its final layers of protection. A series of traps even Indiana Jones would have trouble negotiating, lying dormant in the floors and walls until the triggers were activated. This was the last in the series, so a demonstration was necessary.

'They will, I expect Father Hearne knows all about this, and don't forget they've got magic. This will just slow them down.'

'Well, thanks for the pep-talk Lynn,' Dan said as they made their way back to the wine cellar.

'Sorry, but our best chance is still in finding out what they know, and hoping it isn't where we are,' Lynn said. 'You still up for spying?'

'Yeah, winch me up,' he agreed, pulling himself into the dumb waiter.

'And I'll work out a way to signal the others once we've got something to signal,' Lynn said.

'Speaking of signals, how do I tell you when I want to come back down?' Dan said, making himself comfortable in the dumb waiter.

'Push that button,' Lynn said, pointing to a big red switch inside the box. 'It'll flash this light.' She pointed to an old fashioned bulb set in the wall by the dumb waiter cabinet.

'Nice.' Dan grinned. 'Very helpful.'

'Flash it once to go up a floor, twice to go down a floor, and bash the living hell out of it if you need to come down in a hurry,' Lynn said, closing the hatch. 'Good luck.'

'What is it?' Polly said, scruffing the dogs' heads as they herded her to the gates. 'What's out there?'

The dogs ran out in front, putting themselves between her and the gate.

'Dogs are just dogs Pol,' her granddad said. 'Maybe leave it and come inside. I've put some beans on the stove, we need to make a new plan if we've got no hagstone.'

'I thought we'd agreed to give up and get pissed,' Polly said, turning round. 'What else can we do?'

'I don't know, but we can't give up.' Neville looked up at the thatchcicles hanging dangerously from the roof. 'I get the feeling he's not going to leave us alone, and I don't want to end up oblivious like those poor people in the pub.'

'We can still get pissed though?' Polly said crossing back towards the door.

'Well yes, if you're sure? I don't mind that kind of oblivion, at least it's my own fault.' He raised his whisky glass.

'Well good, I'll drink to that, and you do the thinking.' She took his glass, drained it, and handed it back to him, steadying herself against the porch.

'I find I do my best work with a few drinks in me, so yes. The two are not mutually exclusive.' He grinned and lit a cigarette before pulling a bottle of Black Bowmore from the depths of his jacket.

'I do need to see what they're barking at though, hold them back.' Polly pointed to Fenrir and Cronus and went back to the gate before cautiously opening it.

'Be careful, could be spies.' Neville grabbed for the dogs but as they wore no collars there was nothing to hold on to. They sat for him anyway but he had a suspicion they were the ones holding him in place.

'It's my dogs,' Polly said. 'Sky One, Saxon Two, Grey Wind Three, Ghost One, Saxon Four, Sky Six, what are you doing out on your own?' Six malamutes sat outside the gate looking up with their trademark curious looks.

'I don't think they're your dogs anymore,' Wendy said, coming up from behind with two glasses of wine. 'Check out their eyes.'

The security lights in the barrelworks yard caught the dogs' eyes. They were blue: bright shining blue.

'Shit,' Polly said. 'He's got my dogs. Fuck, now he knows where we are.'

'Not yet,' Wendy said, chucking the drinks in an oversized flower pot. 'They're not telepathic. Get 'em.'

'No way am I grabbing those...' Polly flashed back to Cronus, holding her down in the snow, drool dripping from his maw as he bent to rip out her throat before Fenrir stepped in to save her. He had become top dog, head of the pack once he'd bested him. That wouldn't work this time, it was six against two. 'Stay back Wend,' she shouted, grabbing her.

'But Polly, we can't let them get back to him,' Wendy said, not resisting the arm round her waist.

'You've never been on the wrong side of them, we can't win. I can't do this again,' Polly cried.

'Someone has to.' Wendy held Polly up as she sagged.

Fenrir and Cronus didn't need telling twice, they flew out of the gate, twisting from Neville's grip with ease to get round the other side of the malamutes, penning them in. The malamutes may have been under somebody else's control, but years of obeying Cronus was hard programming to break. The blue of their eyes flickered, but didn't die, as they backed down and retreated into the yard, eyes up, cautious, looking for a mistake from their aggressors, who pushed them further back into the barn until Polly and Wendy could shut the steel security gates that protected Patrick's father's collection of pristine, unridden vintage motorcycles.

'Well, that's bought us some time.' Susan came out swinging a bottle of Rose and Arrow Black Walnut. 'What are we going to do with it?'

What's happened, why have we stopped, why are you drunk?
Mel's voice returned to Polly. She pulled at her finger to remove the
ring only to find it wasn't there.

'How can you do this, without the...' Her worst fears were
becoming reality.

*Never mind that, you need me more than you know. I'm part of
you, and you're lucky to have me.*

'I don't need you, this is not lucky and we're not done.' This
wasn't the time to fight. Lady Melissa was their best hope of getting
out of this.

*Trust me you do, you are, and you're right, we're not. Now fill me
in on what's happened while I've been out. I shouldn't have pulled
that stupid trick, we could have smashed that floor up with a
hammer,* Lady Melissa ranted.

'We've lost. We can't get out to where Sophia hid the hagstone.'
Polly sat on a flowerpot, Wendy sidled back over to stroke her head.

How can you know where Sophia hid it? The disdain was
obvious, especially through this psychic link. Polly felt nothing but
pity for herself, siding with Melissa. She shook her head and tried to
sever the link.

'I've read Nathaniel's diaries, I know the history, I deduced it. I
found the lump of granite in Thomas Sumner's old bedroom after
that clue wrapped up in his old tankard, and I know that the next
clue, or hopefully the thing itself, is on Nymet Tor. Where Nathaniel
first fell in love with you. I may not be Lady Sophia, but Nathaniel
and I had a connection, while I was locked up in your bedroom, his
portrait was the only friendly face I saw.'

*You know nothing of Nathaniel but his final rantings and a stupid
picture painted by a stupid woman. Now read me the clue, they were
my lovers.*

'"In the heart of the moors, where true love began, the bones of
the earth hold your most dreadful weapon."' Polly said, hand on hip,
knowing full well she had the right of it.

*You stupid girl. First kisses aren't the same as falling in love,
anybody with a bone of love in their body is already feeling it before
even considering something so intimate as a kiss. Especially back
then, when people had manners, and class, and better hats. Now
Nathaniel, like everybody else including you, however much you*

deny it, loved me at first sight. We're right on top of the answer.

'Can you hear something?' The Traveller said, looking quizzically at the walls.

'No,' Father Hearne answered, shuffling through papers and banging them against the long oak table that took pride of place in the upper dining room. He could hear a creaking in the walls, but chose not to. 'It's an old house, they make noises. Not to mention that it has actual ghosts walking its floors.'

'There's no such thing.' The Traveller banged his fist on the table. 'And I should know.'

'Well, this place has always seemed to look after itself. There's something behind it.' The priest carefully laid his sheaf of papers down, licking his fingers to start working through them again.

'Yes, you, more often than not it would seem.' The Traveller stomped across and grabbed the pages from his hands, slamming them down out of his reach.

'I walk in all worlds, I help all, I am a servant of...' The priest rose from his chair.

'You are a servant of me, and don't you forget,' The Traveller said, pushing him back down. 'You cannot be distracted by old alliances. I have the dogs now, and therefore, I control the town, the weather, you, the Dewer woman, those bloody meddling trustees and anybody else I want.'

'I choose to help you my friend. Not even you can make me do something against my will.' Father Hearne wriggled in his chair, making a squeaking noise on the old cracked leather.

'I expect I could, if I really needed to.' The Traveller leaned in, hot breath foul and stinking in Father Hearne's face. 'Go and check the secret holes in the walls. This house is far too Edgar Allen Poe not to have a few passages – the eyes in that picture are following me around the room.' He pointed up at a smiling portrait of Nathaniel Harker Polly had had moved from the master bedroom. 'I do not wish to have those eyes on me.'

'It was painted that way, it's always done that. Lady Sophia had quite the talent in her later years,' the vicar explained.

'Yes, yes, so I've heard. Fine, I'll check myself.' The Traveller got up and walked across the room, sticking his head into the fireplace to peer up the chimney. 'Those sound like very big mice, and this shithole hasn't had working heating for years. That clicking is something more than deathwatch beetle.'

Inside the dumb waiter Dan was stabbing at the call button trying not to scream.

'What's she saying? Is Melissa back?' Susan stumbled across the yard at the sounds of Polly talking to herself.

'I'm pretty sure she is,' Wendy replied.

'Yep, and she seems to think I might be wrong, and there may be hope,' Polly explained, waving away the drink Susan offered.

'Hope? Oh good,' Jack said from the doorway. 'That's never come back to fuck me over, what good news.'

'Give me a second guys, let me talk to her,' Polly held up a hand to stop everyone talking. They backed off as Wendy helped her to her feet.

'Okay, Melissa, what do you mean? The clue said *"In the heart of the moors, where true love began, the bones of the earth hold your dreadful weapon"*, and that points to the tor where you and Nathaniel first kissed,' Polly explained, leaning into Wendy as she cleared her head.

You're wrong. This is the heart of the moors. Well, just out there. It makes perfect sense, Sophia was in a perfect rage with me when we had the new wall built in the square. We built it with the bones of the earth, granite. We took quite a lot of it from Nymet Tor – which was one of the reasons she was so mad at me, sentimental fool that she was. The new wall covers the exact spot where Nathaniel and I sat on that fateful Oak Apple Day. I can just imagine how smug Sophia was about the double symbolism. She would have had the Bellever Hagstone built into the wall. Probably got Thomas Sumner to help her, they got to be thick as thieves after Nathaniel died.

'You mean after you killed him?' Polly interjected.

Semantics, he killed himself as soon as he betrayed us. He wasn't Dourstone. He never loved me. He loved a lie, and so he had to die. Polly could feel Melissa didn't believe her own words but felt it best not to push the matter.

'Nice, you still haven't read the diaries then?' Polly said.

No, and now is not the time for this. You need to break that wall down, find the hagstone, stop The Traveller and get my town back.

'We will, in our own time, but first you need to...' Polly stopped short, losing herself. She could feel her essence being squeezed out of the way.

'I need do nothing,' Melissa said, cricking Polly's neck. 'I do what I want, and right now that is this.' She ran a cold hand up the inside of Wendy's coat, stroking her fingers down her side and slipping them inside her jeans to caress the curve of her hip. 'I know what you want too darling.' She stared deep into Wendy's eyes.

'Polly? Is that you,' Wendy gasped.

'Ha, she wishes.' Melissa laughed.

Fine, okay. Let me back in control, we'll do it your way, just stop this, Wendy's vulnerable, I like Wendy, Polly begged.

I know you do, you'll thank me later. All yours. Melissa let go.

Polly pulled her hand from Wendy's underwear, blushed and turned to the others. 'We need to knock a wall down, anybody got any ideas?'

'Tell you it's your ex-mother-in-law and give you back that sledgehammer?' Wendy suggested, with a sly grin.

'Ha ha, I could say the same to you,' Polly countered, remembering Wendy's shaky relationship with her dead wife's parents.

'Touché,' Wendy replied, with a friendly touch of the arm. 'But let's try the sledgehammer first yeah?'

'Since we've got it, I'm in.' Jack swung it through the awkwardness, leading the way.

Light spilled into the darkness on the other side of the square from the windows of The Drop of Dew, its inhabitants blissfully unaware how trapped they really were and enjoying the prospect of a snow day. The pub would not be closing on time and the sound of merry-making drifted over the market sheds in the deserted square.

'Okay, let's do this, who's first?' Jack said, slamming the sledgehammer onto the wall with a mighty thunk.

'I believe it's your turn,' Wendy replied. 'Unless you're scared?'

'Scared of what?' he said.

'Being beaten by a girl, you saw Polly in there,' Susan goaded.

'Ha.' Jack swung the hammer back and took a mighty swing. It connected with a loud crack sending shockwaves up his arm without so much as denting the wall. He reeled back, almost falling into the dog poo bin and dropping the hammer.

'That's the wrong place,' Polly pointed out. 'We need to be there, by the tree.'

'What? The Christmas tree?' Jack said. 'In the middle?'

'No,' Polly said. 'The oak in the corner, by the wall, obviously.'

'Are you sure?' Neville asked. 'We don't want to break the wrong bit of wall.'

'No danger of that with Jack swinging,' Susan joked.

'Oh ha ha ha, your go next then.' Jack picked the hammer back up and passed it to Susan.

They moved to the right part of the wall and everyone but Susan hunched down behind the circular bench around the tree, peering over the top. 'I never noticed that plaque before,' Wendy said.

There was an old plaque at the base of the tree, raised letters on rusting iron spelled out 'For NH, never forgotten, SD.'

'Who are NH and SD?' Neville asked, squinting in the dark.

'Nathaniel Harker and Sophia Dewer, the other two points of Lord Elias Dewer's love triangle,' Polly explained.

'And this Lord Elias was your friend Melissa a century ago?' Neville continued.

'Yes Granddad, I thought I'd explained all this?' Polly sighed.

'You did, but I'm just checking, it's a lot to take in.' He lit another cigarette, and offered her a whisky bottle.

'I know, sorry.' She waved the bottle away, she needed her head clear again.

'And you killed them last year, but they're living in your head because of that creepy-arse ring you insist on wearing?' He pointed at the coffin nail ring, back on her finger.

'Yes, though it seems like she doesn't really need that ring, and, in my defence, she did kill Patrick and try to steal my Lizbet away,' Polly said.

'Okay, so how come this Sophia had this little meltdown over Nathaniel?' He stashed the bottle away in his coat.

'That I don't know,' Polly continued. 'I know Melissa killed Nathaniel the same way she killed Patrick. I can only assume Sophia, who I always thought was completely behind it, was not.'

That's putting it mildly, she was against it from the start, she wanted me to let him live. Keep him with us forever. Stupid girl had no concept of forever, I think she just got a bit over-excited over her first cock.

'But,' Polly tried to ignore the voice in her head as she spoke to her granddad, 'Melissa never told me, even though it would have been very useful information to have before this evening.'

I just did, as much as you need to know anyway. We don't have time, and you don't need to know.

'And she still won't,' Polly finished.

Nathaniel never knew how she felt. She didn't want him to know, her loyalty was to me, and he was entirely mine – until he met that Sumner. Her love was unrequited, and after he died she forgot how little he noticed her and concentrated on blaming me. It overwhelmed her, she lost all reason. I was glad when she died. Is that enough for you?

'A little too much,' Polly replied, taken aback. She knew she shouldn't be surprised at how hard Melissa had made herself over the centuries, but her lack of feeling was still hard to swallow. Especially when it affected her own chemical balance.

'Okay, well if you two are finished bickering, I think I've got it now,' Polly's granddad said, standing up and brushing dust from his knees. 'Are you ready to swing girl?'

'I am,' Susan said, letting the girl slide. She grinned and took a swing at the wall but staggered backwards, knocking a hole in one of the sheds. Jack's schadenfreude was eclipsed by the daunting nature of the task ahead.

'Fuck, anybody else want to try?' Susan said, pulling the hammer back out and demolishing the rest of the shed wall.

'Doesn't seem worth it does it?' Neville said. 'That rock won't break like shiplap, any more bright ideas?'

'Do you think Mel could have a go at magicking it down?' Wendy suggested.

'Do you think you've got any more in you?' Polly asked.

I'll give it a whirl, let me up.

Polly's eyes rolled back again and suddenly there was Lady Melissa.

'Hello there,' Susan said. 'We've missed you, are you feeling better now?'

'Cut the bullshit,' Melissa said. 'You just want my magic.'

'No, we really have,' Susan said.

'And cut all this out.' Melissa knocked Susan's wine glass out of her hand to smash on the ground. 'You're drinking for two now.'

'I'm what?' Susan gasped.

'Pregnant, sorry I didn't notice earlier, but we've been a bit busy.' Melissa took the Rosé bottle and swilled it about her teeth.

'Who, who…' Susan stammered.

'Is the father?' Melissa grinned. 'What do you think I am, a DNA test?'

'Okay, can we focus here?' Wendy stepped between them.

'Yes, sorry.' Melissa took a deep breath and closed her eyes. She raised her arms, feeling her way towards the wall, trying to capture and change its essence, persuade it that it wanted to go home to the moors and stop getting in everyone's way. Granite proved as stubborn as you'd expect and she sat back down, shuffling along the bench to Wendy. 'No good, I can't, too much, too soon, too difficult. I'm sorry, no magic bullet this time. See you.' She collapsed across Wendy's shoulder, putting her arms round her and dropping Polly's head against Wendy's neck.

'So what's plan B then?' Polly said, jumping up and away from Wendy's delicate scent. 'We need to end this, our kids are still on the other side of that snow wall.'

'Yeah, if nothing else, Katie will be charging overtime for every hour we're not with them.' Susan lit a cigarette that Jack immediately snatched from her hand and ground out with his heel.

18

Lynn had her ear to a listening tube. She could make out the sound of a conversation from above, but not any details.

'Oph-mee-a ad oome alens in er bader veers,' came the muffled garble from a tube labelled *Dining Room*. She'd quite lost track of which floor Dan was on at the moment, but had an idea it was near there. Hopefully he was getting a better idea of this.

She twanged the tube back and it rattled off the wall to echo down the passages. There had to be something more practical for spying down here, Melissa was a sneaky old bitch. Lynn was far too practical to be scared of the creeping solitude, even in the very place she had nearly bled to death. There was a cupboard on the wall opposite the tubes, maybe it held some kind of periscope, or a magic mirror. Melissa was magicky, or so she claimed. She pulled it open and stuck her head in. No good, just long pole brushes to clean the tubes, and amplifying trumpets. She pulled one out to try it.

'Em am rne rnn efuef.' The trumpet may have been louder, but it was no better defined. She pulled it off and threw it at the wall. It clanged against the ear-pieces and disappeared into a web of tubing beneath. She tried to reach for it but her hands slid across an unexpected gap. There was another room behind, hidden by the mechanism. She pushed through and found herself surrounded by mirrors, it was eerie, like a piece of her soul was being pulled away. There were loads of them, all on wheels, manoeuvrable and lightweight. She had no idea what the Dewers could have wanted with so many mirrors, undoubtedly some kinky sex thing. Lynn had a terrifying memory of being stuck in a maze of mirrors in the Trocadero centre when she was small, every way out leading to another wall of glass, every reflection of her mother an illusion. She shook her head in case the nightmare became true.

She stalked back to the dumb waiter where she saw the light flashing. Had she imagined the buzzer she expected to hear? She must have, for there was none, just the light blinking furiously. She tripped over a trumpet that had rolled out from under the tubes unnoticed and skidded face first along the floor. Dan was in trouble, and it was her fault for getting distracted, getting lost in that maze again. She struggled to get to her feet, crawling on all fours in the dirt all the way there, where she pulled herself up on the cabinet. She grasped the wheel to pull Dan down, but it was stuck fast.

'Got it,' Jack said, coming back up from the sheds behind the Old School Hall, brandishing his prize.

'Now you're talking.' Susan grinned as Jack leaned the pneumatic drill against the wall. 'Bagsy first go.'

'You're welcome to it,' Wendy said, looking it over with a practised eye. 'I used one of them when we were redoing the house. It bloody hurts, couldn't grip anything for a week.'

'Wuss, they're brilliant fun, I helped Clive's dad break up the yard with one. He wouldn't let me use it for long, because I'm a girl, but he's not here now.' Susan's eyes lit up.

'Rather you than me,' Wendy said. 'If you're sure you know what you're doing?'

'Pointy end at the breaky thing, hands on the handles, give it some welly,' Susan said, grabbing it to demonstrate.

'There's a bit more to it than that, I'll run you through it,' Wendy said.

'She's drunk Wendy. You can't let her do it, it's dangerous, especially in her condition.' Jack took it from Susan, running his fingers down the controls. 'I'll do it.'

'Not like that you won't.' Wendy laughed, Susan joined in.

'Well, no, obviously not.' Jack blushed, dropping the drill and taking Neville by the arm. 'Quick mate, can't lose face here, what don't I know?' he whispered.

'I don't think we have time for a full list, I only just met you, but you're not old enough to know everything, not even much of anything I don't reckon.' Neville's eyes gleamed. 'Now can you narrow it down?'

'What don't I know about this jackhammer that those two do?' Jack's eyes were pleading.

'You need a compressor to run it. Big petrol one I'd imagine, you see a thing like a big oil tank where you found it?' Neville relented.

'Yes, but it's huge, I can't carry that.' Jack's face turned white.

'Must be something to tow it with round here.'

'Okay, do you think they've realised I don't know what I'm doing?'

'We're right behind you. We heard every word.' Susan cackled. 'You're every bit as pissed as I am.'

'Ah shit, I just didn't want...'

'Us to lose our respect for you?' Wendy said. 'Think less of you?'

'Jack, Jack, Jack,' Polly said, strutting up to him. 'We couldn't possibly think any less of you.'

'Mel?' Jack said.

'Nope, all me.' Polly booped his nose.

'Fine, I'll be back in a second,' Jack said. 'As you heard, I need to get the compressor, so I'm going to have to hotwire Chris's tractor.'

'I'll give you a hand.' Neville clapped him on the back. 'I'm pretty good with a bit of wire.'

'Thanks,' Jack said, not bothering to pretend he actually knew how to hotwire anything.

The men went off and Polly began tapping along the wall with the sledgehammer, hoping to learn exactly where to start. It clonked and thunked against the very solid wall, as she hunted for the hollow ringing that would mark a cavity.

It will be there, Melissa shifted Polly's eyes, drawing her attention to a point on the wall directly opposite Sophia's plaque.

'I didn't know you could do that,' Polly gasped, twisting the ring on her finger, very aware she needed to stay in contact with Melissa, but scared she might take her over at any minute. More sure than ever the ring was nothing more than a stage prop, a fake safety button. No more use than a padlocked fire escape.

It was just a nudge, stop worrying. The difference between what I can and will do is vast. I won't hurt you, you need to trust me. We're on the same side. Now give that bit a tap.

Polly tapped at the wall and finally heard an echoey thunk, rather than the solid thud she had been hearing.

'It's here,' she said, and gave it a hefty whack with the hammer now she had found the thin bit. It still didn't make a dent in the Dartmoor granite.

'Pol, what are we going to do with those dogs?' Wendy asked, coming back from the house with a bowl of beans. 'I know they're the bad guys, but can we just leave them there, locked in that barn?'

'Yeah, they've got food, they've got water. They're malamutes,' Polly answered.

'And so have you, eat this.' Wendy pushed the food into her hands. 'You need it.'

'Okay, okay,' Polly admitted. She sat down and spooned the bland, sticky orange goo into her mouth. Baked beans always reminded her of home, when she'd had to cook for her brother and sisters almost every night, a memory as bitter-sweet as the beans. 'Malamutes aren't like other dogs: Sky One refused to eat for three days once because her bowl was in the wrong place. They don't mind doing nothing and they're extremely hardy, not to mention stubborn. I've seen Cronus do nothing but eat, sleep and fart for a week.'

'Yeah, but they're a bit...' Susan said, staring at her own bowl of beans.

'Possessed and odd yes,' Polly said. 'Not themselves, but it's not their fault. Locking them up here until we've fixed this is the kindest thing we can do.'

'But maybe they can...' Wendy pushed up against Polly, who could feel her flesh give against her own beneath their thick coats. She hoped her flushed face looked like it was a result of the beans.

'Get out on their own, attack us, let The Traveller know where we are, rip us to pieces? One of those?' Polly grinned.

'I thought maybe they could spread the infection to Fenrir and Cronus, put us right in the shit?' Wendy said, holding on to Polly for warmth. 'But I don't like your suggestions either. Thanks.'

'I don't think they can, no. It didn't happen to Fenrir last year,' Polly said.

It might, but there is always a bargain. Like the one you made when you took my ring, like the dogs do every year when they take the heart. There is a price and an acceptance. I'd like to think these two are loyal enough not to take it. But they're just dogs. I don't know what will happen if they face his alpha and lose.

'So you don't know either?' Polly said out loud, putting down her empty bowl and slumping against Wendy's shoulder.

'What doesn't Melissa know?' Susan asked, fiddling with her

wedding ring.

'Whether we can trust the dogs or not, sorry,' Polly replied, sitting back up straight.

'Just watch the eyes then I guess.' Wendy folded her arms and pushed her bum right back into the bench. 'And eat your beans Susan. If you're going to chuck that drill about pissed you can at least soak up some of that wine first.'

'Fine,' Susan said, and poured the bowl into her mouth in one, chewing it down with a wry grin.

A horn tooted a jaunty tune, as smoke blasted from the front of a tractor struggling through snow and ice to pull up by the wall.

'Ready?' Jack said, jumping down and trying to connect compressor hose to drill.

'Would you like some help with that?' Susan said, trying very hard not to laugh.

'No, I'm sure I can...' he tried to front it out. 'Okay, you got me, I don't know what I'm doing. Are you happy now?'

'Very, thanks,' Susan grinned. 'I don't know much more about it than you, but I'm sure Neville here can teach us, right Nev?'

'Not really, never handled one of these. Seen a few other guys work them though,' Neville explained. 'I know where the tubes go, and what most of the buttons do, but I was always too scared for my hands and ears to do it myself. I'm a musician, an artist, and too drunk to be trusted with one of these.'

'I can, give it here, we'll figure it out between the two of us.' Susan took hold of it, fondling the controls.

'Well I'd say you're probably too drunk as well, but I'm not arguing with a lady holding a jackhammer.' Neville backed off.

'Me neither,' Jack said, handing over the limp hose.

'Very wise of you both,' Susan said, with no trace of a slur in her voice. 'And I'm fine, I've always been able to outdrink all of you.' She straightened up and winked. It looked a lot like she had been acting more intoxicated than she actually was.

Jack sloped over to Polly and Wendy, and aimlessly poked the wall.

'It's right there,' Polly said, hopping back off the bench and kicking the spot she had found. 'There's nothing more we can do without that.' She pointed back at her grandfather and Susan, connecting hoses and priming motors with the odd whoop.

'I better check on them,' Wendy said. 'I think I'm the only person here with any experience of...'

'Okay, let's do this, get the fuck back, all of you.' Susan strutted through, wielding the jackhammer like a weapon.

'Hang on Suse,' Wendy said. 'You can't hold it like that, you'll lose a tit.' She grabbed her friend to refine her grip. 'That's better. Now you'll stay hot.'

'Thanks Wendy,' Susan replied before using the correct grip to hold the jackhammer up as if she had the power of Greyskull.

'Safety first miss,' Neville shoved it back down and stuck a hard hat with a visor on her head. 'That stone won't come out easy, and you don't want to lose an eye.'

'I know, I know, I just wanted to make an entrance. I was going to put the hat on,' she said, carefully putting the drill on the ground before donning thick protective gloves and adjusting her visor. Once she had checked all her gear, she gave Neville a thumbs up. He fired up the compressor and a loud throbbing filled the air. 'Right you pricks,' she shouted. 'This time I mean it, get the fuck back.' She powered the drill into life, giving it a few experimental revs in the air and taking out a chunk of Christmas tree.

Polly, Jack and Neville ran to the opposite corner of the square for cover. 'Be careful Susan!' Polly shouted, poking her head up from behind the wall. 'We don't want the hagstone pounded into a million pieces.'

'I'm not fucking stupid,' Susan screamed back over the roar.

'No you're not, but are you ready?' Wendy said, taking it back, turning it off and giving the connections one final check.

'Yes, now run, I'm going in,' she said, firing it up again. Wendy went to monitor the compressor.

Susan strode to the wall and gently nudged the tip in. The granite was as hard as promised and the vibrations of the jackhammer were every bit as painful as Wendy had warned, but the power was thrilling. It was difficult not to get carried away, but she knew she could not damage the precious hagstone inside. A hard push found a weak point, and then it was through, mortar and rock crumbling aside like extra mature cheddar under the wrong knife. A small hole, just enough to gauge the thickness of the hollow panel before she attacked it longways, so as to only remove the cavity wall, not the actual wall. Once she had made a hole wide enough to get a hand inside, she carefully trimmed the edges, with minimum pressure, like a troll surgeon. Once she was happy with the hole she turned the drill off and wiped the cloud of dust from her visor with her sleeve.

'Well?' Neville was first to reach her, as the howling tailed off, Cronus and Fenrir joining an unhappy choir of their former comrades at the dreadful sound.

'Don't know yet,' she said, panting from the exertion. 'I forgot how heavy those bastards are. Never held one up off the ground like that for so long.'

'Good job,' Neville patted her shoulders. 'Is that it?'

'Yes,' Polly said, reaching in and pulling out a fist sized stone with a hole in, copper wire and iron horseshoe nails arranged in pentagrams on both sides. 'It's the Bellever Hagstone, Mel says so.'

'Finally!' Wendy said. 'So what do we do with it?'

'I don't know yet.' Polly stroked the stone reverently, wondering how it could possibly be so important.

I'll fill you in on the way back to the Manor, Mel said. *Rub your thumb around the wire.*

Polly did as she was told and the hole changed, became darker, glowing an ultraviolet purple. 'What the hell's that?' She immediately stopped what she was doing and it went back to normal.

It's a gateway. Bigger on the inside, get me home, now.

'We need to get back to the Manor,' Polly said. 'Unhook that compressor, we'll take the tractor.'

19

Dan jabbed the button. He could hear footsteps clunking across the floor. Could The Traveller hear the gentle clicking? Probably, but what choice did Dan have, if the dumbwaiter stayed here he was caught. If he was caught then who knew what The Traveller would do? And the only way to move was to signal Lynn. Why the hell wasn't he moving? What was she playing at?

'What is that noise?' The Traveller was saying. 'Rats? Deathwatch beetle? This place was rotten enough last time you were here, and it's had a long time to rot since.'

'I've been here all along,' Father Hearne objected, 'and Polly's been putting a lot of money into renovating the place, it's in remarkably good condition...'

'I wasn't talking to you,' The Traveller said. 'Where is that coming... of course.'

His footsteps stopped, and the dumb waiter door rattled. Dan tried to hold the latch inside closed but it was too well-engineered. It clicked across and the hatch began to slide upwards.

Suddenly the world dropped away, and Dan felt himself falling. His last-minute getaway wasn't quite fast enough, however, and the last thing he saw was a pair of coal-black eyes locking on his.

'There's a cripple in the dumb waiter Arthur, did you know there were people here?' The Traveller said, tossing a walnut in the air and catching it again.

'I had no idea, I thought all the rats fled with their leader, I'm so sorry.' The priest's voice floated down the shaft as Dan continued his descent.

'Don't be sorry, help me get them. He must be headed for the cellars, in which case, so are we.'

The hatch at the top slammed shut as the dumb waiter thudded into the cellar with enough force to knock Dan's hat off.

'They're coming, what do we do?' Dan said, as Lynn pulled him from the tiny box.

'We can run, or we can hide.' Lynn bundled him back into his chair.

'Which were you doing while I was stuck up there jabbing that fucking switch?' Dan moaned, shifting his bum around in the chair.

'Looking for an upper hand, I thought the dumb waiter had a buzzer.' Lynn shrugged. 'And then unjamming that wheel, it hasn't been used for a long time. Sorry.'

'Well, I'm okay, for now, what did you find?' Dan asked.

'I think we might have one last trick up our sleeves if they get through the gate and the traps.'

'You mean when they get through,' Dan said.

'Yes, I'm rather afraid I do, but we won't make it easy for them,' Lynn said, taking the handles of Dan's chair and pushing him towards the speaking tubes. 'Have you ever seen *The Man With The Golden Gun*?'

'Are you sure we've tried everything?' Kerry asked Clive. They stood in a pile of broken tools, blow-dryers, tables, cages and some of the ancient ironmongery that hung about the place: all of which had been hurled at windows that refused to break.

'Nearly,' Clive said. 'Trouble is we can't get enough force to knock the fucking windows out. I've only got one hand, and you're a...'

'Don't you dare say I'm a girl you lanky streak of piss,' Kerry said. 'I could take you in a fight any day, even back when you had two hands, remember when we were kids?'

'Yes, I do. You're five years older than me Ker, that was bullying,' Clive said. 'But you're right, it's not us. It's these bloody windows.'

'There's still this.' Kerry pointed to the stainless steel grooming table that took pride of place in the middle of the room. 'I reckon we could give it some beans if we done it together.'

'Fine, what have we got to lose?' Clive agreed, taking one side. 'Left window or right?'

'Door first, then windows,' Kerry said. 'I've got a good feeling about this.'

They lifted it on end, and gave it a test, letting it fall against the door under its own force. It took some paint off as it slid to the floor with a crash.

'Again?' Clive asked.

'Again,' Kerry agreed. 'Hang on, what's that noise?'

There was a loud rumbling and the walls came crashing down before they had a chance to jump clear.

'How do we get past the... oh.' Jack stopped talking as Polly drove the tractor directly at the dogs standing in their way.

Fitting five people and two very big dogs into a tractor cab had been quite the task. Jack's idea to leave the compressor hooked up to the back as a trailer had been ignored, so Fenrir and Cronus were jammed in behind the big chair into which Polly and Jack were squished. Susan and Wendy clung to the doors to try and stay on the side ladders while Neville held fast to the back peering past the dogs and shouting encouragement through the open window as Polly gunned the engine, screaming round corners and sliding across ice. It was amazing they had made it to the Manor gates without anybody falling off.

Jack lowered his head, as if that would protect him, while Polly slammed her foot to the floor. Tractors seemed so slow when he was stuck behind them on endless winding Dartmoor lanes, but sitting behind that massive engine, staring at an ever-closer pair of very solid-looking gates it felt a lot faster than the 120 miles an hour he had once squeezed from his beloved Mazda MX5.

The Traveller's guard dogs stood their ground until the last minute, when they split up, running around the back of the agricultural monster to give chase, easily keeping pace but unable to jump high enough to reach their prey. Cronus and Fenrir barked from the cab, unwilling to jump down.

'Okay, but what do we do when we reach the house?' Jack said. 'We'll have to get down, how do we get past them?'

He'd seen what the pack could do. Cleaning up the remains of victims from the altar stone on Wish Weekend Sunday morning was one of the jobs he'd been given as a more junior member of Dourstone's inner circle. He didn't fancy being reduced to a few leftover chunks of organ and bone.

'I've fooled them before, I can do it again,' Polly said, clinging tight to the wheel, fingers turning white. 'They're the same monsters inside, be they malamute or… poodlemann? Doberoodle? Whatever the hell that thing is.' She nodded at a huge mongrel. 'Anyway, I've got my boys to help me' – she hugged Fenrir's head to hers – 'and we've got more to worry about than a few dogs, look down there.'

'What? Oh.' The Traveller's wagon was on the wrong side of the gates, taking up valuable real estate in the courtyard.

'We're going to need more than just a pair of dogs to do this, he's in the house isn't he?' Jack slumped forward, grabbing his head in the hand that wasn't clinging on for dear life.

'Yes, I'd say he is,' Susan said, jamming a foot up into the cab as she changed grip. 'God I hope Clive's okay.' It was the first time she had expressed concern for her husband.

Jack looked surprised.

'I've got a better idea than a doggy stand off,' Wendy said, clinging precariously to the open door. 'Besides, these two mean well, but they won't hold that lot off for long.' She scruffed Cronus' ears with her free hand and outlined her plan. They sped up the driveway, accumulating dogs.

'Okay, good,' Polly said as they got to the end. 'Shit.'

The inner gates had been closed and barred. Even being the rightful owner and having the keys was no good against that.

'Oh come off it Pol,' Jack said. 'Surely you saw that coming? I could see that before we even got to the bridge. I thought you had a plan!'

'Plan!' Polly screamed. 'We're all just winging it, I was hoping that…'

'Hoping what?' Wendy asked, swinging her head into the cab.

'Nope, no. Melissa says she's all out, nothing more in the barrel,' Polly said. 'I'd hoped for another bit of magic demolition.'

'We had this problem back at the siege of Gondolin,' Neville shouted, up on his tiptoes to get his head through the back window.

'No you didn't, you weren't there Granddad.' Polly sighed. 'Nobody was, apart from the elves.'

'Okay, maybe it wasn't in Gondolin, maybe it was a disagreement with Esau's scrapyard, but the theory holds, ram the fucking gates girl.' He pointed ahead.

'They're very strong gates Granddad,' Polly said.

'Maybe, but so were Esau's, and we broke them with a Ford Fiesta, this is a Massey Ferguson. Pull back to the top of that slope, get your toe down and give it some beans. This isn't my first tractor parade.'

Polly shrugged, it was either this or drive back to the stone circle, crawl through the passage and hope nobody had thought to bar the cellar doors.

'Okay, hold on.' She reversed back through swarming dogs, who jumped at the sides to snap at Wendy, Neville and Susan's ankles. She gunned the engine again, revving enough to make the dogs move before slamming her foot down and sliding up the gears to full speed.

The ancient Massey Ferguson threw its bulk along the tarmac to collide with great oak gates that had held intruders at bay for centuries. They were no match, and both they and the gnarled bar behind splintered into shards of antiquity.

'That's going to cost so much money, I think they were listed,' Polly complained as they crunched ancient history under their tyres.

'Okay, head to the right, and full side on,' Wendy screamed as they hit the cobbles, almost punching Polly in the side of the head to gain her attention.

Polly dutifully pulled the tractor into a handbrake turn and pulled up underneath the great window of the drawing room.

'Hang on.' Wendy put her foot on Polly's thigh, scaled up the side of the cab and jumped on the tractor's roof. 'Yes, I thought I had...' She got her fingers underneath the sash window, heaved it open and climbed into the house. 'Come on, you're lucky I didn't have time to lock up properly before we ran off.' She reached back across and beckoned them over.

'Why was the window open in all this snow?' Polly said as Jack helped her out of her seat.

'Air circulation, stops the damp. These old buildings are rife with it, you'd know that if you spent any time here,' Wendy explained as she reached down to help Polly in.

Polly had spent plenty of time breathing in damp while Lady Melissa kept her drugged and tried to steal her child. She had to break this spell, get back to Lizbet. Why couldn't these monsters leave her alone?

'Shove the dogs up,' Polly yelled down once she was inside.

'Really?' Susan said, standing on the roof, hand on hip. 'You're saving the dogs before us, nice.'

'They've got no hands to climb, they need help, better to do it while there's three of you down there to push, Cronus weighs a ton.' Polly and Wendy held their hands out.

'Well that explains why you went in first.' Neville grinned as he and Susan managed to heft the ancient malamute to window height.

'Funny, and it wasn't,' Polly answered, nuzzling her head against the dog as he scrabbled against the windowsill. 'It's harder to pull him than it is for you two to push. I'm doing you a favour.' She held his front end while Wendy pulled at his sides. It wasn't easy and the three of them ended in a tangled mess of fur on the floor.

'Sorry Wendy.' Polly blushed.

'Nothing to apologise for, come on, let's get the wolfhound in.' Wendy pulled Polly's hand from inside her jumper and grinned as they got back to their feet.

Jack was hanging off the side of the tractor, shoving dogs away with a stick. Now it had stopped moving they were finding it easier to climb. 'Hurry up, will you, I can't keep pushing these dogs away, there's too many,' he shouted as he nearly lost his footing.

'Nearly done,' Susan said from the other side as she and Neville struggled to lift a wriggling Fenrir. 'Jesus Christ he stinks, has he rolled in foxshit?'

'Probably, it's his favourite, sorry,' Polly apologised as she wrapped her arms round him.

'Done, they're in, get up here,' Wendy announced as the dogs skittered over polished floorboards.

'Get in, I won't be a second,' Susan shouted, jumping back down to the tractor, having helped Neville and Jack through the window.

'What are you doing?' Neville shouted, reaching to grab her. 'Those dogs will get you, it's not safe.'

'You're right, that's why I have to do this,' she replied before reaching under the seat for the brick she knew Chris always kept there for just this purpose. She revved the engine, and spun the tractor round, reversing it hard against the wall. 'Okay, get ready, I'm coming,' she called, climbing out of the door and balancing on the wheel arch, plastic bending under her weight. She took a deep breath and dropped the brick on the accelerator before leaping for the window. The tractor bumped across the courtyard, scattering dogs, before taking out a substantial amount of stable wall as it keeled over on its side.

'Little help?' Susan clung to the windowsill by her fingertips, legs failing to find purchase on the wall. Polly grabbed her hands and pulled, Susan weighed more than she expected.

'I'm coming, hold on,' Jack called, scrambling across from his ungainly landing place. He added his strength to Polly's to wrangle Susan inside where she landed on her face.

'Ow! That hurt!' Susan said, as Polly slammed the window.

'Sorry,' Polly said. 'At least you're in though. What did you do that for?'

'Those dogs would have got in if we'd left the tractor there. It was like a massive ladder.' She twisted her head against the deep piled Persian rug she was splayed out on. 'I hope there's not too much damage.'

'You're alright,' Polly replied, helping her to her feet. 'I wasn't going to reopen the grooming salon anyway.'

'Good. I would have thought we'd have some kind of reception committee, where is everyone?' Susan asked.

'Are we sure he's in here?' Jack asked. 'Maybe the others put up a fight, maybe they took his caravan?'

'What, with all the dogs against them?' Susan replied. 'And then just wandered off?'

'No I suppose it doesn't seem very likely.' Jack dropped his head. 'He's in here somewhere then.'

'He's here, no two ways about it,' Polly explained. 'Mel can feel him.'

'Ah fuck, we're back in trouble then,' Jack said. 'Why couldn't we have stayed in the pub, amnesiac and happy.'

'Because we're better than that.' Susan took his hands. 'We can do this.'

'And anyway, he's not expecting us,' Wendy said, clapping her hands. 'He'd be waiting here if he was. We've got an advantage, and not just the hagstone. Maybe he can't feel Mel the way she can him?'

'Where is he though? And what's happened to the others?' Susan turned white. 'You don't think he's...'

'Don't go jumping to any conclusions,' Neville said. 'We don't know anything yet. Where would you go if you were an evil spirit from the dawn of time hell-bent on revenge?'

'I'd be looking for whoever I wanted to be revenged upon,' Wendy said. 'Or failing that, the source of whatever made them tick, if I knew what... oh fuck. They're in the cellar.'

'How do you know that?' Jack asked.

'Look at that.' She pointed to the dumb waiter hatch hanging open as the waiter itself carried an Exeter Chiefs beanie aimlessly from floor to floor.

'Okay, cellars it is, have you got the hagstone?' Polly asked.

'Yep,' Wendy answered, holding it up. 'Right here.'

'Pass it over, Mel should know what to do,' Polly said, cupping her hands.

Wendy threw it over arm and Polly snatched it one-handed from the air.

'Thanks.' Polly's eyes had turned silver, with a face that brooked no arguments. 'To the cellars, time to stop that fuck before he ruins everything. But first...'

She opened the front door to a rush of dogs, throwing themselves at a tiny gap, snuffling, barking, howling and scratching. Lady Melissa grabbed the first one and dragged it through before slamming the door on the rest.

'Quick test,' she explained. 'Sorry Saxon Five.' She looked the malamute in its eyes, holding it at arm's length by the scruff as it scrabbled against the wooden floor, desperate to reach its prey. She closed her eyes, chanted something nobody else could hear and ran her thumb around the Bellever Hagstone's wire pentagram. A strange blue light poured out and the dog went limp. Its eyes changed back to their usual dirty amber and it stopped struggling before lying down in front of Lady Melissa with one paw in the air and its tongue hanging out. 'Good boy,' she said, rubbing his belly. She got back to her feet and flicked him a biscuit before striding towards the cellars. 'Come on then.'

'Oh dear, they've locked the gate,' The Traveller said with a laugh at the bottom of the cellar steps. 'How will we get to them?'

'If they're even still down here,' Father Hearne said. 'You might have imagined it.'

'I did not imagine a man in my dumb waiter,' The Traveller said, opening the gate with a wave of his hand. 'What are you implying?'

'Nothing, you're not paranoid.' Father Hearne followed him into the cellar where he stood on a raised brick and automatically ducked, then pushed The Traveller behind him as two rusted circular blades fell out of the walls, spinning sadly and wobbling to the ground in a clatter.

'Oh, that's a little more inconvenient than the gate I suppose,' The Traveller said. 'Mind how you go Arthur.'

'Will do,' the priest said, moving off carefully.

20

'What was that?' Clive said, clawing through rubble. 'Are you okay?'

'Tractor,' Kerry answered, already on her feet and helping him up. 'Big fucking tractor – looks like Chris's.'

'Why has a tractor come through the wall?' Clive asked as they left their prison and stood blinking in the moonlight.

'I don't know, but it's got your wife written all over it. Maybe it's the cavalry, should we go and help?' Kerry said.

'I'd rather go home, but okay. How are we getting through them?' Clive pointed to the pack of dogs between them and the house.

'Piece of piss,' Kerry said, firing up a blow-drier.

'We must be nearly through it now,' Father Hearne said, brushing tiny blow darts from his suit. 'I don't think they're even here still.'

'Oh they are,' The Traveller replied. They had got through all the traps with ease, a mixture of protective spells, cunning and malfunctioning mechanisms had kept them unscathed. The final blast of tiny poison darts had not had the force to pierce skin or clothing and were just a nuisance to remove from the crevices they had landed in. The poison on their tips had long been neutralised and both traveller and priest were feeling confident they would be fine.

'Well, I'm sure they'll listen to…' Father Hearne was cut off as he felt another trigger go under his foot and a net came out from nowhere, strapping him and The Traveller tight together where they stood.

'Not so cocky now are you?' Lynn said, appearing in an archway.

'This won't hold me for long,' The Traveller said, smirking at Lynn's triumphant face. He ran a finger along the edges of the net.

'What about me?' Father Hearne wheedled, tearing at a hole that gave no relief. It was a strong net. He didn't like to think what it had been made for. 'Will it hold me for long?'

'I might, if you don't shut up,' The Traveller hissed before slicing the thick cables with his bare hand. 'What did you hope to achieve?' He reached forwards to grab Lynn but his fingers folded up against a mirror. She wasn't there. 'Oh, very clever. Don't think I can't find you. I know this place every bit as well as any of you. I have walked these halls. I walked this ground before there were any fucking halls. This ground is mine.' His voice began to rasp with anger.

'What does it matter where I am,' Lynn called out. 'If you're so unstoppable, we're nothing to you.'

'I could leave you, but you're like an itchy tattoo scab. A thing I can't leave alone, and I want my new home free of vermin. I want no taint of the Dewer woman left, and you stink of her. I shall flush you out and collapse the tunnels. I know all the secrets of this place. Nobody shall get in without my knowing. Arthur, go and fetch my dogs.' His leering smile reflected across the mirrors. 'All of them.'

'Of course, if you could just?' Father Hearne tapped at the web that still held him.

'Oh for God's sake, here you go.' The Traveller snapped his fingers and cables exploded into dust that sparkled as it scattered.

'Thank you.' The vicar ran off past snapped off spikes, unlaunched arrows, punji pits that had failed to fully open and murder holes that poured nothing but dust towards the exit.

He pulled up short as a shadowy figure appeared. Reinforcements, the others were back. All the breath left his body and his lungs refused to pull any more in.

'Oh good, you're still here,' Melissa said, looming from an alcove. 'You can help us, is he here? Are you safe? Where are the others?'

'I don't know, we got separated, but yes. He's down here, what are you going to do?' he bluffed, relief flooding his system and pumping his lungs. Of course, they hadn't been in contact, communications were dead. They didn't know what he had done and the longer it took for them to work it out the better.

'I'm going to fuck him up, you better get out of here.' Melissa twisted Polly's face into a vengeful scowl that made The Traveller's evil grin seem a happy toddler's smile.

'Okay, thanks, I think the others are over by the dumb waiter. Not sure where he's got to.'

'Where are you off to?' Melissa narrowed Polly's eyes. 'All on your own?'

'I figured somebody should infiltrate the house while we know he's down here. I've got a few tricks left up my sleeve.' Father Hearne edged away.

'Good man, glad to have you on our side.' Melissa clapped him on the shoulder. 'Though it looks like you've already used most of the tricks.' She waved at the circular blades lying forlorn on the ground.

The vicar ran up the steps to fulfil his promise, heaving a sigh of relief. He had never been a match for Melissa, and was terrified what she would do when she found him out.

Susan, Jack, Neville and Wendy emerged from their hiding places and the group moved warily in the direction from which Father Hearne had come.

'Susan?' hissed a voice from the blackness. 'Is that you? Thank God you're back.'

'Dan?' Susan whispered, walking through a dark archway towards the disembodied voice.

'It's me, did you find it?' Dan grabbed her arm.

'Yes, we have it. Melissa's in control and we're going to finish this.' Susan held Dan's hand for a beat.

'Good, very good,' Dan answered. 'Now, more importantly, we've lost Clive and Kerry.'

'Where?' Susan shrieked.

'If we knew that they wouldn't be lost would they, one thing at a time please,' Lynn said, stepping out of the shadows and checking an invisible clipboard, as if chairing a Trust meeting. 'And The Traveller's down here. He's trying to get into the bone throne room, but I've locked it.'

'Clever you,' Wendy said.

'Not really, it won't hold against him for long. That one didn't.' Lynn waved at the remains of the lock on the iron gate. They wouldn't be able to use that again.

'How did he get in?' Melissa asked. 'There's some very clever magic over this house that really should have stopped him. If I do say so myself.'

'That bastard vicar double-crossed us,' Dan explained.

'Oh, well that would get round my spells yes. Hang on, Father Hearne?' The colour drained from Polly's face. 'My Father Hearne?'

'Yes, he's around too,' Lynn said. 'The cowardly shit.'

'Oh bollocks,' Neville said, slapping his forehead. 'We just let him past. We let him go.'

'But that means...' Lynn began.

'Dogs, way too many dogs, right behind us, move, move move,' Kerry shouted as her and Clive ran through.

'Where did you spring from?' Susan asked.

'We were locked in the stables, until somebody broke us out,' Clive explained.

'You're welcome honey,' Susan grabbed him, hugging him like she wouldn't ever let go.

'What a touching reunion,' Lynn remarked, looking at Jack who rolled his eyes and shrugged.

'Put him down Susan, weren't you listening?' Kerry shouted, grabbing Dan's chair handles, kissing the top of his bald head and running off in one smooth move as dogs swarmed through the cellars, all glowing blue eyes and snarling mouths.

'I hear you, my pack, you shall not leave my side again. Find them, find her, fix this,' The Traveller's voice carried through the tunnels. 'I know you're here Dewer, I can feel you.'

Melissa waved Polly's hands in a complicated motion but nothing came of it. 'Damn it, still nothing. You're useless girl, where's all that strength you used against me last year, why can't I access it?'

Sorry, I guess it doesn't work like that, I expect I could access it though...

'Don't go getting any ideas. You'll be out again soon enough.' Melissa stamped her foot. 'Sorry everybody, no tricks left.'

'Well, that's it,' Dan said. 'Leave me for bait and get yourselves out. We've lost the Manor, we'll lose the town. Tell the kids I...'

What about the hagstone? Has all this been for nothing?

'Oh yeah, sorry, forgot this,' Melissa said, rummaging through her pockets and pulling out the hagstone. 'They're good dogs Brent.'

'They're his good dogs now, even yours, haven't you realised?' Lynn stuttered.

'They belong to no-one. He never understood that and neither did Polly, however many times I told her. That's how we ended up in this mess. I should never have trusted this place to that silly girl.' Melissa held everyone back, standing in the centre of the archway as dogs filled the passageway. Lynn's mirrors made them appear to be coming from all angles.

'You know nothing. They belong to me,' The Traveller's voice came down the tunnels.

'They are their own dogs, you just have to know how to talk to them, and you never could, could you?' Melissa raised her voice to carry through the air.

'The evidence says otherwise, Lady Dewer. Your time is done.' The last word echoed about the walls, distorting and evolving to sound like doom, doom, doom, doom.

'They are...' Melissa closed her eyes and held the Bellever Hagstone in both hands above her head. Eerie blue light spread from it as she spoke unintelligible words under her breath. The power from the ancient gateway revitalised Melissa's spirit, bringing Polly's body back to full strength. The malamutes carried on towards her, unrelenting, unstoppable.

'Melissa, don't let them take Polly, you can't, please no,' Wendy threw herself between woman and dogs.

'Careful you stupid...' the hagstone flew from Polly's hand into a dark corner and the blue light vanished.

'Sorry, I just wanted to help,' Wendy cried as she disappeared beneath fur and claw.

'Find it, help her, somebody.' Polly reasserted herself, crawling across the floor in distress.

'On it.' Dan span his chair into the dogs, scattering them from Wendy. 'It's fine, can't feel it anyway,' he said as dogs clawed his paralysed legs.

'It's fucking not,' Kerry said, wading in with a bat as they began to bite.

Polly looked over, wanting to leap in and save Wendy, but knowing her best hope was the hagstone. 'Why did you let me back through?'

I'm not good at looking for things, usually I'm all "Accio Hagstone" *and things come to me. This is more your thing*, Melissa explained, unwilling to let Polly know she'd broken the spell all by herself. She didn't think it was a good time for Polly to confront the depth of feeling she had for Wendy. *What's that?*

Polly saw a gleam in the dark and threw herself towards it. She fell to the ground and pulled it up, preparing to let Melissa finish the job. But it was an old branding iron, stained with blood from her duel with Clive on this spot the year before. 'Fuck, I can't do this!' she shouted.

'Polly, catch,' Lynn shouted, throwing the hagstone across.

She fumbled the catch and it vanished in the gloom a second time.

'I'm okay,' Wendy shouted from the floor, holding two dogs by their throats with each hand and using them as shields against the rest. Dan and Kerry kicked, punched and batted the others that stalked in, but they would soon be overwhelmed by sheer numbers. Clive, Jack and Susan were leaning against mirrors propped against the archway to block the rest of the pack. 'But I don't think we're going to hold out much longer.'

Polly bent down, grabbed the hagstone and felt Melissa flow back.

The mirrors gave way, the weight of dogs too much for the dried out rotten wood. Clive, Jack and Susan sprang away from an explosion of malamutes, mongrels and broken glass.

Polly's arm went up, Melissa's voice chanted, and blue light exploded as a malamute leaped for her. The hagstone fell again, light fading, as she was pinned to the ground by filthy paws.

'Hello Sky,' Melissa said, grinning all over Polly's well-licked face. 'As I was saying,' she continued, louder, 'the wisthounds are their own and you cannot keep them. You do not understand them, so they are gone, leaving these animals to be their own.'

There was no reply.

'Come on then, let's finish this.' Melissa stood up, stroking the dog's neck. 'Where the hell are Cronus and Fenrir?'

They quickly made their way to the throne room where their question was answered. The dogs were trapped, The Traveller's pack of mongrels had them pinned in a corner, Wotan at the front, saliva dripping from his massive jaws.

'I may not have your stupid sledge dogs any more – why did you stop keeping hounds Elias, I liked them,' The Traveller said, sitting on the throne of bones. 'But I still have my own, and they outnumber your useless creatures.'

'They are not useless, they are extremely good... oh my God.' Melissa stopped in her tracks as she saw The Traveller properly for the first time. 'But you can't be? How can you be him? It's not... it's not...'

'Oh but it is, and he hates you every bit as much as I,' The Traveller said.

21

Is that? Polly said, recognising the only friendly face she had known during her long weeks of imprisonment in Lady Melissa's bedroom. *Is that who I think it is?*

'It's not him, but it's his body, same as this isn't you, but it is yours,' Melissa explained. She turned to The Traveller, 'How can you be in that body? He died, we gave him to the dogs.'

'I found him, I offered him a deal. His life, for a price.' The Traveller picked at his nails, one leather booted foot propped on the opposite knee. 'He was willing, he so wanted to live, to rescue his child. And yet he could not return here any more than I. We came to a mutually beneficial agreement.'

'Let him speak, let him tell me. Not you, release control, let him back, let me...' Melissa's voice cracked.

'Very well, we are of one accord still are we not?' He paused, listening to his internal dialogue. 'It seems we are, Arthur.' He addressed Father Hearne who stood just outside the door. 'Keep an eye on these people, make sure there are no tricks, and ensure he does not outstay his welcome.'

'Can do,' the priest replied, aware that he was just one person with no real weapons.

'Oh God, they don't know who you are do they?' The Traveller laughed. 'They think you're just a man. Oh well-played. Far be it from me to out you Arthur, you've always played your part so well. Forget I said anything, he's just a priest.'

'I know what – and who – Arthur is,' Melissa said. 'I've always known who he was, whichever face he has worn, and I always suspected he might be a traitorous shit, but that's irrelevant now, however true it is. Let me speak with him.'

'Fine.' The Traveller's black eyes rolled back and there he was. Older than when she had last seen him, greyer, and with that awful beard, but there were those flashing green eyes she had fallen for.

That ready smile and easy manner could not be far behind.

'Hello Elias,' Nathaniel Harker said, without smile or welcome. 'You didn't expect to see me again, did you?'

'Of course not, I thought you dead, I thought you gone forever. Forgive me, I have tried to make it right. I kept an eye on our child, I made sure he and his descendants were not lost, made sure they were okay.' Melissa stumbled towards him, arms outstretched.

'Ha,' he spat. 'I know you did that for you, to claim the next Dewer woman for yourself. So malleable, so easy, so nice. So willing. Not like this one you've had to borrow. How the mighty have fallen.' He shuffled in his seat. 'Arthur told us how she tricked you, used your own dogs against you and now denies you the very thing you worked so hard for. The child we have removed from you with one little storm. Tell me, are you scared?'

'No. She will be mine, no matter what you think,' Melissa said.

This was not the Nathaniel she remembered. He had so much hatred in his eyes, was so bitter, so twisted. Surely that kind, gentle soul she had so ill-used was still there somewhere?

At the mention of Elizabeth, Polly woke up and battered at the walls in her mind. She could not break through, not this time. Melissa's passion was stronger and pushed her down further and further until she could only watch what was going on, unable to interact.

'Always so sure of yourself Elias, always. But that girl destroyed you. You're weak, and we're here to finish you. You're not the only one who loves this place, it's ours now, and once we are rid of you we can make it the paradise it should have been had you not jealously hoarded it so long.' It was Nathaniel's voice, and Nathaniel's face, but those words did not sound like him.

'I'm sorry for what I did to you Nathaniel,' Melissa said, standing with one foot on the bottom step of the dais. 'But you broke my heart. I was jealous of what you had with Thomas, I was frustrated at the useless boy child you had given me, you and Sophia had a bond I never had with either of you. You mortals have it so easy, you never understand. Never.'

'So you left me for dead.' He gave her the accusing look she remembered from the night she had done exactly that.

'Yes. I am sorry.' She dropped her head, looking to where the remains of her old body had been kicked about by dogs.

'Well luckily for you I was saved.'

'By him?'

'Yes, when you had forsaken me, left me for dead, splayed out on that rock, just waiting for your hounds to come and take my useless, broken heart from my chest, a stranger came. A stranger who offered me a deal.' He smiled.

'That's not possible, he couldn't cross the boundaries. The protection, the dogs, it should have held then, even if that stupid girl has broken it now.' Melissa looked up at the others, hoping for support.

'Oh no, he couldn't. It wasn't him. It was a priest, travelling from Iddesleigh, with a willing sacrifice.' Nathaniel sat forwards, pointing with clasped hands.

'You?' Melissa turned to Father Hearne. 'Restored so soon?'

'Well, yes, I admit I had a hand in it. I only want what's best for all of us, this stupid fight had already been going on long enough. After you had the townspeople burn me out of my church and throw me to your dogs I was lucky enough to find a sympathetic host quicker than usual, with a little help.' The priest skipped across the floor, away from the conflict.

'Of course, you two have been in league longer than I imagined.' Melissa slapped Polly's forehead. 'Carry on then Nathaniel, how did you escape?'

'The priest told me he would take me away if I was willing to make certain concessions. By that time the cold was about to kill me, the dogs were certain to arrive soon and terror led me to grasp at any olive branch. So I accepted his offer. Obviously, without any idea what it would entail.'

'Obviously.' Melissa folded Polly's arms.

'And then he cut me free from your cart and I switched clothes with his willing sacrifice. I asked no questions of how he found somebody willing to die in such a terrible fashion. Perhaps I should have, but I was in no condition to be questioning my salvation. He told me later on, when there was nothing I could do about it. But by then I knew who he was, and what he was like. Anyway, we bound the poor man to the stone before the vicar and I walked away from Dourstone, past the boundary cross and far away.'

'Why not just take Nathaniel and break my magick?' Melissa asked.

'I refused his request,' Father Hearne answered. 'As I keep telling him, I am not on any side, I only wish for an understanding.'

'Very noble,' Melissa said. 'Carry on Nathaniel.'

'Thank you. He was in a bad way when we came to him, had not found a new host for a long time and the one he had was rotting from the inside. He told me that if I allowed him to ride in my body then he would help me be revenged. That while I might not return to Dourstone soon, our paths lay the same way. He promised me elongated life, more time. He forgot to mention that I would never again see my son, or live a normal life.

'He terrified me, quite frankly. Despite everything I had been through with you I wasn't ready. He was in a ruined house on a desolate part of the moor, dressed in a long damp black robe with tattered sleeves. His skin was sloughing from his bones, even his face, his nose had gone completely. On the bright side, I had been expecting to meet the reaper that night, so to find I could bargain with the fellow was a pleasant surprise.'

'Quite,' Melissa replied. 'Who doesn't want to play with Death himself?'

'I know, it was like being in one of Sophia's ghost stories. Anyway, I have no idea what would have become of me had I refused, since in keeping my life I had already received my part of the bargain, but I was so grateful I allowed him in. The poor creature he had been inhabiting crumbled to nothing before my eyes, and we have been together ever since. United in our hatred of you.' Nathaniel banged his fist on the skull that tipped the chair's arm.

'Well, isn't that cosy,' Melissa said, stepping back. 'Everybody wants me dead. How the tables have turned.'

'Not everybody,' Susan appeared at her shoulder. 'We are with you.'

'Are you?' Melissa said. 'I mean I've heard you all this last year, badmouthing me to Polly every time you're worried she won't give you what you want.'

'No, not entirely,' Wendy said. 'We don't owe you any loyalty. But we don't want any harm to come to Polly – at least I don't – and you're still in her.'

'Well then, let's see whose dogs are better when they're all just dogs.' Melissa raised the hagstone, unleashing that blue light on The Traveller's pack, turning them back to nothing but a horde of hungry mongrels. 'Fenrir, Cronus, see these intruders off my property,' she said. The two dogs advanced on Wotan in a series of barks, working together as a team.

'It's still two against...' Nathaniel's words clogged in his mouth as malamutes appeared in answer to Cronus's call. The distraction was enough to give Fenrir the edge over the big black beast. He knocked him to the ground and Cronus joined in. It took short work for the huge bear to get back to his paws and give his rebuttal. He pushed Fenrir aside and went back to Cronus, holding the older dog down and going in for his throat. The other malamutes rushed to the defence of their leaders, but Wotan was able to shrug them off as they attacked one by one through the narrow gap he had forced Cronus into.

As Wotan went in for the final bite, Cronus growled, wriggling ineffectually underneath the weight of the dog, fighting to the last. Wotan's huge maw gaped teeth dripping saliva. Cronus snapped back, but couldn't get his head to the right angle. As all seemed lost, the huge black beast squealed and flew backwards. Fenrir and Saxon Five had a back leg in each of their mouths and were pulling him from their friend.

Wotan pulled himself loose, and sprinted away, butting off his attackers. The wolfhound ran after him, and the dogs left the room in pursuit. The fight had swept away all that remained of Lady Melissa Dewer's physical presence, crushing the crumbling bones to dust and scattering them to the corners of the room.

'So would you like to be yourself again, and nobody else?' Melissa asked Nathaniel. She walked to the top of the dais, and leaned close to him, holding out the hagstone.

'Don't be ridiculous,' The Traveller said, back in control once more. He stretched forwards and licked Polly's cheek as he grabbed her thigh. 'He's a hundred and fifty years old, do you think he'll survive if I let go? He might make a lovely addition to your chair, but that's about it. If you love him, you need me inside.' He released her thigh, reaching higher.

'What makes you think I love him?' She stood back, slapping his hand away.

'I know you, I've known you a long time. You didn't slap me away half as quick as that girl you're in wanted you to.' The Traveller laughed, picking at the bones of the chair as if nothing had happened. 'I've watched you all down the centuries, waiting for you to slip up. And you never did, not until you met him. You loved a mortal, and you picked one that could never truly love the body you were in, one that only loved the facade you projected; who could not endure your femininity. So deliciously ironic. I never thought any of us could truly love another, especially one with such a brief existence. But you did, and look where it's led.'

'I'm okay.' Melissa stomped to the bottom of the dais, out of reach.

'You're all over the place, and you can't use the one weapon you have. You won't knock me out of Nathaniel, because you won't kill him again. I've seen his picture, hung in pride of place in your finest room. All these years and you've never forgotten him. I've seen nothing of Sophia, of the many wives, lovers and others you've kept over the years. Just him. You won't do it.' The Traveller took up his slouched position again, arrogantly crossing one leg over the other.

'No, maybe you're right.' Melissa sat down on the steps and tossed the hagstone from hand to hand.

'I will though, give it to me,' Wendy said, striding towards Melissa and snatching it from the air. 'This has gone on too long. We need to get back to normal. We need our children. To be able to leave town and start a new life. Now how does it work?' She ran her fingers over the stone to no effect. 'Maybe I can knock you out of Polly at the same time.'

'You won't be able to work it and I've done enough. You can keep Polly. He was right the first time.' Melissa dropped her head and whispered something inaudible. Wendy's hand jerked open and dropped the hagstone. Melissa caught it without even looking up. 'Promise me you won't harm these people, or this place. That you'll look after it. Promise me Nathaniel.'

'Fine, they can stay,' The Traveller said, rising from the chair to walk down the steps.

'Then do what you will, take me, leave Polly, and leave her dogs. Here.' Melissa stood up and held out the hagstone, staring him down.

'I'll leave the woman, but you're asking a lot,' The Traveller said, close enough to feel Polly's breath on his face. He reached for the hagstone and she pulled it away.

'Just one more request,' she said. 'Give me one last night with

Nathaniel – if he'll have me – let me make it up to him, then you can do what you want. I promise not to hurt you while he's in control.' She stared into those eyes, all wrong in that face, and held the hagstone out of his reach.

'He says that's agreeable. That the two of you have much to talk about. Arthur!' he barked at the priest. 'Make sure nothing goes awry while I am under. I will be there myself anyway, underneath, you know that don't you Melissa? I can watch.' He grinned. 'I can come back at any moment and stop – or join in with – whatever you're doing. Not that you can do anything to me without killing him. I have won, you are utterly defeated, please never forget that.'

'Yes, that's fine. Whatever, it's not about me. I am done with this world. Take me where you will.' She placed the Bellever Hagstone in his hands and bowed her head.

'Back upstairs all of you,' The Traveller ordered as his mongrels returned, triumphantly herding in malamutes. Fenrir and Cronus ran to Melissa's side, heads bowed.

Lynn, Clive, Susan, Dan, Kerry, Neville and Wendy were escorted from the room by Father Hearne and a group of dogs, defeated and unsure of their future.

'The Dewer woman and I will join you once I have restored my pack,' he shouted as they left.

'Leave Polly's escort untouched.' Melissa folded Polly's arms 'We agreed.'

'I don't think so,' The Traveller said. 'I don't recall agreeing to any dogs being left. Just your poor little friend in here.' He tapped her forehead with a long yellowing fingernail.

She looked imploringly at him. She couldn't bear to see Fenrir and Cronus turned, they were too invested in Polly. It was bad enough watching her other dogs go. She couldn't leave, knowing she hadn't done all she could.

The Traveller shook his head.

Melissa grudgingly let go of the dogs. With a wave of The Traveller's hands they moved, against their will, to either side of the dais.

'I want to make sure you see what happens to these two,' he said, as ropes snaked from nowhere to secure the dogs. They pulled at their restraints, scrabbling at the steps and trying to reach each other.

They looked to Melissa with trusting eyes. There were no more places to hide and she was the only person they could turn to. Their mistress would save them. Polly had rescued Fenrir from his prison at Battersea and Melissa had kept Cronus at the top of his game these long years. The two of them together must be able to save the dogs they loved. They sat down and offered paws like good dogs did when they needed help. But there was nothing more to be done. Hers and Polly's heart broke knowing what was to come.

The dogs clawed at their bonds, whimpering.

'And now, I shall have my infernal pack restored.' The Traveller raised the hagstone above his head, closed his eyes and muttered to bring forth another blinding blue light. The dogs stopped milling around, their eyes turning that shining shade of blue. They turned to Wotan, who barked once, then turned to The Traveller for instruction.

Melissa watched Fenrir as he stopped pawing at the floor, trying to reach his friend on the other side. His tortured howl caught in his throat and his face went neutral, blue covering his eyes and a serene calm coming over him. Cronus watched in horror, as Polly saw him follow suit from deep inside her own head, even more unable to help than Melissa. He blanked, then his eyes turned blue and he sat down like a good dog, no pawing, no whimpering, no more fear in his face.

The Traveller lowered the hagstone with a sneer, a wave of his hand released the two dogs, who marched into the throng to be lost in the pack. Just two more dogs waiting for a command.

Their heart finished breaking and they wept together through Polly's eyes, they could take no more and wished beyond wishing that they were two people able to comfort each other physically.

22

The evening room of Dourstone Manor was an oddity, an extravagance not often seen in country houses. Most would be happy with a morning room, a drawing room, a dining room, a lounge and a billiards room and although Dourstone Manor already had those rooms and many more, the Dewers had felt the need for one optimised for the last light of day and had created a room at the top of one of its towers. It was not a formal room, they did not entertain there, it was solely for the use of the Lord and Lady of the house and as such had a bed for those evenings when they did not feel like leaving. It was not a day bed, though it was occasionally used as such. It had, being so far from the hustle and bustle of the main house and prying eyes, been a favourite place for Nathaniel and Lord Elias.

'I haven't spent time in here for over a century,' Melissa said, standing in the window, sipping at a Penfolds Grange 1951 and gazing at the view she would never again contemplate. 'I couldn't separate it from you.'

'Feeling a little guilty for killing me were you?' Nathaniel replied, standing in the doorway, unwilling to re-enter this room with all its memories.

'If we're going to be honest, and there's little point in being anything else now, then yes.' Melissa turned, a standard lamp lit up the black halo of Polly's hair, fresh grey strands glinting in the tight black curls. She had dressed up for the occasion: if this was to be her last night of corporeality then she wanted to look nice. Polly wore a black 1930s evening gown with green and red birds embroidered through silk that she looked most striking in. Melissa agreed, it accentuated her skin tones and rippled around her in a way that made Melissa's eyes keep straying to the mirror.

'Then why? We could have been happy. We were a family.' Nathaniel looked appraisingly at Melissa. It was definitely his Elias, all the mannerisms were there, the folded arms, the tilt of the head. The way he would stand, favouring his right leg over his left. But here he was in the body of a young woman of colour. He had always had to look past Elias' basic biology. Nathaniel was not attracted to women, just this one creature that defied gender. It did not matter what body they inhabited. He loved them unequivocally.

'It was the nineteenth century Nathaniel,' Melissa said, collapsing onto a deep leather sofa by the big circular window and spreading Polly's legs as wide as the gown allowed. 'Even the aristocracy had to preserve ourselves from scandal.'

'Are you saying you gave me up to save your reputation Elias?' Nathaniel sat on the arm of the sofa, respecting the niceties of social propriety. He had no history with Polly, only his Lord Elias, and had no wish to upset the young lady.

'No, no, of course not. I'm sure we could have found a cover for you, another Sophia, a home in the Manor, a way for us all to have been together, but...' Melissa ran fingers through Polly's hair.

'But what?' He looked imploringly into her eyes.

'But you left us, never forget that. We loved you, and you betrayed us.' She reached across and grabbed his leg.

'You two slept with everyone, you had those… those… orgies. The sex parties you threw after the sacrifice, all that flesh, all those willing partners. And yet you begrudge me one dalliance.' Nathaniel stood up and stalked across the floorboards to the fireplace.

'It was so much more than one dalliance. You loved Thomas Sumner.' Melissa pulled her legs together and drew herself up on the sofa.

'I admit that I did, yes. But you loved Sophia. We were not exclusive to one another.' Nathaniel poked at the fire, causing its centre to glow a bright red before flames leaped from its zenith.

'But you also loved Sophia and she loved you; we loved each other. You and I were not exclusive, but I thought the three of us were, in our own way. We had an accord, a trust, we had – as you said – a family. You broke that.' Melissa got up and walked across the rug towards Nathaniel.

'I cannot understand you.' Nathaniel replaced the poker with a satisfying click.

'Sex and love are not the same thing. Those people we used in our games were no more to us than the contraptions we used in the bedroom. A means to an end, not a meaningful relationship. Not like you had with Thomas. I knew, I saw you, I heard. I felt it and it hurt.' Melissa folded her arms, tightly hugging her chest.

'You must have had thousands of lovers over the centuries Elias, are you telling me you never betrayed any of them? That none of them betrayed you? That you had never before been hurt?' Nathaniel raised his voice, turning to look her in the eyes.

'Not the way you did. I had never loved a man before.' Lord Elias Dewer's steely grey eyes stared out from Polly's face, sucking Nathaniel into a feeling he thought he had been rid of before the war to end all wars. Melissa took a deep breath before continuing, 'Men had only ever been a means to create new vessels. I had been in love, yes, with many a girl who ran away and left me for the first man to offer her respectability. A way to avoid the scandal of the Dewer name, once they knew what I really was. Plenty loved me for the same reasons as Sophia, to be themselves and remain respectable. A woman everybody thought to be a man? What perfect cover for their sapphic desire. Their gratitude for my position afforded me lifelong loyalty. But they bored me, I wanted rid of them all before they finally died, or left. Eternity may be a long time, but even a mortal lifetime gets boring very quickly, especially when they get to the less flexible end.' Melissa winked and gave a filthy laugh before swigging her wine.

'We had less than five years together, and yet you had me murdered.' Nathaniel poured himself a large brandy from a cut glass decanter on the well-stocked drinks trolley. 'You speak in terms of my betraying you, you would coax guilt from my heart. You left me for your dogs – twice no less – my heart in place of what you lack. And you claim it was my fault!'

'The fault was mine Nathaniel. Not a day since has passed that I haven't regretted my actions. It was done in haste, I was stubborn, pig-headed, angry and hurt, and I lashed out. I should not have killed you any more than I should have killed your great-great-grandson last year. Polly may be right, perhaps we should end this cycle of death.' Melissa sat back down, placed her drink carefully on a side table and cradled her head in her hands.

'Admirable sentiment Elias,' Nathaniel replied, his voice quieter, less angry. 'If a little late.'

'I know, I am sorry, I will keep saying it until you believe me,'

Melissa continued. 'I kept up the ceremonies of sex after sacrifice for a long time after you died. Hoping to meet another like you. But eventually it brought no solace, I have not held such a party in many years. Sophia hated me. Blamed me for your death. It was fair, it was my doing, but when I realised I had made a mistake she offered me no comfort. She resented me for the rest of her days, made sure I realised the extent of my guilt, and removed the one weapon I had against your friend from my possession.'

'She had already planned that before I was gone,' Nathaniel said. 'We feared you would use it recklessly, she thought you might harm yourself in your post-natal madness, I agreed, but never thought she would do it. I never thought she would have need to.' He sat next to Melissa.

'She did not have need. The stupid girl didn't need to do any of the things she did, I regret not being kinder, at her end, but her decisions were her own.' Melissa shuffled a little closer.

'For the love of God Elias! Take some responsibility. Even now, after all this time, when you've been beaten, you are still so proud. So sure nothing is your fault, so...' He waved his arms in frustration.

'Everything is my fault. I accept that, and I am sorry. She was a good woman, you were a good man...' Melissa grabbed one of his arms, holding it to her chest to stay its motion.

'I still am.' He did not fight.

'You are no longer yourself, he… we, I mean... we affect the people we take. And they in turn affect us, it is a two-way street. Polly has made me far too sympathetic, for example, and I have made her somewhat bossy.' She let go his arm and he slowly took it back.

'I'm sure you are right, but there's enough of me left to know who I am, what I want and who I have always been.' He looked at his arm as if he hadn't for a long time.

'What do you want?' She reached across and placed her hand on his chest.

'I want to go back, I want us to have never fallen out, for the baby to have lived with us, for us to have produced the heir you needed, for you to have loved me. For you to have used a murderer or rapist, anyone other than I, for your dreadful sacrifice. For us to have lived the life I dreamed of and I to lie satisfied and content in my grave.' He smiled, taking her hand in both of his. 'What I want is the impossible, though I have seen so much of the improbable, I'm no longer sure anything is.'

'Well, I'm afraid what you wish for is. That was never possible. Even if we could turn back time. The dogs are not evil, they do not feed on evil. The bargain requires a good heart, once a year as the weather turns to bad. I could never tell the people, but...' Melissa pulled Polly's hands from Nathaniel's and lifted her drink. 'But now, it seems it doesn't matter. Polly knows now, if she ever manages to find a way back from this, she'll need to remember that, the only way to keep the town is to lose good people. Her Patrick was a good man. You. You were a very good man, I am sorry.'

'I know all that, I'm so damned steeped in doglore from my time wandering. I never discovered how your criminals kept them, how did you do it?' He walked across the room and refilled his heavy brandy glass.

'Isn't it obvious? I lied. I made it up, I found good people, slandered their names, turned the town against them and fed them to the dogs. I had to, it was the only way.' Her voice sounded more than ever like the arrogant Lord Elias Nathaniel remembered. She finished her glass, and held it out.

'But the priest?' Nathaniel stepped back slowly towards the sofa, his own full glass in one hand, wine bottle in the other.

'Oh, that was okay, that was just Arthur, always popping up, trying to prick my conscience, make peace between us all.' Melissa's face broke into a smile and her tone lightened. 'I've lost count of the amount of times I've thrown him to the wolves. He always picks dithery, well-meaning holy men, so they're almost always good, even if he isn't. I still don't know why I haven't thrown this latest "Father Hearne" to them yet. I must be getting sentimental.'

'They burned the church, because of you.' Nathaniel poured wine into her glass as she held it steady. He didn't smile.

'I never wanted a fucking church and I much prefer it open to the sky. It has more atmosphere. Will he still have the Midnight Mass tomorrow?' Melissa asked, knowing she would never see it.

'He says he will, to mark the beginning of the new Dourstone.' Nathaniel took the bottle back to the drinks trolley.

'I suppose that's something. He's over his plan to raze it from existence then?' Melissa spread Polly languidly over the sofa and patted the other seat.

'That was never his plan. You misunderstood him. You never...' Nathaniel came back over but remained standing.

'Enough about him. I can do nothing more.' Melissa patted the sofa more firmly.

'I can.' Nathaniel sat down with a creak, making Polly's slight body bounce on the old springs.

'You can't, you only think you can, he is stronger than you. He'll make you think his plans are entirely your own idea and you'll be so pleased with yourself. I cannot bear the cross-contamination, it is not right.' Melissa slapped the sofa arm.

'So that's why...' Nathaniel looked up, light dawning in his eyes.

'Why I took innocent babies, why I only truly connect with Dewer girls? Yes. We struck a deal, a long time ago. I do not hurt them and they don't fight like this one.' Those silver eyes lost their sparkle as Melissa looked at the floor, cradling her glass. 'Poor Melissa had to live so much longer than she should, with no life but mine, not that mine isn't quite fun – as you know.' She raised her glass and winked. 'But I feel guilty for every one I have had to use. Just as I feel guilt for every life I have had to end to keep him away. And all for nothing, he has returned, and all this will vanish. I have failed utterly, and I am sorry.'

'I have taught him to love this place, he will keep it. As I will keep you in my heart, even once you are gone.' Nathaniel put an improper hand on her leg.

'You mean...' Melissa put her glass down and clasped his hand.

'I forgive you. I shouldn't, but I see the good in you. You mean well, even if your actions say otherwise. I loved you from the moment I saw you. I have never loved a woman, but then you are not really a woman, are you? You are sexless.' He covered her hand with his.

'Oh, I wouldn't say that,' Melissa replied, winking Polly's eye.

'You know what I mean.' Nathaniel blushed.

'Oh come on, you've lived through the 20th century, the sexual revolution, you can take a little old-fashioned innuendo, surely?' She shuffled closer.

'Not the way you have. We travel, we plot, we scheme, we stay mostly outside society, and he keeps me inside, unable to interact. I have been... wanting for certain things.' He avoided her gaze.

'Certain things like me?' Melissa crushed against him, stroking his thigh.

'Well, now it comes to it, yes.' He put his arms around her, pulled her in and they kissed for what felt like an eternity.

'Since this is my last night in a mortal body, do you think we could..?' She eyed the bed.

'That depends, how does your host feel about it? I've been made to put up with some very uncomfortable situations since last we met and would not like to force myself upon your young lady.' Nathaniel pulled back.

Her eyes flashed from silver to brown. 'I feel I know you Nathaniel. You have my blessing, let your Lord Elias work through me, if this is the only good that comes of all this, then I will do all I can. Don't hold back on my account.' She took his face in her hands and pecked him on the cheek. 'Get in there lad.' Silver eyes returned and Melissa grinned through Polly's face.

'Well, I suppose if Polly doesn't mind,' he said. 'Then I would...'

'Damn straight you would.' She laughed. 'God I've missed you.' She kissed him.

'Do you still have those – contraptions?' Nathaniel asked, breathlessly.

'Oh my dear, give me five minutes to fetch my toy chest. You wouldn't believe how far things have come since our day. Latex has been a genuine fucking revolution.' Melissa ran from the room.

23

Polly and Nathaniel stood on the front steps of Dourstone Manor; Cronus, Fenrir and Wotan keeping guard. At the bottom were Clive, Susan, Kerry, Dan, Lynn, Neville, Wendy, Jack and Father Hearne. A thick semi-circle of dogs prevented escape.

'Any last words Lady Dewer,' The Traveller said, now firmly back in control of Nathaniel Harker.

'Could you not reconsider, and let me fly free, hostless and harmless?' Melissa said, it was hard for her to look at the man she had been so joyously reunited with. That beautiful full lip curled in such a distasteful sneer. His arrogant pose so unlike the kind, humble man Melissa had missed for so long. She was not afraid of what lay ahead, but did not want to leave her lover in the hands of such a cruel being.

'I can't take that chance, sorry. You're staying where I can make sure you never fuck up my plans again, right in here.' He tapped the hagstone. 'Forever and ever.'

'And you'll look after the town and the people, and take down these ridiculous barriers?' she said.

'Yes, we have an accord.' The bright skies of morning had already made a dent in the snow and one or two of the courtyard's cobbles were poking through.

'Arthur, hold him to his promise. Look out for Polly and Elizabeth especially, I have no reason to trust you, or you me, but please, for the sake of our friendship?' She held her arms out towards the priest. 'I think we both hold the same values, at heart.'

'I will, and I do, never fear,' Father Hearne said. 'I thought I was acting for the best. I had hoped for better.' He bowed his head. 'Sorry.'

'Okay, let's do it then, bye bye baby.' The Traveller leaned in, grabbed Polly and kissed her mockingly.

'I'm sorry to all of you, but I can't let Nathaniel die. I hope you can forgive me, and that this creature holds up his side of the bargain and leaves you alone. I'm sorry. I could have done better.' She turned to face the people she had let down. 'I should have done better.'

'No, you couldn't. I've beaten you, finally, I did better, so much better.' The Traveller held the Bellever Hagstone in the air, triumphant and spinning on his heel.

I understand, Polly said from inside. *I would have done the same for Patrick. I did all I could to save him from you, though it wasn't enough. For what it's worth, I forgive you.*

Thank you Polly, that means a lot. Melissa said, steeling herself. *Look after Elizabeth, remember, there's a little piece of me in that girl.*

You spent so much time with her after she was born it's hardly a surprise. Polly answered. *I know you were trying to steal her, but we might not have made it without your help.*

You wouldn't have needed help if it weren't for me. I'm sorry too. Keep her safe. Melissa pushed Polly down, she didn't want her near the surface for what was coming.

Melissa, I... Polly's words went unheard. Melissa looked to her beloved Cronus, he did not recognise her. Did not see her.

'Enough.' The Traveller stopped cavorting. 'It is time. Goodbye to you Lord Elias, Lady Melissa and the long line of the Dewers. Dourstone is mine.' He flourished the hagstone in Polly's face and muttered a few words before blue light exploded, encompassing her body. It span wildly round her, sucking at her very essence and pulling at her skin, her hair, her clothes, her everything. Her mouth opened wide in an unheard scream which may have been hers or Melissa's. She dropped to her knees, arms outstretched, legs spread wide in a star on the top step. The light surrounding her got brighter and brighter until they could no longer see Polly through the glare. Then, as quickly as it had appeared, it was sucked back through the hagstone.

Polly collapsed to the ground, even her knees unable to support her. She felt empty, as if she had lost something important: something she needed, something that had been a part of her for so long she wasn't sure how she would be able to cope without it. As if an organ had been torn from her abdomen.

'I... I need to go, can we go now?' she said, reaching for her dog.

Fenrir growled, and snapped at her hand. 'Have you quite finished with us?' She took her hand back, looking imploringly at the wolfhound. He gave a curt bark, his pose indicating she should not come any closer.

'Why yes, but any of you living on my estates will have to take your things and go. You have 24 hours, I'm not a monster.' The Traveller turned on his heel and headed inside, followed by the dogs, Cronus and Fenrir part of the pack behind Wotan. Polly called them both, hoping they might remember, hoping there was some kind of imprint on them, but nothing. This close to The Traveller, not a single dog could be swayed from his intent. The big hole inside her doubled, then tripled, threatening to engulf her.

Wendy ran up the steps as soon as the canine guard left. She dropped to her knees and took Polly's head in her lap.

'Are you okay, are you hurt? Is she...' Wendy stuttered, unable to ask what she knew she had to. 'Is she gone?'

Polly nodded. Not wanting to say it out loud.

'I am sorry for all of this,' Father Hearne said to the assembly. 'I thought they could come to a peaceful accord, I thought...' He stood at the bottom of the steps, hands held up, surrounded by members of the Patrick Sumner Trust.

'You thought he wouldn't invade my property, steal my daughter's inheritance, toss us all out on the streets and kill my...' Polly pushed Wendy aside, dragged herself to her knees, and crawled to the edge of the steps. She couldn't finish her sentence, never before realising the truth she had to admit. That the creature possessing her mind had been her best friend. Being without her hurt. The pain she felt was not just from the ordeal of the hagstone, though that had taken its toll physically, it was loss, grief. When had her emotions become so complicated?

'No, I didn't,' the priest said, helping her back to her feet. 'Come to the church tomorrow night. We can heal, Dourstone was always more than just the Dewers, it can be again. Sing with me. Sing with the people, help me rebuild this place.'

'I don't think so Mr Vicar,' Neville said. 'Look what you done to my granddaughter. It'll take more than a bit of a sing song to right this.'

'I know, I know, but I can help.' He put his hands to Polly's temples, and her pain went away in a shimmer of light. Her physical pain anyway, she wasn't sure what she could do about the aching inside. 'Better?' The priest asked.

'Yes, a little. Is that..?'

'Magic, yes, I'm like her – and him,' Father Hearne explained, letting Polly walk away. 'In case you hadn't figured it out.'

'Well, dur,' Wendy said, putting an arm around Polly to help her down the steps. 'Clearly a lot more like him, you picked the wrong side.'

'I was never on either side,' he said. 'I wanted what was best for both of them. They couldn't ever see it, the bigger picture, both so stubborn. Anyway, I suppose it's too late now, unless that impossible woman has one last trick up her sleeve.'

'I think she's all out of sleeves,' Wendy said. 'I hope you're happy.'

'I'm not, but I could be.' Father Hearne turned to the door. 'You two go and look after your babies. The children are the future, after all. Do reconsider coming to Midnight Mass.' He went through the door, closing it behind him with an attempt at a consolatory smile.

'Well, at least the snow's melting,' Lynn said. 'There's always a bright side. Shall we take the tractor?' She pointed to the wrecked stable block.

'It was hard enough with just five, I don't think we can fit us all on, not without somebody falling off,' Wendy explained. 'Maybe you could hang on to the back, have a tow?' she said to Dan.

'Yeah, maybe, that doesn't sound at all dangerous,' Dan replied.

'Good, maybe you could take a couple of us on your lap?' Jack suggested.

'Maybe you could fuck off mate, I'm not a trailer.'

'Okay, sorry, sorry,' Jack said. 'Just a joke.'

'Doesn't matter anyway,' Clive said from the other side of the machine. 'Unless one of you can fit a new axle. There might be one round here, and some tools. I've changed bits of tractor before, back when I had two hands, but I've not got a great track record with farm machinery and lost limbs.'

'Yes Clive, we know, we get it.' Lynn sat on a granite mounting block. Clive would take any excuse to tell the story of how he lost his hand to a thresher on his dad's farm. 'No tractor.'

'There's always the sledge,' Wendy suggested.

'We're all out of dogs, remember?' Clive rubbed tractor dirt into his jeans. Susan nudged him in the ribs and eyeballed meaningfully towards Polly, hoping he might learn some tact in the face of a woman who had just lost her dogs. 'Unless you want to pull it yourself?'

'Ha ha,' Wendy replied. 'Are you calling me a dog?'

'No, no, nothing of the kind,' Clive backtracked. 'What about the Land Rover?' He pointed over to the rusting red 4x4, still skewed across the yard where Polly had left it after her first abortive escape attempt.

'On it.' Jack pulled the door open and hopped in. 'Keys?'

'They're in the ignition, genius,' Wendy shouted.

'You want to be careful with that thing son,' Neville said. 'Polly worked that old engine way too hard. I don't think it's...'

'Oh, so they are, hang on.' He turned them. There was a horrible graunching noise and a puff of smoke from under the bonnet. 'I'll just give it another...'

'I said, you might want to be careful with...' Neville began, stepping away from the car.

'Fucking no, stop. Stop now.' Wendy leaped in and pulled the keys out. 'You gun that thing one more time and it's going to...'

'Get out!' Lynn screamed.

Wendy pulled Jack from the driver's seat and they rolled across the yard, landing in a very uncompromising position. The engine caught fire, screaming its last breath to blow the bonnet over on to what was left of the tractor.

'Fine, we'll leave the Land Rover then,' Jack huffed, pulling himself up from underneath Wendy, and removing his hand from her chest with an apologetic grin. 'Very sorry, that was an accident.'

'I know, I'm not your type,' she said.

'I wouldn't say not my...' he began.

'I would, don't push it.' She stomped away from him and took Polly's arm. 'What else have we got to get home in?'

'Fuck it. I'm rolling, who's with me?' Dan said, setting off across the cobbles.

There was a mutter of agreement as they looked at the ruined vehicles.

'Are we going to put that fire out?' Lynn asked.

'No, if he wants it all, he can have it all, on fire, or not on fire.' Polly huddled into Wendy and they tramped after Dan.

24

It was just before midnight on Christmas Eve and snow fell gently on the ruined church's ancient flagstones. Pyres made from abandoned market sheds lined the former aisles, providing heat for the townspeople gathered at this altar to the sky. Scarves were wrapped round necks, woolly hats perched on heads, and it felt a lot like Christmas.

'I got us drinks,' Jack said, pulling bottles from a back pack. 'Lovely warming ones.'

'Not as warming as this,' Wendy said, opening a steaming thermos of mulled wine. 'Ho ho ho.'

Polly hugged Elizabeth to her chest as a family walked past wishing them a merry Christmas and making the appropriate oohs and aaahs Elizabeth always elicited. Polly reached down to stroke their labrador. It might be nice to get a dog, she thought. She'd always wanted one, but there had never been time for dogs. She was so busy, what with one thing or another.

'You alright Pol?' Susan said, mixing Jack's bottles into plastic cups. She had found an alcove that was probably used to store holy water or something before the church burned down. It seemed appropriate to turn it into a cocktail cabinet. 'Cheer up, it's Christmas Eve. And don't worry about your granddad, I'm sure Clive will get him back in one piece.'

'I know, thanks for lending him out, especially so late. I would have driven him back but the car's in the garage. It's really good of you.' Polly reached down to stroke a dog that wasn't there, then shook her head, wondering what she was doing.

'Not a problem, I'm glad to be rid of him,' Susan laughed. 'And it wasn't your fault we lost track of time. It's been a really weird day.' She steadied herself against Jack as she slipped on an icy stone. He caught her by the waist and helped her back up, his hands lingering just a little too long and high not to be noticed. Lynn shot them a filthy look as she took a cup of Wendy's mulled wine.

'Yeah, I couldn't believe how fast The Midnight's crept up on us,' Jack said. 'I'd have driven, but I was already over the limit. Lucky Clive's always wanted a go in my MX5.'

'I can't believe you let him borrow it, you love that car,' Lynn said.

'Yeah, I do, but my snow chains didn't fit his Focus, and we're mates. Mates share what they love.' He looked at Susan.

'Yes, yes they do,' Wendy said, stifling a giggle.

'I suppose so, yeah. Thanks anyway.' Polly stared into the sky at the thick stars, barely dented by firelight. The street-lights had been turned off for atmosphere, the town was lit the old-fashioned way, smoke spilling from pyres that lined the route to the church. She was sure she was forgetting something important, but she couldn't put her finger on it. Elizabeth wouldn't settle and kept jiggling about, burbling to herself.

She bounced the child on her knee, trying to calm her down. Her stay at Dan and Kerry's had unsettled her. But why had she been staying there? Did that have something to do with it? She couldn't remember that anymore than she could remember what happened to her Land Rover. She hadn't been able to tell Susan it just wasn't outside the cottage. She didn't want to admit she didn't know where it was. It didn't matter anyway, this was Dourstone, there was always somebody on hand with a car to lend or a lift to give. It was a proper community.

'Here, get this down you.' Wendy handed her a mulled wine, other hand on Polly's back. 'It'll warm your cockles before the singing starts.'

Polly leaned into Wendy, accepting a hug and letting the child swing free in her sling. Elizabeth burst into fresh tears.

'I don't know what's got into her,' Polly said as Wendy stroked the baby's head. 'Or me. I feel... like I'm somebody else. Like there's something missing, something... Oh I don't know, listen to me, I sound proper mad!' She laughed.

'It'll be your hormones, stop breast-feeding her, you'll be better.' Wendy gently grabbed Polly's boobs. 'I know I was once I stopped.'

'Yeah, maybe,' Polly muttered.

'And the only thing wrong with her is that she's sick of your company and doesn't want to be out in the middle of the night,'

Wendy continued. 'Honestly, I don't know why you didn't leave her with Katie.'

'Stop it, she's okay, she normally sleeps right through anything.' Polly knew she hadn't needed to bring her along, and while she accepted it was late for a baby, for some reason she couldn't bring herself to leave her. But she didn't want to have to explain that to Wendy.

'Not long now, here they come.' Lynn clapped them back into order and pointed to the bell tower – the only part of the church still intact – where The Traveller and Father Hearne walked through the arched doorway, shaking hands and making their presence felt.

Polly drank her mulled wine, looking over at the priest. He seemed nervous, but she couldn't think why. He and Lord Nye had hosted the Midnight Mass together every year for as long as anyone could remember. They may not sing the most conventional carols, but it was always beautiful. A cold starlit winter's night, surrounded by warmth, fire, friends and music. Long may it stay that way and long may Lord Nye remain such a generous benefactor.

The brass band started up 'The Holly and The Ivy' and everybody pulled out their hymsheets, trying to find the words, since it had been printed in the wrong order. Most of the townspeople were utilising the school assembly mode of singing: staring at the ground, mumbling or soundlessly moving their lips in time, but there was a small group at the back – who had evidently had more than a couple in the Drop of Dew during the afternoon – who more than made up for it and were even doing the actions. A lot of people are unaware of the actions to certain Christmas Carols, but this group knew them well enough to be perfectly synchronised. Not every note they sung was pitched correctly, and not all of the words were the right ones, while most that were were in the wrong place, but they made a joyful sound and lifted Polly's spirits.

Why would her spirits need lifting? It was Christmas, Elizabeth and her had their lovely warm cottage to spend it in, good friends to spend it with, and Lord Nye had opened the Manor up for the townspeople to celebrate together over the traditional eleven days of yuletide. His ancestral home, filled with warming fire, where his family had lived for generations. The gardens were decorated for the season, Santa had an actual grotto, and there was to be a celebration every night of the Yule: each themed differently and elaborately catered. It would be a magnificent season. Elizabeth pulled more strongly at her arm, but she pushed her down and swung her from side to side in her sling.

Polly saw Anna scanning the crowd and moving with purpose towards them as she sang. Anna was singing loudly and with some actual talent, much to the consternation of the people she passed on her way across. She slotted herself in front of Jack and looked back with a smile. He nodded and moved in closer behind her, raising his voice in song just as it ended.

'Friends, fellow Dourstonians, people. Thank you for coming to our little service,' Lord Nye said, standing up at the altar and spreading his arms wide. 'Yule is a special time of year. The dark will soon be leaving us and the days of light shall return. With that, I have an announcement. In the spirit of rebirth, we shall be knocking down these old ruins and replacing them with a brand new shining multi-faith worship centre run by a full-time vicar. Father Hearne is being relieved of his duties to the other dioceses and will be remaining here with us full time. Isn't that wonderful?'

The announcement was greeted with a round of applause and excited muttering. Lord Nye would always do what was best, they trusted his judgement. A multi-faith worship building was just what the town needed. Lynn shushed the crowd back into silence so The Traveller could continue.

'It will be accompanied by a whole raft of regenerations. We have such plans for this place, we shall push forward into the 21st century it has lingered so long upon the edge of. The centre of town will be covered over with a new, more modern shopping and leisure experience. We shall bring the tourists in, I have planned a Dartmoor visitors' experience to go over the old market, and the square will be its sister. The outdated and unloved Drop of Dew will be brought up to date, I have had word from the people at Wetherspoons and expect big things. Then we shall remove these old crumbling buildings and replace them with new, shining structures. Costa, Burger King, Wagamamas, Cafe Rouge, and even Starbucks have expressed an interest. We are at the dawning of a new era. This town will boom like never before!' He raised his hands to rapturous applause.

The group in the corner linked up in a group hug, Elizabeth squeezed between them warm and safe. All of this was such good news. Polly had missed being part of society since leaving London. Bringing Dourstone into the 21st Century was a good thing. The people would be happier, more prosperous, it would bring jobs, tourists, money, all the things that promote growth and a booming economy. The Traveller would protect them, make everything better. The future looked bright.

Elizabeth began to scream louder.

'Fuck, Nev, what are you doing?' Clive shouted as Jack's MX5 skidded onto the pavement. 'We nearly hit that bald bloke with the traffic cone on his head.'

'That's Charles Kingsley,' Neville explained, releasing the handbrake. 'He always has a traffic cone on his head.'

'I don't think that's much of an explanation,' Clive said, checking none of his bones were broken. 'What did you do that for?'

'They're in danger boy.' Neville snapped his seatbelt against his chest, glad of its protection. 'We need to get back.' He tapped his hand on the dashboard like a driving test examiner after an emergency stop.

'What are you talking about?' Clive said, running steel fingers through his hair. 'We're almost there. You're nearly home.'

'I ain't going home boy,' Neville said. 'Polly's in danger, and your missus, and all of them. How did we forget?'

'Forget what?' Clive shook his head.

'Forget him,' Neville said, grabbing Clive's collar and pointing to a cloud, shaped like a deadman's hat atop an eyeless face, lit by moonlight.

'What, Lord Nye?' Clive said. 'But he's… he's…' Images of dogs, blue light, and a hagstone wrapped in copper wire flashed through his mind. 'Oh fuck,' he said.

'Remember now do you?' Neville nodded.

'Yes, we need to make sure we don't forget again before we get back, think of a plan Nev.' Clive gunned the little sportster back to full speed and screeched off past the Christmas Eve revellers on Bideford Quay.

'So good to see you, Polly, are you well?' The Traveller shook her hand by the church gate as they headed out to the square.

'Yes my lord, I'm well, thank you for asking,' she replied. Elizabeth began kicking and punching in her sling. 'I'm so sorry, she usually sleeps right through anything in this but tonight…' She shrugged.

'No matter,' The Traveller said, smiling and waving his fingers in the baby's face. Elizabeth's two teeth snapped viciously at them, her face set in defiant glare. 'Oh, isn't she a feisty one?' He laughed and wandered off to another group, who welcomed him with open arms and smiling faces.

'Polly,' Father Hearne said, shaking her hand and leaning in to whisper urgently in her ear. 'You have to remember.'

'What, to put the turkey on in the morning? It's okay Arthur, I've set alarms, it's marinating as we speak. It will be delicious, I take it you'll be joining us all at Clive and Susan's like usual?' She giggled, trying to calm Elizabeth with a bouncing motion.

'Polly, I've never had Christmas lunch with you in my life. This is all an illusion. Wake up, please, this isn't what I wanted.' He grabbed her shoulder and stared into her eyes, a faint corona of purple glowing from his irises.

'I don't…' Polly had a fleeting glimpse of being trapped under snow.

'Oh but you do,' Father Hearne grinned. 'I think you do.' He gripped her hand tighter, not letting go of her shoulder as he looked down into Elizabeth's eyes. 'Have her eyes always been that silver colour?' he said, craning his neck to check Lord Nye was occupied.

'No she's got her father's…' Polly said, staring down into her child's face. Her eyes were silver, she had thought them hazel. She bent her head closer and Elizabeth stopped struggling. A knowing look way beyond her years spread across that tiny face and she locked Polly's eyes to hers. Polly's mind exploded with a thousand different lifetimes; all lived here in this place. And in every one, this priest, over and over and over again. Sometimes a village wise man, sometimes a witch, sometimes a monk, once as witchfinder, occasionally a nun, or itinerant washer-woman, but always here. Always badgering about the same thing. Making amends.

'Polly, kiss your child. For God's sake, and mine, kiss Elizabeth.' Father Hearne broke his hold.

She lifted the baby's mouth to hers and kissed her lips.

All those memories, all that emotion, welling up at once and exploding into something real, something familiar, something that filled the hole she had been unable to decipher. Something that pushed her way down to the back of her mind, possessing her completely and reminding her who was in charge.

'Oh my fucking God that's better, what's wrong with you girl? How could you let him pull that woolly mind trick bullshit? Did I not drop enough hints? Were you not paying attention? I've always been in here, I just needed you to remember.' Melissa's voice poured from Polly's mouth before she gasped for air.

I'm so sorry Mel. I don't know how I forgot, how I could let you down. Why didn't you just tell me what you had planned?

'I couldn't, he'd have figured it out. You know we can do a bit of mind-reading? Not easily, and he might not have thought to. Anyway, probably my fault, not yours, I didn't really want you to know I'd been lurking in Elizabeth, you get kind of antsy about her,' Melissa explained.

So you've been split across Elizabeth and me all along, without my knowing?

'Yes Polly, do keep up, most of me is still on the other side of the hagstone, and he's not going to let that go so easily. We've got a bitch of a job ahead.' Melissa hugged Elizabeth to her chest, now quieted and content in her sling.

Risky plan. I forgot that you existed, everything that happened. My whole reality was changed, could you have done that? Have you done that? Polly asked, worried that even this reality was a lie.

'I could, but I don't,' Melissa said. 'I like to think I'm kind enough I can gain people's loyalty without resorting to spells.'

Yeah, maybe try it without slipping them one of your 'herbal' drinks. Polly hadn't forgotten how her mind had been altered by Melissa's brews.

'A small localised trick is different,' Melissa said. 'I'm sorry. Anyway, No harm done, we've got time. We can do this. I can't let him turn my town into Plymouth, it'll end us. This place is special. Do you have a plan Arthur?' She turned to the priest.

'I've got more than a plan, how do you think you got back?' Father Hearne said, offended. 'It's not like Polly hasn't touched Elizabeth since this morning. I had to give it a bit of a kick.' He looked around to check The Traveller was nowhere near before pulling the hagstone from a tweed pocket. 'I do believe this might help.'

'Of course, of course, well done.' Melissa stared hungrily at the rock in his fingers. 'I suppose he trusts you the same way I trusted you. Now give it here. There's not that much time left, and I'm not so stupid as to trust you again, no offence.' Melissa grabbed the hagstone.

'No, no, none taken. I wouldn't trust me either, but look, see what he's doing!' Father Hearne indicated the happy townspeople. 'They're completely hypnotised, I can't sit by while he does this. It was never part of my plan.'

'I can't believe you had a plan, look at the mess you've made. All this trouble, just because you wanted a happy ending.' She raised an eyebrow and poked his chest, then fiddled with the hagstone. A glowing blue mist poured from the darkness on the other side and she inhaled it hungrily. 'That's better, I feel a lot more myself. You, take this, and look after it.' She passed Elizabeth to Wendy and stalked off. 'This could get messy.'

'No, thank you, it was my pleasure to help,' Father Hearne muttered under his breath as he followed. 'So glad you're back.'

25

'You,' Melissa shouted at The Traveller as he stopped to talk to everybody in the square, acting the part of the genial landowner down to the last fake smile. 'Here now.'

'Why Polly, what can possibly have upset you so much?' he said, making excuses to Adrian the butcher and strolling towards her.

'You know I'm not Polly as well as I know you're not Lord Nicholas Nye.' She held up the hagstone. 'This is going to end, now.'

'Remind me to get rid of that useless, double-crossing, sentimental old priest.' He eyeballed the stone in her hand, shaking his head. 'Anyway, nothing has changed, you can't use that on me.' He laughed. 'Remember, it will kill Nathaniel, he'll be gone, forever. No more.' He wiggled his fingers in the air.

'Well, that might have been true, but things are different now,' Melissa said, weighing the granite in her hand.

'How so?' The Traveller lurched back mid finger wiggle.

'Some things are more important, maybe I don't care if he lives or dies now?' She tossed the hagstone in the air and caught it again. 'I'm going to need my town back. Here's your chance to leave peacefully. Like last time. No fuss, no arguments, just head off and leave these people alone.'

'You don't even have the dogs. Where's your leverage? You have nothing, you won't kill me, I can see it in your eyes. You're all empty threats. I have the town and the dogs. They love me, not you.'

Susan, Wendy, Jack, Dan, Kerry and Lynn twitched as the spells went deeper. They stared blankly at Polly as if they no longer knew her.

Do something, I thought you had all your power back, why is having you and Father Hearne here not blocking his spell? Polly's voice screamed.

I am still much reduced. Melissa explained. *Getting back has taken a lot from me. I can't pull anything more from you or the child. If you hadn't...*

You can't blame my killing you for everything Mel, isn't there something more you can do? Polly said. *Just let people remember.*

This is different, this is more solid, he has used a more powerful memory charm, it needs... She tailed off, trying to recall the counter-measure.

Quickly, if he's controlling Wendy's mind then... Polly's suggestion roused Melissa to action and she snatched Elizabeth from Wendy's arms before anything could happen. The crowd advanced, putting themselves between her and The Traveller. He disappeared up the hill with a laugh. 'You're finished Dewer, I'm more powerful than you. You have nothing.'

'I have everything,' Melissa muttered. 'You will understand soon.' She looked around for the priest, recalling the words that would unlock the Bellever Hagstone's full power, allowing her to break any and all surrounding magick. She would have no trouble murdering Nathaniel a second time, it had been easy the first and, while it had always been a profound regret, it had been for the good of the town. This was an even bigger crisis, The Traveller had gone back on his word. He didn't care for the town, he would destroy it, not with his original plan of hellfire and brimstone, but replacing it with a modern vision of hell. She could sacrifice Nathaniel again, she had to.

While distracted by this comparison, Cronus appeared at her side. She absent-mindedly bent to stroke his head and he grabbed the hagstone. She could not defend it and keep a hold of the baby so the turncoat thief ran away. She cursed her stupidity and tried to run after him, but he was quickly swallowed by the unmoving crowd. 'Fine, I have nothing,' she sighed, sitting heavily on the wall. 'Arthur! Where are you?'

The priest appeared. 'Have you got a plan?'

'Not yet – well, nothing that'll work – are you with me?' she asked, hugging the baby.

'I've always been with you,' he said, sitting next to her and putting an arm across her shoulders.

'Funny way of showing it,' she said, leaning in.

'You and he are the same. I wanted you to settle your differences, stop fighting. End this ridiculous feud. He told me he wanted it too, I believed him, right up until he killed you. Nice trick by the way – I didn't believe it would work until I saw it.' He doffed his immaculate homburg hat.

'Not really a trick, if you'd known anything about me you'd know most of me was inside this baby. It still is.' She bounced Elizabeth up and down. 'How did you think it was going to work?'

'Honestly I had no idea. This was the last thing I expected, I can't believe you'd leave yourself that vulnerable?' His mouth gaped in astonishment.

'No, not ideally. Usually the transition is easily handled from mother to daughter, joined together as me and only me. Polly fucked that up last year, I can't fully bond with her, there's no genetic imprint. She is not a Dewer. I thought you and he knew that, I thought that was why you cut her off from the baby. To weaken me. None of this would have happened if we'd been together.'

'You mean?'

'Yes, I will be running at at least 75% of my previous strength now I have her with me – once we've got over that little resurrection trick. I wasn't even close with just Polly to work with.'

'So?' The priest waved his arm to indicate the crowds of mindless people advancing on them, Anna at the front, arms linked with Jack and a murderous look on her face.

Please Melissa, you can do it. Polly's voice cut through, panicking at her former friends' blank faces.

Susan and Lynn flanked Jack and Anna. 'Who are you?' they asked. 'We don't take kindly to strangers just turning up to our Midnight Mass.'

'No,' Wendy said. 'We don't.' She took a flaming plank from one of the braziers and the transition from crowd to mob was complete.

I told you I can't remember the… Melissa said. *Oh. Actually, yes this might just...*

'Any time you like,' Father Hearne said as he stood between the mob and the mother and child it threatened. Dan had pulled a large spanner from under his chair and was thwacking it against his hand.

'I know, luckily Polly's just jogged my memory, hang on. Do you mind if I?' Melissa grabbed the priest's hand.

'No, not if it helps, go on.' He nodded back.

'Ta,' she muttered a few choice words then looked up. Father

Hearne sagged back onto the wall, hair visibly greying. 'Sorry, I know you like this one, but you'll need to replace him sooner than you thought.' She patted his hand before spinning a new web of spells with hands and words.

'Not the first time you've shortened my lifespan; but no matter, well done,' the priest said.

People shook their heads with confusion, stopping where they stood as reality came back, eyes clear and full of fear as they realised they had had their minds played with so easily. Some group folk memory made them turn to Polly, an understanding that their ancient liege lord lived in her. The representative of the Dewers of Dourstone would know what they should do.

The members of the Sumner Trust were first to her side, apologising and making a big show of solidarity.

'Ummm… sorry, sorry, not sure how I got here,' Anna said, extricating herself from Jack and striding off down the hill. 'Message me, or I'll message you. Whatever.'

'Yeah, I will, sorry,' Jack called after her as Susan and Lynn advanced on him from both sides.

Melissa stood, pushing Father Hearne back down when he tried to follow suit, and passed Elizabeth to Wendy without a word.

'People of Dourstone. Go, go home, hide, run, do whatever you need. But it's going to be dangerous out of doors tonight. Even more so than Saturday night, I assume you remember that now? Sorry, and I'll explain later.' Melissa said. 'I don't suppose any of you managed to grab a weird-looking hagstone from my dog on his way past?'

There was a great shaking of heads.

'Bollocks, would have been too easy,' she said. 'Right, what have I got to work with?'

'I'm with you, as I should have been all along,' Father Hearne tried to stand, but fell back down. 'Sorry, just need to get my strength back.'

'You won't be much use for a while, but you have been, thank you,' Melissa said, putting her hand on his shoulder. 'And you will be, take a bit of time to find your strength, I didn't use all of it.'

'Wouldn't blame you if you had,' he said.

'Arthur, Arthur, Arthur, we've had our differences over the years, and I may have killed you a few times too many, but I think you've turned a corner.' Melissa walked away. 'I'm not going to kill you

189

again unless it's completely necessary. Not now you've shown me as much trust as you just did. You're not bad, just misguided.'

'Thank you.' He slumped back down.

'Now, what have I got to work with that isn't completely fucking useless?' She grinned, turning to the Sumner Trust.

'You've got us again, I'm so sorry you lost us.' Susan strode forward and took Melissa's hand.

'Not your fault, he's very strong and I wasn't. I am now though – thanks to Arthur and Elizabeth – and the three of us are going to finish this.' She shook the offered hand and pshawed her away.

'Where? And should you be taking that baby?' Kerry asked.

'Up to the stone circle, where all this began. And yes, I have to take the baby.' Melissa made to take the child. 'I am, as you may have gathered, nothing without her. None of you need come.'

'We're coming,' Wendy said, holding Elizabeth away from her. 'At least I am. I promised Polly I'd take care of Lizzybet if anything happened, I meant it. We all remember what happened last time you ran off with her.'

'This is different and more dangerous, but yes, I could do with some help.' Melissa stopped trying to get to Elizabeth.

'Fine, I'm not leaving you in control of Polly with nobody looking out for her, and the baby stays with me, deal?' Wendy said, hugging the child close.

'Deal, thank you.' Melissa smiled.

'I'll go back and make sure the kids don't get left alone again, unless you've got me that all-terrain wheelchair I asked for for Christmas?' Dan turned to Kerry.

'I have not, sorry,' Kerry confirmed, patting Dan's shoulder.

'Then I'll say goodbye, anybody want to keep me company?' Dan looked at Jack.

'You're on mate. We should leave this to the women,' Jack said, looking to the ground. 'I've already proved I'm not much use in a crisis.'

'Coward,' Lynn said. 'But that's no surprise.' She flicked her eyes to Anna's blond head just visible through the departing crowd, then Susan. Jack shrugged, giving his best winning smile. He was never going to pick just one.

'So we're sending the girls up there to certain peril yeah?' Dan said, chuckling.

'I don't need all of you, the more people I take, the more chances he has to take hostages and kill friends.'

'I'm coming too,' said Lynn. 'You'll need somebody sensible – and not so emotionally involved.' She gave Wendy a knowing look.

'I'm not emotionally involved,' Wendy objected. 'It's a child, all children matter.'

'And that beautiful – almost certainly bi-curious – piece of arse that Melissa's wearing has nothing to do with it?' Lynn said.

'Maybe a little.' Wendy blushed. 'You think she's curious?'

'I know she is.' Melissa winked.

'She can't hear me can she?' Wendy slapped her hands to her cheeks.

'Not if I don't want her to,' Melissa replied. 'Do you want her to hear?'

'No, no. This isn't the time, it wouldn't be right. I don't even fancy her, you're being a twat Lynn. Let's get on with it.' Wendy paid close attention to Elizabeth as the colour in her cheeks rose.

'Fine, she won't hear it from me,' Melissa agreed.

You lying cow, Polly said.

You'll thank me later, whether you're interested or not.

I'm not gay Mel, Polly insisted.

You forget who you're arguing with, Mel pointed out. *I have evidence you're not straight either. And Wendy's hot, if you're not interested, I might have a pop.*

Can we drop this now, we've got more important things on.

Fine with me.

'Right. Anyone who's coming: with me.' Melissa pointed up the hill. 'Bring the baby, guard her with your lives. Everybody else, go home and keep your ears open and your kids safe. Are communications back up?'

'Yeah, I've got 4G,' Kerry said, checking her phone. 'Hit us up if it all goes wrong.'

'Either of you got cars nearby?' Wendy said.

'No. No cars. This is old business and old business needs to be done the old way. We're walking.' Melissa wiggled her fingers in Elizabeth's face, making her giggle, and led the way.

26

Lady Melissa Dewer appeared on the horizon with the full moon shining behind her. It may have been Polly's body, but that swagger was unmistakeable. The long centuries had given Lady Dewer a way of moving that Polly would never have the confidence to pull off.

She stepped off the road and made her way over a thick crust of snow to the standing stones. There was no point in hiding, they would always find each other, it was destiny.

'I don't know why you think you can win this time,' The Traveller said, without looking up. He sat atop the old altar stone, restored to its former position at the centre of the circle.

'Because you haven't changed. You went back on your word,' Melissa said, standing at the edge, alone.

'I fail to see how that can help you win? You still won't kill Nathaniel, even if you had the means to remove me.' He threw the hagstone in the air and caught it with a grin and a wink. 'Good boy,' he added, scruffing Cronus's head. The enormous malamute leaned into him, the same way he used to lean into Melissa.

'You're a little too sure of yourself,' she replied.

'Why wouldn't I be?' he said, clicking his fingers. Fenrir padded softly from a crush of dogs sleeping under a ragged patchwork shelter. 'I have the dogs at my beck and call, I have the Bellever Hagstone, I have the town and its people and I have you.' He hugged the wolfhound into his other side.

'In what way do you have me?' Melissa replied, hand on hip.

'You are quite alone, nobody is coming to help you. I have stripped what few friends you have away and spending a little time being dead must have weakened you.' He jumped from the altar stone and stalked towards her.

'Yes, it must have,' she replied, not moving.

'How did you get round that by the way?' he asked. 'You should still be in here.' He fingered the hagstone, flicking the gateway on and off. 'That's a very neat trick.'

'That would be telling.'

'Fine, time to die.' He raised his hands and Melissa froze, but did not run. He ran his thumb around the wire pentagram in preparation of its killing blow. 'Maybe you'll have the decency to stay dead this time.'

A Mazda MX5 crested the hill and screeched off the road without warning. It knocked down two stones before hitting The Traveller who lost his grip on the hagstone as he went down, flinging it up in a graceful arc towards the woods.

'Catch it!' Clive shouted, leaping from the driver's side into the snow once the car had come to a halt. The stones had taken all the paint from the passenger side and it had enough dents in it to give Jack a heart attack. It was small mercy he wasn't there to see it.

'Damn you, you meddling idiot,' The Traveller said, his hands weaving complicated magicks before thrusting out two balls of glowing blue energy. Nobody's eyes were on him though, Clive and Melissa's were on the hagstone as its parabola peaked and Melissa ran to catch it. But the tiny stone was too far away, falling through branches before she had even crossed the treeline.

'No! Clive, get out of the way!' Susan bolted from the woods, distracting Melissa from an energy blast that sent the Lady of Dourstone sprawling in the snow at the base of an ancient oak.

'Susan?' Clive turned in slow motion.

'Why don't you ever watch what you're doing?' she said as she threw herself into his arms, in time to take the second projectile in the back, knocking them both to the ground.

'Shit, why you get out the car you stupid boy?' Neville muttered, tugging at his seatbelt, head down. He was trapped in Jack's midlife crisis, and a sitting target were he to poke his head above the door.

The Traveller wandered towards the car. His immediate threats had been dealt with, Susan and Clive were out of the game and Melissa wasn't moving. He had time to check the vehicle for any more unanticipated distractions.

Neville didn't. He could see three options and none of them were great. Option one: he could slide across into the driver's seat – provided he could get the seatbelt off – get the car going – provided it would start after all that excitement – and drive away – provided the wheels could get out of all this snow and The Traveller didn't send some deadly spell to finish him off.

Option two: again, provided he could get the belt off, he could get out, make a stand and join the fight. From what he had seen he reckoned he could get a good twenty seconds of resistance in before one of those glowing energy balls took him out of the game.

Option three: stay where he was, try not to be seen, and hope for the best.

He pulled a blanket from the back shelf and covered himself up, squishing down as far as he could when he heard the crunch of The Traveller's boots. There was no way of telling if he had been spotted: if The Traveller even cared enough about an old man to bother. Neville was no real threat after all, just another mortal in the way. Neville held his breath under the blanket as he felt a boot kick at the driver's side tyre.

'Shame about this car,' The Traveller muttered. 'Maybe I'll fix it up, this chap won't need it now.' He must have meant Clive was dead. If it was only Neville left, then it was all up to him. His hand hovered over the sticky seatbelt release, he prayed it would work, resigned to option two even if it meant certain death. If it bought his granddaughter some time it would be worth it.

'Oh, what's that?' he heard The Traveller say, hand on the door handle and probably looking straight at Neville's blanketed head. This was it. Time to do or die. He thumbed the seatbelt release, it clicked, but did not release. He braced himself.

'You'll regret that.' He heard Melissa shout. 'They were under my protection, you've made me break my word. I don't like having to do that.'

'Are you joking?' The Traveller laughed, letting go of the car and turning to Melissa. 'Your word means nothing.' He twisted the air and she stopped where she stood.

Neville breathed a sigh of relief and untensed his rigid muscles.

An invisible hand pushed Melissa onto the altar stone, spread-eagled and unable to move, staring up at the stars. 'I keep mine though, and I promise you will never leave this circle. Maybe it's time I fed you to the fucking dogs. See how you like a taste of your own medicine.'

As if on cue the pack surrounded her in a snarling ring of frothing saliva and hot flesh. Cronus and Fenrir stared without recognition, no love in their eyes, just pure glowing blue hatred.

'I don't think so,' Melissa said, shrugging off his spell. 'You've never really been a match for me dear. You seem to have forgotten.' She pulled herself up to sit on the edge of the altar stone, one leg crossed over the other as if having a little sit down on a country walk.

'But... but...' Doubt spread to The Traveller's face and he threw another ball of blue flame. She spread her arms and grinned as flames beat against an invisible shield to melt a perfect circle in the snow. The dogs ran towards her but bounced harmlessly from the edge, unable to penetrate her protection. She bent her arms up behind her head and lay back on the altar stone on her own terms. She looked to the moon and grinned before getting up and shaking her limbs out.

'Anything else?' she asked. 'Or is it my turn?' She fixed him with a hard stare, grin never leaving her mouth.

'Oh hell yes. There's plenty more where that came from. I've always been the strongest, always. You're nothing but a mewling bitch.' He became a whirling dervish, spinning his arms, chanting and flinging every kind of spell, but all to no avail. Lightning bolts and fireballs and hailstorms of tiny but deadly sparks all ricocheted from her shield. She walked purposefully towards him through the maelstrom; Polly's face set with Melissa's eyes and icy vengeance writ large across both of them.

'We're two bitches together thank you,' Polly and Melissa's voices came in stereo as The Traveller flew through the air to come crashing down on the altar. 'Stronger, faster, more powerful, mother goddesses intertwined in one. Your cock-stroking, show-boating bullshit won't help you this time. We will be your end. How's that for mewling?'

'Look on this face. You won't kill him,' The Traveller said, his back held fast to the stone.

'I wouldn't do it without permission, no. Let me have a chat.' She leaned in close and ran a finger down his cheek. His eyes bulged and he gasped for breath.

'What, what are you doing? You can't, nobody can...' His black eyes rolled and came back green.

'So Nathaniel, my darling. What say you? Are you ready? Have you lived long enough?' Melissa stroked his cheek as she spoke, not releasing the hold on his body, in case The Traveller proved stronger.

'I have lived long enough without you. Now we have made our peace I think… I think I can go. It seems a shame, finding you again, finally forgiving you, and having to leave.' Tears fell from his eyes. 'At least it will not be for nothing. I would do anything for you. Even this.'

'He would never let us be together, and without his spirit inside, the universe will catch up, all your years will settle at once. It is not pleasant.' Melissa recalled the loss of her last body. 'Centuries in seconds, destroying your flesh from within.'

'I have died for you before, at least this time I do it willingly.' He looked into her eyes, before closing his and nodding acceptance. 'Farewell Elias, I pray we meet again on another plane.'

Polly's lips kissed Nathaniel's and tears fell from her eyes, rolling down to mix with his own in his thick black and silver beard.

'Arthur, Wendy,' Melissa shouted, standing up. 'Bring the child and the hagstone to me. I need all the power I can muster. Lynn, check on those fools over there.'

'These fools saved your life woman – and my Polly's – have a little humility,' Neville said, free of the car and kneeling in the snow by Clive and Susan.

Father Hearne, Lynn and Wendy appeared from the trees, bearing Elizabeth and the recovered hagstone. Lynn rushed to Neville's side to help the fallen, while the others headed for the altar stone.

'Did you tell him your plan?' Father Hearne asked.

'Didn't want to get his hopes up,' Melissa replied.

'It might not work, Lady Dewer, it is just a theory. I beseech you not to. Is there no reconciliation to be had?'

'Let's find out, you can come out now.' She released her hold on The Traveller and his eyes rolled. 'Could I be friends with the Eye Shaking King? Would you be friends with me? Live here together in peace and make it better for everyone?'

'Reconciliation, with you? Never, I would die first.' He spat at her, but his projectile landed on his own face.

'See, he would die first, I told you.' Melissa planted Polly's legs wide and took the hagstone from Wendy. 'And he will. I pray this works.'

'Who to?' The Traveller laughed.

'You know full well who. You should as well if you value your immortal soul.' She bent to The Traveller and stripped him of his jewellery. 'Sorry, but no tricks,' she said, removing his clothes with a wave of her hand. 'To make sure, I will burn all of this later. No trace, no secret stash.'

'I'm not like you, I don't need to hide myself in things. You and your whore-crutches.'

'Do you mean Horcruxes?' Wendy asked. 'Like in Harry Potter?'

'I know what I mean,' The Traveller said. 'I am all things. You cannot finish this, you must know that?' he said, struggling naked against invisible bonds in freezing snow.

'I can try though.' Melissa began to chant softly, tapping and stroking complicated riffs on the hagstone as her volume gradually increased. The Traveller's face turned a ghastly shade of green and his eyes glazed over.

Fenrir and Cronus left the pack, coming to the altar stone to stand guard, they looked adoringly up at their mistress with their own eyes. Melissa's spells were complex, but thorough.

The rest of the dogs remained outside the circle even though Melissa's protective spell no longer held there. Her power was all concentrated on extricating The Traveller from Nathaniel. Cronus and Fenrir stood, eyes blazing next to their mistress, and none would dare take them on. Not even Wotan. Their current alpha was being challenged, and pack rules meant they could not intervene.

Melissa cried out and held the hagstone above her head, blue light spilling out to fill the circle and cause Father Hearne to leap away with a frightened yelp.

The Traveller's eyes span in his head and he screamed: an unearthly sound that came from the very depths of his ancient soul to carry across the moors. Herds of deer woke and looked up from the trees and grass, rabbits stopped in their burrows, all of nature froze at that sound. They knew what it meant.

Melissa drew a deep breath, and kissed the hagstone before beginning a different chant, stroking and twisting it in the opposite direction. 'Arthur, please, I can't finish this alone.' She straddled the rigid, screaming body of The Traveller, leaning close to his face.

The priest grudgingly entered the blue light and laid hands on the hagstone. Polly's eyes rolled back and forth, changing from brown to silver and back again, while The Traveller's scream was suddenly cut off and Nathaniel's body lay limp.

'Now, fast, now, NOW!' Melissa screamed, covering Nathaniel's frozen mouth with her own. The scream ended with a crack that sent clouds scurrying away from the bright moon. Polly's body collapsed into the snow and silence returned. Wendy's chest heaved with a violent sob. She quickly covered the ground between them and fell on top of Polly, weeping.

The dogs howled as one into the night. Now restless, masterless and confused, Cronus rounded them up, nuzzling against Wotan. The enormous dog accepted the offer of friendship, bowing his head to Cronus, then Fenrir, in turn.

'What, what happened? Why am I still here?' Nathaniel sat up and saw Wendy desperately scouring Polly for signs of life. 'I was supposed to die, not her. This is all wrong.'

'You need to take this,' Father Hearne explained, removing the coffin nail ring from Polly's cold finger. 'Then you may understand.'

Nathaniel took it and pushed it over his little finger, it only just fit.

'Oh,' he said, eyes opening wide.

We can be together now my love. Maybe not forever, but there are ways. Other magicks, older spells, there is always hope. Melissa's voice sounded in his head. *I'm sorry I did not seek permission. I couldn't lose you again.*

'I would like nothing better, except maybe some clothes,' he said, trying to hide his nakedness.

'Sorry Nathaniel, but we have to burn all his things,' Father Hearne said. 'You can have my coat for now.' He passed him his herringbone overcoat.

'Thanks,' Nathaniel said, gratefully covering his shivering body.

'Please, please tell me you can help,' Clive called from over by the MX5, where he and Neville knelt over his wife in the snow. 'It's Susan, I don't think she's going to make it.'

Nathaniel's eyes rolled into his head, coming back shining silver. Melissa stood up gracelessly as she got used to his heavy body. 'Oh,' she said. 'New teeth, that's always difficult.' She staggered to the car. 'What's the problem then?'

'She got hit, by that ball, it was meant for me, can you do some magic? Make her better?' Clive was weeping into his wife's hair as he begged.

Melissa bent down and inspected Susan's limp body. 'Ugh, this itchy beard will have to go, it doesn't even suit you,' she muttered. 'I could restore her, but there would be a price.'

'Anything, anything you want,' Clive said. 'She's pregnant. I can't let the child die.'

'Told you then did she?' Melissa asked.

'No, but I can tell.' Clive gripped his wife's hand. 'Thanks for confirming it.'

'You know she's been fucking Jack don't you?' Lynn said. 'It might not even be yours.'

'Yes. But it doesn't matter whose baby it is. It deserves a chance,' Clive said.

'I think you know the price. She is going to die.' Melissa put her hand on Clive's good right one. 'That means to bring her back, somebody else must take her place.'

'I understand.' Clive nodded, eyes glistening with tears as they widened in realisation.

'But the child isn't even a person yet, just an embryo,' Lynn said.

'Maybe, but I can't live without Susan, whatever she's done. She'll be okay without me, and our children need a parent, not a husk.'

'If you're sure.' Melissa closed Nathaniel's eyes.

'I am, do it.' Clive bent down to Susan, kissing her cold forehead.

Melissa took their hands and began to chant, drawing life from one to pour into the other. Eventually she stopped. 'You should say your goodbyes now. I haven't left you long Clive. You brilliant, brave, lovely man. I will miss you.' She kissed him, then left them alone.

'Tell the children I love them,' Clive said, holding Susan to his chest.

'You can tell them yourself you twat,' Susan said, opening her eyes. 'Lucky I jumped in to save you. Why didn't you get out of the way?' She hugged him.

'I didn't see it coming. Thank you for saving me, but I kept the receipt and Melissa's helping me return the gift. I love you.'

'But... but... you're here?' Susan began to cry. 'We're here, we're together, we're alive. Why can't she keep us that way?'

'It doesn't work like that. Balance, life for a life, and this way I'm saving two.' He sniffed, wiping snow from his face.

'How did you know? I didn't know?'

'You've been crying at gravy adverts since November, that only ever means one thing. You were the same with the other three.' He smiled.

'But Clive, there's something you don't know, I...'

'Have been cheating on me, I know. As long as you came back to me, I never cared. Even with Jack, he's my best mate, and I'm honestly happy to help him get over Edwina. Whatever it takes. Whatever you've done, it's a privilege to be able to give you more time. You are my life – literally now.' He laughed ghoulishly and fell to one side. 'Ah, that'll be it.'

Susan moved to hold him up. 'You beautiful, stupid man. You're so fucking stubborn, always so sure you're right.'

'I don't like it, being right, I don't want to be, I just am. Sorry. I love you.' He coughed, then was still.

'I love you too you fucking twat,' Susan said. The last words she would ever say to him, ugly crying now with a face smeared in snot and tears. She hugged his body close, holding him away from the snow, away from the destruction, and willing these last moments not to end.

'Okay, you dogs. I know you can hear me, and I know our accord has been broken, but I ask for a new deal. I know the price,' Melissa said, breaking the silence. 'And I am prepared to pay it.'

'Hold on, you're not going to?' Lynn looked to Elizabeth.

'No, not the baby, I still need her.'

'Not Clive!' Susan screamed. 'Please not my Clive.'

'No,' Melissa said. 'I wouldn't do that. Besides, it needs to be a living heart.'

'Well, I suppose mine's got a couple of good years in it yet,' Neville said.

'Maybe as a last resort.' Melissa winked. 'I'd still like to check it out first.'

'Well, now you're not in my granddaughter...' Neville pulled out a cigarette.

'No, I'm not,' Melissa replied.

'Surely you couldn't?' Wendy hugged Polly's unconscious body closer, Jack's car blanket wrapped around them and Elizabeth.

'No, of course not. I need a good heart, not that sneaky bitch. She's already got more than enough blood on her hands.'

'Is she going to..?' Wendy didn't dare ask. She had done everything she could remember from her first aid training, but this was a magical injury.

'No, she'll be fine, get up,' Melissa ordered. 'We're leaving.'

Wendy passed Elizabeth up to Lynn then gently lifted Polly. She weighed so much less than she had before Melissa left her, Wendy could easily carry her over to the car.

'Wait here, and we shall be back my friends, there is still work to be done but you shall have your price,' Melissa promised the pack. They bowed their heads and Cronus led them into the woods, leaving the people alone.

Fenrir leaped into the driver's seat of the MX5 and licked Polly back to consciousness.

'What, what happened?' Polly said. 'Why do I feel so..?'

'Alone dear?' Melissa said leaning in. 'You are your own person once more.'

'Oh. So you're in Nathaniel now?' Polly didn't know quite how to feel about that.

'Yes, and not for the first time.' Nathaniel's face broke into a filthy grin.

'Is that a good idea?' Polly asked.

'It's the only one I've got, so it had better be. Get out dog.' Melissa shooed Fenrir from the driver's seat and he hopped into the back.

'Right then, to town, then the Manor.' Melissa gunned the engine to life after a series of false starts as she got the hang of her new legs.

'Are you sure you can drive?' Polly grabbed the wheel.

'I'll be fine, are you lot okay to walk?' Melissa shouted.

'I don't suppose we've got any choice have we?' Lynn replied. 'Here, I believe this is yours.' She passed Elizabeth to Polly who showered her with kisses and held her like she would never let her go.

'You could wait here until I can find somebody to drive up and get you?' Melissa suggested.

'We will, we'll wait with Clive,' Wendy said.

'Very honourable of you,' Melissa agreed. 'I shall send young Daniel and his van once we get back. Look after Susan will you?'

'Of course.' Wendy nodded.

'Thank you,' Polly said, holding onto Wendy's sleeve. 'For looking after me.' She pulled her down and kissed her. 'That's a yes by the way, I am very curious, if you'll let me.'

'Oh.' Wendy kissed her back. 'I'll definitely let you.'

'Well, I'm very happy for you both,' Neville said. 'Any chance of a lift to Appledore? Since I cut the last one short to come back and save you?'

'I'm afraid not, no space in this ludicrous dick extension. Maybe later,' Melissa explained. 'Oh and can somebody tell Jack we're going to need that pretty young girlfriend of his.' She shoved the car into gear and pulled away. 'She seems nice.'

'Yes,' Polly agreed. 'Anna looks like she has a good heart.'

'That's what I'm counting on,' Melissa said as they sped down the hill towards Dourstone.

THE END

UNTIL WICKER DOGS BOOK 3
ARRIVING WISTHOUND WEEKEND DECEMBER 3RD 2021

If you finished this book then please could you leave a review on Amazon as it's the single most important way for us authors to gain visibility. You don't have to write more than a couple of lines, and I won't hold it against you if you hated it – as long as you're honest.

Amazon UK

Amazon US

If you would like to delve further into Dourstone, then sign up to my mailing list at daholwill.com/sign-up/ to receive your free copy of *The Stalking of Lady Sophia*

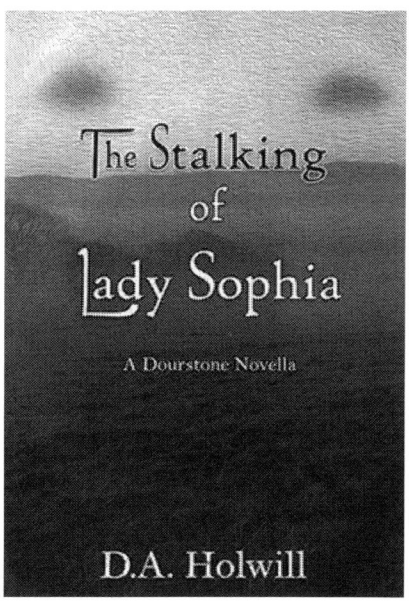

Long before Polly, Patrick or even Nathaniel Harker came to Dourstone, a young woman meets an enigmatic stranger at her father's funeral.

Sophia has lost her lover to an arranged marriage and her father to a drunken fall from Westminster bridge. When she sees a black dog from her bedroom window she does not believe the omen can make things worse.

Unfortunately for her they can, and circumstances force her and her mother to beg charity from estranged family in Devon.
With no way back to high society and her beloved, the only respectable person that will give her the time of day is the enigmatic Lord Elias Dewer.

Could he be her saviour, or the cause of all her misery?

Turn the page for a preview chapter of
Wicker Dogs Part Three: Jack Sharpnails

1

'Watch out!' Cole shouted, dragging her knees up to curl into a protective ball on the back seat of the big Volvo estate.

'We're fine, don't worry,' Maurice, her dad, said from the driver's seat in front, slamming on the brakes to skew the car across a narrow, potholed moor road, the front left corner pushing a spindly gorse bush at a sharp angle. It had been a long drive and the sudden appearance of a pack of dogs had taken him by surprise. Not least because he had thought they were sheep.

'Be careful.' Victor, Cole's stepfather, looked round anxiously to the pile of luggage in the boot that Ben, the baby, was balanced on. 'Are you all alright back there?'

'I'm fine,' Cole said, unfurling her faded grey skinny-jeaned legs. 'She hasn't even woken up.' She nodded her head towards her stepsister, Frankie, drooling into her long blonde hair on a travel pillow.

'Yes, but what about Ben?' Victor said, with a huff.

'Barely noticed, he's so squished in by all these coats we could go over a cliff and he wouldn't feel it.' Cole spared her baby brother a glance, but since he wasn't screaming for once, she assumed he was okay.

'Where did those dogs come from anyway?' Maurice said, running a hand through his shaggy greying hair before restarting the engine.

'It's Dartmoor sweetie.' Victor leaned across and planted a kiss on his bearded cheek. 'There was a sign about livestock, remember, we laughed at the "Take Moor Care" pun. You're going to have to start watching the road instead of looking at me.'

'Funny,' Maurice replied, taking in Victor's smooth southern European features and shaved head. 'I wasn't looking at you, I was watching…'

'The scenery Dad,' Cole interrupted, scratching her scalp through short-cropped brown hair before readjusting her nose stud. 'Same as always.'

'Yeah, maybe, sorry.'

They still couldn't head off as the dogs refused to leave the road.

'Are you people alright?' A rap on the windscreen surprised everyone, apart from Frankie, who rolled her head to the other side with a mucus-infused snore.

'Yes, sorry, didn't expect to be set upon by wolves,' Maurice joked, winding down the window.

'They're not wolves, they're…'

'Alaskan malamutes,' Cole joined in. 'Yes, I recognised them, I work, sorry worked, at a vets. Lovely dogs.'

'Thank you,' a clean shaven man with long dark hair pulled back in a ponytail said, turning his attention to Cole and leaning in to her window. 'Most people think they're huskies.'

Cole had been working at a veterinary practice in Bristol after dropping out of university and, because she had been studying with a view to getting a veterinary nurse qualification, she could tell an Alaskan malamute from a Siberian husky. The pack was mostly Alaskan malamutes, along with a lot of mud-covered mongrels, and, if she wasn't mistaken, an Irish wolfhound at the head.

'Malamutes are bigger though, aren't they?' Cole shrugged.

'Yes they are,' the man said, grinning from ear to ear. He pushed back a battered brown leather hat and straightened up. 'Nathaniel Harker, pleased to meet you.'

'I'm Cole, those are my dads, Maurice and Victor, that's my step-sister, Frankie, and baby Ben up on the back shelf.' Cole stuck her twig-like arm out of the window.

'Pleased to meet you,' Nathaniel replied, shaking the offered hand. Cole found herself staring transfixed into gleaming silver eyes as he held her gaze with a wry smile.

'Maurice Hawlings, likewise,' Maurice said, shoving his hand out. Nathaniel turned to give it a perfunctory shake before returning his attentions to Cole as his long wax jacket flapped in the breeze.

'And this is Polly,' Nathaniel said, as a young woman came hurrying across the moors, tight black curls bouncing round her face.

'I wish you'd not run off ahead like that all the time, it's alright for you with your… oh.' Polly stopped talking as she realised they had company.

'Polly, this is Cole, and…' Nathaniel tailed off.

'Maurice,' Cole's dad prompted. 'And Victor, Frankie and Ben.' He indicated each in turn with a wave of his arm.

'Hello,' Polly said, gasping for breath. 'Pleased to meet you all, this is my little Lizbet.' She spun on her heel to show off a toddler strapped to her back.

'Elizabeth,' Nathaniel said.

'Hello you.' Cole waved. 'Aren't you cute?'

'She is not,' Polly laughed. 'She's a horrid demanding monster.'

'Should get on well with our Ben then,' Maurice replied. 'I don't suppose either of you know the way to Dourstone Nymet – I'm worried we might be a bit lost.' He pointed to a phone mounted on the windscreen that had lost signal and stopped giving directions miles ago.

'Why yes we can, in fact, Lizbet here owns most of it,' Polly explained. 'Technically she's the Lady Elizabeth Dewer of Dourstone Nymet, but I'm her mum so I'm looking after it until she's big enough.'

Nathaniel's lip curled and he gave a little snort.

'My lady.' Maurice bowed, as much as one can bow in the driver's seat of a Volvo.

'I'm sure she's charmed.' Polly gave a little bow in return.

'We'll probably see a lot more of you then. We've bought the Drop of Dew – moving in today,' Victor said, leaning across his husband.

'Why have we stopped?' Frankie shouted, juddering into wakefulness. 'Are we there?'

'Nearly,' Victor said. 'We are nearly there aren't we?' He stage whispered to Polly.

'You are, just keep going straight, turn left at the big old stone cross, head past the stone circle and you'll get to town. You can't miss it,' Nathaniel interrupted.

'That's a lot of stones, I thought we'd left all the stoners behind in Bristol!' Maurice joked.

'Okay…' Polly didn't laugh. 'Anyway, you're only a minute or two from town.' She stroked the head of a big Irish wolfhound nuzzling up to her impatiently. 'We'll probably see you later, it's a small place.' She waved and walked off across the moors, dogs forming up in lines to follow in her wake.

'Yes, see you later.' Nathaniel directed this at Cole, not so much as glancing at the others.

'Well, they seem friendly,' Maurice said, pulling the big Volvo away.

'Brilliant,' Frankie muttered. 'Just what we need, bored nosy bloody locals with nothing better to do poking their nose in.'

'Frankie,' Victor sighed. 'We need to make the effort to fit in. It's a proper community. Not like home.'

'Yep. Brilliant.' She pulled out her phone and started scrolling. 'Why are you doing this again?'

'We needed a change, this pub needed buying – we all have to do our bit. Village pubs are closing in their thousands, everything's been hit hard by the last few years. It is our patriotic duty to move to the countryside, buy a substantial property at a knockdown price and use it to sell alcohol.' Maurice braked sharply again as a turning by a stone cross took him by surprise.

'Patriotic, yeah, sure.' Cole smiled and looked out of the window.

'Nobody forced you to come,' Victor said. 'You're old enough to get your own place.'

'I'm old enough to get my own place,' Frankie muttered. 'Just can't afford it yet.'

'You can do what you like when you've turned eighteen and finished your A levels this summer,' Victor said. 'But until then you're here with us Francesca. It's beautiful here, you'll love it.'

'Yeah right.' Frankie put her earphones back in and stared out of the window.

Cole was happy to get out of Bristol, not all of it was as progressive as it gets painted, and their unorthodox little family attracted a lot more hate than it deserved. On the other hand, she didn't think coming to the depths of Dartmoor was going to make that any better, even if they were going to be running the only pub in town. Maurice said it himself, it was a dying industry, pubs were disappearing by the second. Since everybody realised they could buy cheap booze from the supermarkets and socialise virtually from the comfort of their own homes, the pub was becoming obsolete.

It was her dad's dream though, and she was here to support him – whether he cared or not. It helped that she'd been dreaming of a countryside veterinary career, all livestock and working dogs, rather than the fat cats, pampered lap-dogs and ill-thought-out reptiles she had seen in the city. Hopefully she could find a paid apprenticeship, since Maurice had made it abundantly clear there was no budget for her or Frankie at the pub. They were ploughing everything they had into the purchase and expected renovations.

A stone circle hoved into view, that was cool. The clouds parted and a shaft of sunlight hit a large flat stone in the centre that glowed a deep red, as if drenched in the blood of long centuries. Polly and Nathaniel sat on the rocks, framed by deep woods. Nathaniel was smoking a pipe. He tipped his hat and winked as they passed.

Cole shuddered. Nathaniel's face had the shape of one from the dreams she had been having this last year. Since the last time she had heard from Anna. Only in her dreams he was older, much older, with an untidy silver and black beard, an old-fashioned deadman's hat and burning black eyes. It couldn't be the same man, that was impossible. Every night she closed her eyes and saw open moorland, dogs running freely over it towards some unseen prey. Sometimes heading deep into the woods, to a river, pitted with small islands, lined with sharp rocks and flowing through deep pools, treacherous shallows and muck-filled weirs. And then he would appear and she would wake. In spite of him, it had awoken a desire to see the moors for real, so when Maurice had suggested she join them in their new venture she had jumped at the chance. It wasn't often that Maurice included her in his life, she had always felt like an afterthought. Given that her mother had all but left her to bring herself up she was keen to establish a better relationship with him. Especially when it transpired they were moving to the very place Anna had last been seen.

The moors called to her, this was where she was supposed to be, she was sure of it. The missing piece of her life she had waited so long to find. A vast expanse of granite and green to explore and enjoy. She looked to the other side of the road, where open moorland glistened in mid-day sunshine. She knew each of the peaks she could see puncturing the horizon had a name, and hoped to have time to learn them all. She could remember Yes Tor and High Willhays, but couldn't pick them out of the lineup.

'What do you think then?' Polly said, nudging Nathaniel.

'I think you should remember who actually owns all this,' Lady Melissa Dewer said from inside him. 'Know your place, this is not yours.'

'It is Elizabeth's though, legally, and I'm her legal guardian, so you know…' Polly grinned. 'It is kind of mine.'

'You never used to be this scheming.' Melissa sighed, puffing on her pipe.

'You made me this way,' Polly replied, throwing a stick for Fenrir, her Irish wolfhound. 'And you left it all to Elizabeth in your will. So you've only yourself to blame.'

'I hadn't planned on you killing me,' Melissa said, watching the Volvo trail off towards town. 'Oh, they've turned the wrong way…'

'They'll still get there, just the long way round,' Polly said, taking the stick from Fenrir as he bounded back.

Melissa nodded, coughing as she relit her pipe. 'I wish I didn't have to feed your filthy habits,' she muttered.

'Can't you get him to give up?' Polly asked.

'Not without having to go through the withdrawal myself, no. This body won't last long enough for it to matter anyway. Not worth the effort.'

'But what about Nathaniel, won't he die if you leave him?'

'If he doesn't stop moaning I'll be glad of it,' Melissa said.

'Seriously?'

'No, you're right.' Melissa hung her head. 'But there might be a way for him to survive.'

'Might?'

'Yeah, only might, but it's better then nothing.' Melissa's gaze followed the Volvo down the hill. 'Of course we'd need to find a willing host…'

'Not again thanks,' Polly said, getting back up and chivvying the dogs into order.

'No, the feeling's more than mutual dear, and there are other complications. I would need to make peace with an old friend.'

'I didn't know you had friends?'

'I don't any more, as I said, I need to make peace,' Melissa said. 'And Jack Sharpnails hasn't walked above ground for a long time.'

'I don't think I want to know do I?'

'Not if you don't want to help no.'

'Good, I don't. New hosts, tributes for the dogs, how are we going to get away with all these people going missing,' Polly complained.

'Same way we always have, you'll see. It'll be fine.' Melissa knocked the ash from her pipe. 'Nobody's missed Father Hearne yet have they?'

'No, I suppose not.'

'Or that girlfriend of Jack's, what was her name?'

'Anna.' Polly shook her head. 'Her name was Anna, they all have names.'

'Sorry, yes, they do.' Melissa put a hand to Polly's shoulder. 'Anyway, there's been no trouble over either of them. We'll be fine. I've been doing this a long time.' Melissa swept off over the moors.

'Yes, I suppose,' Polly said to nobody. It was true, all the trouble from the Christmas before, when The Traveller had cut the town off with a wall of snow, had been put down to freak weather. There had only been one official casualty, and the registered cause of Clive's death was careless driving. She got to her feet and followed behind with the dogs.

'Okay then, home sweet home,' Maurice said, pulling up in a picture postcard perfect town square. Thatched cottages and large Victorian brick buildings surrounded a walled-off area with trees and benches. Somebody had taken a huge chunk out of the wall near one of the trees, Cole noticed with a hint of sadness. Vandalism still happened, she supposed, wherever you go, though she had to admire anybody who could knock such a big hole in such a solid-looking wall.

She opened the car door and got out, stretching her legs in the March sunshine. The Drop of Dew was big, she had not realised from the photographs her dads had shown her. Its long front took up all the lower side of the square, holding a gateway big enough to drive a car through and, as Victor pushed it wide open, she realised that was exactly what it was there for. None of its many windows were aligned on the same plane, and the thatched roof undulated along a curve as if it had been built round a sleeping dragon. The largest windows on the first floor had iron balustrades, wide enough to call balconies if you stood on tiptoe. Chunks of render were missing from the frontage and the peeling, faded, sign hung at a wonky angle from one chain, the other dangling uselessly from its bracket. They had a lot of work to do.

'Come on then, since you were too busy to come and see it before, I'll give you the tour.' Maurice was bursting with pride as he stood on the threshold: living proof that love is blind.

'Let's get the car and the baby in first, shall we Mo?' Victor said, pinning the gateway open.

'Yes Dad, we don't want to anger the locals by adding to all this do we?' Cole indicated the roadway, already blocked with badly parked traffic all over the pavements. There was no way anything could get round their double-parked Volvo.

'Okay, okay. Haven't got the keys yet anyway.' Maurice got back in and reversed the car carefully in. Frankie gave Cole the finger from the back seat for no reason other than she could. Cole rolled her eyes and ignored her. She wanted them to get on together, like sisters should, but it was hard. Their fathers had been together since the girls were at primary school, so it wasn't like they hadn't had time. Cole was a few years older than Frankie, but had been treated as an interloper every time her mother got fed up of her and sent her to stay with her dad. Cole had spent her childhood being batted between the two like an unwanted shuttlecock. Frankie had lived with Maurice and Victor full time, Victor being her one surviving parent, and had not taken kindly to having to share her dad with Maurice, let alone her home with another child. Cole hoped that being stuck together in this remote place might finally be the push they needed to become proper sisters. After all, they were older now, it was time.

'Hello, are you the new owner?' A man in a wheelchair wearing an Exeter Chiefs beanie rolled up. 'Aren't you a bit young?'

'Ha ha, no, I mean, yes, I mean…' Cole stammered. 'Pleased to meet you, I'm Cole, and my dads have bought the pub.'

'Dan, likewise, pleased to meet you that is, I'm all out of dads. I hope yours have got nothing to do with Endeavour Hotels,' the man said, holding his hand out.

'No, never heard of them.' Cole shook the proffered hand. 'Dad's doing this off his own back. Free House, no ties. Always been his dream.'

'Good to hear,' Dan said. 'We need the pub back, it's been shit without it. Those Endeavour bastards have been buying up all the pubs round here, running them into the ground and selling them off for second homes.'

'No danger of that here, none whatsoever my dear fellow.' Maurice came charging back through the gateway. 'I wish to be a proper landlord, in the countryside, in this – dare I say it – magnificent old inn.'

'You may dare, it is magnificent.' Dan nodded. 'Oi, Jack,' he shouted across the square. 'They're nothing to do with Endeavour.'

'I told you that,' a tall man with floppy brown hair said, striding towards them with two sullen children in tow. 'I wouldn't sell this place to just anyone would I? Good to see you again, Maurice.' Jack held out his hand.

'You too, do you have the…?' Maurice asked, shaking the offered hand.

'Yes, of course, here you go.' Jack gave him a huge bunch of keys. 'Good luck.'

'Do you know what you're doing?' Dan eyed Cole suspiciously.

'I don't have to,' she said. 'Dad's in charge.'

'Oh yeah, you said, I thought you looked a bit young,' Dan said. 'Any experience?'

'What do you mean?' Cole said.

'Not you, he means your dad.' Jack flicked his fringe from his face before turning to Maurice. 'This is my mate Dan by the way, I tried to shake him off, but when I said who I was meeting, he wouldn't leave me alone. Dan, Maurice, Maurice, Dan.'

'Please to meet you. Have you run pubs before?' Dan asked.

'Well no, I've never run a pub before, but I have run many theatres to great success, and it can't be all that different.'

'If you say so,' Jack replied, brushing one of his kids from his leg and pushing it into the square to play with the other. 'But my estate agents service is always available if you need to cut your losses.'

'I'm sure it won't come to that, but thank you very much,' Maurice said.

'Any chance of a beer then?' Dan asked. 'Now you're here.'

'Going by the smell coming from the cellar, I'd say no.' Victor came out of the gate. 'It's going to take a bit of work before we can serve anything – probably need all new lines.'

'This is my husband, Victor,' Maurice said. 'Sadly he's usually right about these things. He served time behind the bar at the

Admiral Duncan in Soho.'

'Never heard of it,' Jack said. 'Do you want to join us for a drink in the square later, if the weather holds? We usually have a couple to watch the sunset and mourn the pub.'

'That sounds great, hope to see you later on then, nice to meet you,' Victor said. 'Right you two, we've got work to do, enough gabbing.'

'See you later,' Cole said, waving as they went inside.

Jack Sharpnails
Wicker Dogs Book Three
Coming Wisthound Weekend
2021
(December 3rd)

D.A. Holwill is online at:-
www.daholwill.com
www.facebook.com/daholwill
www.instagram.com/dave_holwill
and @daveholwill on twitter

AUTHOR'S NOTE AND ACKNOWLEDGEMENTS

I typed the last few words of The Bellever Hagstone's first very very rough draft whilst forced to self-isolate with a runny nose in the middle of March 2020, glad of a few days at home to get the final confrontation nailed down. Little did I know what was to follow (and I don't just mean the realisation I'd have to go back and rework Wicker Dogs for the 8000th time when I read it through afterwards).

Covid also pushed some of my favourite beta-readers out of the picture since they work as teachers (though I did get one Doctor back) and, contrary to what some people might tell you, they had to suddenly work four times harder than usual. Despite all this, I tried very hard to keep the pandemic out of it, and Tim Brooke-Taylor selfishly dying and ruining a really good gag in chapter nine gave me a great excuse to set it in the before times.

I need to thank my wife, Netty, as always, for being the first to read it and helping make sense of a thoroughly directionless first draft. Nobody else could put up with my ever-changing moods as I fight the writing demons. I also need to thank Lou Mitchell, Kerriann Speers, Sarah Squire and Sophy Layzell for hacking their way through a far superior later edit and helping me focus on the wood while I was being distracted by trees.

I'd also like to thank James Brogden (another teacher) for providing the blurb that now graces the cover of Wicker Dogs. And my stepkids Adam and Rudi – even if Rudi's helping me check the final proof of Book One while we were drinking meant the paperback version spent a whole month in the wild with completely mad page numbering. And finally, my mailing list, and especially the launch team who I am confident will help this book, and its predecessor, find its audience.

I hope you'll join me in December for book three to find out what happens next.

Printed in Great Britain
by Amazon